"You and I, Jennifer, are ~~most~~ ~~good~~ ends ..."

Through a mist of emotion, she looked into his face. "How can you possibly know what is in my heart?"

"You have not spoken ... but your eyes do not conceal the truth."

Hawk's soft declaration flooded her face with burning color, and she brought up both hands to cool her cheeks. "I'm very grateful to you for saving my life, of course ... but beyond that ..."

"We care much for each other," he insisted.

"You put words in my mouth," she argued feebly.

He arched a raven brow. "It is useless to deny what I can see for myself."

She took a shallow breath. "All right. We care for each other, but I'll admit to nothing more. We've faced death and danger together. Such things can charge the emotions. In a few days, I'll be gone, and soon after ... we'll forget."

He held her gaze in a timeless moment.

"And does one so easily forget the sunrise of the heart?"

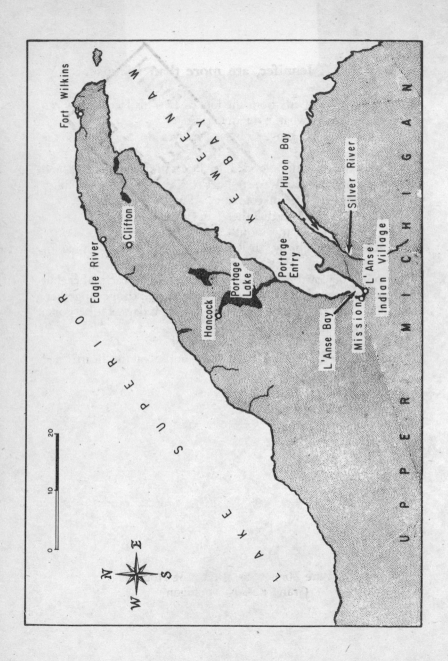

Jenny of L'Anse Bay

DONNA WINTERS

Serenade/Saga
BOOKS
of the Zondervan Publishing House
Grand Rapids, Michigan

A Note from the Author:
I love to hear from my readers! You may correspond with me by writing:
> Donna Winters
> Author Relations
> 1415 Lake Drive, S.E.
> Grand Rapids, MI 49506

JENNY OF L'ANSE BAY
Copyright © 1988 by Donna Winters

Serenade/Saga is an imprint of Zondervan Publishing House,
1415 Lake Drive, S.E., Grand Rapids, MI 49506.

ISBN 0-310-47651-8

Scripture quotations are taken from the King James Version of the Holy
Bible.

Edited by Anne Severance
Designed by Kim Koning

Printed in the United States of America

88 89 90 91 92 93 94 / DP / 10 9 8 7 6 5 4 3 2 1

To Fred with love

Notes and Acknowledgments

This novel is a work of fiction. Names, characters, places, and incidents are either the product of the author's imagination or, if real, are used fictitiously.

I would like to thank Clarence J. Monette for his advice and for his local history series of books about the Keweenaw Peninsula. Without his inspiration, this story would not exist.

A special thanks to Pat Cavner of the Caledonia Library for her willingness to request countless volumes from other libraries.

I am grateful to Howard Creswick, who graciously provided the map.

The French word, *L'Anse,* is properly pronounced *lŏnce*. The English pronounced it *Lē ŏnce*. Keweenaw is pronounced *kē' wĕ naw*. Ojibway is accented on the second syllable.

chapter
1

June 1867

THE DUST ROSE IN THICK WHORLS—choking, stifling dust. Through the gray haze, she could barely make out the ample figure of Grandma Jen, who was wielding her carpet-beater with a vengeance.

"That's right, dearie, whack away! We'll rout the dirt this very day!"

But the child standing behind her was lost in the pungent cloud that sent her into a spasm of coughing—

Jennifer Crawford stirred, slowly coming to full consciousness. So it had been a dream, after all. Her beloved Grandma Jen was dead, and that five-year-old child who had helped with the cleaning had seen twelve more springs come and go since that long-ago day.

She took another moment to gain her bearings. This was not Clifton, the bawdy copper mining town of her childhood, but Eagle River, perched on the sandy harbor facing Lake Superior. Here, her father had started his general merchandise business, which was thriving as the town grew.

She struggled up in bed, unable to shed the uneasy sensation that something was wrong. Though the last chimes of midnight still echoed from the mantel clock in the parlor, the room seemed unusually bright. Perhaps there was a full moon tonight.

Odd. What could have disturbed her sleep? There was no sound aside from the steady ticking of the clock and her parents' even breathing in the room across the hall. She rubbed her eyes, which stung as if irritated from the dust in her dream.

Her curtain fluttered in a sudden breeze, and she caught an acrid odor drifting through the half-open window. Jennifer crawled out of bed and drew aside the filmy lace.

For an instant she stared, not comprehending the horror that met her gaze—like a fever-dream come to life. To the west the sky glowed red. Panic tore through her as she recognized the foul smell.

Smoke!

Huge dark clouds billowed along the street, carrying live sparks and bits of ash. They drifted everywhere, some burning themselves out, some smoldering, ready to ignite.

She breathed in a shallow gasp of fright. Most of Eagle River was built of wood . . . the houses, the public buildings, the places of business . . . the second-floor apartment in which she stood and her parents' store below. The entire town was in danger of being engulfed in a fiery inferno!

On bare feet Jennifer raced across the hall to her parents' room. Belle and Clinton Crawford were deep in sleep and burrowed away from her insistent hands.

"Mama! Papa!" she screamed. *"Fire! We must get out!"*

"Ummm . . . Not now, Jennifer . . . What's that you say? Fire?" Her father pulled himself to a sitting position, shaking off sleep.

"Hurry!"

Clad in only a thin nightgown, Jennifer returned to her room. She grabbed a brown serge work dress and pulled it on, skipping stockings and petticoats, then fumbled for her shoes.

While she worked her bare feet into the shoes, she kept her eye on the open window. A spark drifted inside like a flaming butterfly, igniting the delicate white lace of her curtain. She ran to the window and slammed it shut, then grabbed a quilt, throwing it against the curtain to squelch the flame. But the tongues of fire had already licked up beyond her reach. She threw the quilt aside and turned to her dresser, yanking open the drawer and grabbing a handful of handkerchiefs, which she threw into the wash basin.

As she scooped up the dripping cloths, pandemonium broke out on the streets below. Shouts and the incessant clanging of the fire bell propelled her across the hall to her parents' room. Through the haze of smoke that filled the room, she could see her mother grappling with her wrapper, her father buttoning his trousers, both coughing and choking.

"Cover your nose and mouth." She pushed the wet cloths to their faces.

Her mother gasped. "I can't breathe . . . can't see. . . ."

Jennifer grabbed by the hand. "Hold onto me. Papa, are you all right?"

"hI . . . hI be all right," he managed between fits of coughing. Though twenty years had passed since he had left Cornwall, Clinton Crawford still spoke with the misplaced h's of a typical "Cousin Jack."

"Hold on to Mama and follow me!"

Jennifer's eyes were stinging, watering. Her lungs burned. Groping her way along, she led her parents through the hall to the stairway, then down the sixteen steps to the first floor. The three of them stumbled out the back door, falling in a heap on the sand in the alley.

The sky was a lurid, billowing red. A strong gust of wind whipped erratically between the buildings, driving sparks before it. Cinders from Crawford's General Store took flight, settling on the building next door.

Nightmare, Jennifer thought, her emotions numb with shock.

A bucket brigade was forming, and Jennifer dragged herself to her feet and found a place in line.

"hI'll be back," Clinton called, "just as soon as your mother be safe."

Jennifer watched as the fire consumed her father's store, their home, everything they owned but the clothes they were wearing.

Why, Lord, why? was the question she hurled at the heavens as a tiny spark of anger fell, smoldering, into her heart.

Hot, soot-covered, and weary, Jennifer concentrated on putting one foot in front of the other. The Woodworths' home, where her mother was waiting, was only a block away, but it seemed more like a mile. Soon, the sun would break over the horizon to rise on an Eagle River now in ruins—twelve homes and businesses, gone.

Trudging beside her father, Jennifer looked up into the Cornishman's face. Dark smudges across his cheeks and forehead bore testimony to his valiant struggle to save their earthly belongings, but his blue eyes were clear and undefeated. "What are we going to do now, Papa?"

"The Lord will show us. He'll provide, hI reckon." Though his voice was strained with fatigue, there was no hint of resentment. It seemed Clinton Crawford had lost no confidence in his God.

How do you know? He's just given us a taste of hell. Do you think now he'll show us a glimpse of heaven? Jennifer thought bitterly, not daring to say the words aloud.

Three days later Jennifer stood on the shore of Lake Superior. While crying gulls soared free over the lake, Jennifer felt imprisoned by her bubbling, churning emotions. Her bitterness over her loss had not diminished with time. On the contrary, it boiled hotter than ever.

From force of habit, Jennifer reached for the silver locket which usually hung around her neck, but it was gone, melted in the heat of the blaze. A gift from her Grandma Jen, it had been her most cherished possession, a reminder of the Cornish lady who had brightened the first five years of her childhood.

She would always remember the days when her mother and grandmother had run the boarding house in Clifton. Grandma Jen had brought a measure of Christianity into the lives of the tough breed of miners who came as emigrants from Cornwall without family, and often without knowledge of or dedication to Christ.

Were it not for her, many more of the men would have sought refuge in the saloons and gambling halls.

Now, the locket—the only tangible reminder of her grandmother—was gone, and fresh grief welled within.

There had been talk after the fire, accusations of arson. Though there were no witnesses, everyone believed William Jenkins had set the blaze. He had threatened the magistrate the day before the fire, and had been jailed when unable to prove his whereabouts on the night Eagle River burned. Since then, he had been released for lack of evidence and had fled the area. No one in town expected to see him again.

Still, it was a malicious, vengeful act that had stripped Jennifer of her precious memento—of practically everything she and her parents had owned. Anger gnawed at her insides. Her feeling was irrational, unchristian, she told herself as she struggled to come to grips with her increasing rage.

Since the fire, Jennifer and her parents had been staying with the Woodworths. Brother and Sister Woodworth, as the congregation called them, had once been missionaries to L'Anse, the French word meaning *arch* given to the southernmost area of Keweenaw Bay, but had been assigned three years ago to serve at Eagle River. After the fire, they had insisted the Crawfords take up lodging with them. Jennifer, however, felt uncomfortable with the arrangement. The small frame house was not quite adequate for three added guests. Even so, she knew she must repress any show of dissatisfaction with the cramped quarters, or appear terribly ungrateful.

Jennifer's gaze shifted from the gulls to the white sand on the beach. There played an elongated shadow of shawl fringe, riffled by breezy fingers. Even this reminded her of the licking flames she had fought in vain!

Turning away from the lake, she walked toward the white clapboard house, purposely approaching from the rear so as to avoid passing the rubble she had once considered home. Quietly, she entered the back hall.

"It will be good to see the Bentleys again," she could hear Sister

Woodworth saying as she prepared breakfast. "It's been three years now since they took over our old mission post at L'Anse, and I expect they could use a bit of encouragement by this time. Of course, we'll be eager to see our Indian friends again, too." She paused, a wooden spoon poised over her pancake batter. "Though the chief and his son accepted Christ while we were there, many others remained firmly rooted in their heathen ways."

As Sister Woodworth described the Ojibway village, a half-formed idea began to take shape in Jennifer's mind. She stepped inside the kitchen, drawn by the aroma of freshly brewed coffee and fried bacon.

Clinton Crawford pulled out the chair beside him. "Good morning, Jennifer. Come, sit 'ee down," he invited, offering his cheek for her kiss.

Jennifer obliged, then took the chair he held for her. "Good morning, Papa, Mama. Brother and Sister Woodworth." Her words sounded stiff and perfunctory, even to her own ears.

Sister Woodworth, a white apron draped around her ample girth, carried a platter of fluffy flapjacks and thick slices of bacon from the iron cookstove to the oblong pine table, while Belle Crawford filled coffee cups.

Leveling her gaze on the reverend's wife, Jennifer drew in a deep breath and began. "I couldn't help overhearing your conversation as I came in just a moment ago. May I ask how long you plan to stay at L'Anse?"

The woman's lips twitched in a semi-smile, as if she were not quite sure where Jennifer's question was leading. "About two weeks, dear."

Two weeks. Just right for a change of scenery, Jennifer thought. "Would you and Brother Woodworth . . . mind having a traveling companion?"

Her mother gasped as she returned the coffeepot to the back burner with a clang. Jennifer knew she had spoken brashly, inviting herself along, but this seemed the perfect solution to her growing restlessness. Her help wouldn't be needed in the store any longer, and having heard the Woodworths discussing L'Anse, her curiosity was piqued.

In spite of her mother's reaction, she caught a look of approval passing between Clinton Crawford and Brother Woodworth.

The reverend leaned back in his chair and cleared his throat. "You're welcome to come with us, Jennifer. The Indian canoemen will be fetching us at Hancock on the tenth of July," he explained. "I know most folk extoll the new road to L'Anse, but Anna and I prefer to travel by canoe."

"hIt be a bony road, that one," Clinton Crawford interjected with a wave of his hand.

Brother Woodworth chuckled at the colorful description. "That it is. Travel by water is more pleasant by far, and without the dust. There will be plenty of room for you to join us, Jennifer."

His wife added, "And once we reach L'Anse, the Bentleys will welcome you with open arms. I'll send them a note today, letting them know you'll be coming along. There are two extra beds in the room upstairs, and Edith will want to air it out for you."

"Thank you, Sister Woodworth." Looking down at her brown serge work dress, she made a wry face. "I suppose I'll have some sewing to do before we leave.'"

"Busy hands make light work, Jennifer. We'll do it together."

Following breakfast, Jennifer and her mother helped Anna Woodworth with her laundry while the reverend called on sick parishioners and Clint Crawford returned to the site of his burned-out general store.

Jennifer tried to uphold her end of the conversation as she worked with the older women, but her thoughts kept slipping back to the night of the fire. How could a loving God allow such a disaster? Her parents, especially her father, had labored for twelve years in this town. Before that, it had been the copper mines that had wrung from him his youth and vitality. They had come here, hoping to build a better life.

When all the laundry had been hung out to dry, she excused herself. This time she headed directly for the main street of town, where her father was clearing charred rubble from the site where his store once stood.

His clothing was already blackened with soot. Even so, Jennifer was tempted to hug him as she used to when she was little, but she resisted the urge. Something more important had brought her to the scene of devastation, something she wanted to discuss with him in private as he took a break from his labors and accompanied her on a walk along the beach.

They had strolled a few yards down the sandy shore when Jennifer stopped to face her father. Her dark eyes searched his blue ones. "Papa, why do you suppose God let our store and home burn?"

Clinton Crawford hesitated only a moment. "hI don't know, Jennifer. Reckon 'e has something else in mind for us."

"Don't you resent him, even just a little?"

Jennifer read a succession of emotions as they crossed her father's face—frustration in the set of his jaw, puzzlement in his knitted brows, then peace as he caught her slender hand in his. "No, hI don't resent 'im, Jenny Mae," he answered, using a name reserved for special, tender moments. "The Good Book says all things work together for good for those who love the Lord. There's naught to be gained in resentment."

"Papa, I know you're right, but inside I can't help blaming God."

Clinton Crawford led his daughter to a sun-bleached log that had beached during a storm, brushed off the grains of sand, and invited her to sit beside him. Wrapping his arm about her shoulders, he said, "Jennifer, 'ave 'ee prayed 'bout these feelings of yours? Do 'ee honestly want to be rid of 'em?"

She cast her eyes downward, a feeling of guilt creeping over her.

A moment later, he lifted her chin. "hI'm glad 'ee will be getting away for a while, though hI'll miss 'ee," he admitted. "The trip will be good for 'ee. Brother Woodworth 'as told me many a tale of 'is days with the Ojibways. They've got their troubles, like anyone, but they're trying to improve their lot, and most of 'em appreciate the missionaries. The Woodworths worked among the Ojibways at L'Anse for . . . must be well nigh thirty years."

"Papa—" She studied his face. "What are you going to do, now that the store's gone?"

Clinton Crawford gave a slight shrug. "Go back to the bal," he replied, using the Cornish term for "mine."

"No, Papa, you mustn't!" The words tumbled out before she could stop them. Years of hard labor had stolen his youthful vigor and strength, and she feared for his safety if he should return to the mine. Many a good man had met an early death there.

"When your mother and Grandma came with me to the Keweenaw from Cornwall twenty years ago, mining was all hI knew. hI made a decent living as captain at the Cliff Mine. I put my savings together with the money the women folk made from taking in boarders so we could start the store. Back then, hI wanted to get out of Clifton. A mining town's no place to raise a young girl. But you're grown now, and the store's gone. hIt's time to go back. Now, promise me 'ee won't worry?"

As Jennifer studied the tiny lines radiating from the corners of her father's eyes, she knew she had found one more reason to resent God. "I can't promise you that, Papa."

Her father bent and kissed her forehead. "hI'm sorry Jennifer, but hI reckon 'tis the way things must be." He rose from the log and helped her to her feet. "hI'll be getting back to work now. 'Twill take me a few more days to clean up the rubble from the fire." Together, they walked toward the village, stopping in front of the lot where the Crawford General Store had once stood.

Her father paused, placing his hands on her shoulders. "Don't 'ee worry 'bout the fire, Jenny Mae. Think on your trip to L'Anse!"

"I'll try, Papa." She almost succeeded in smiling.

The next few days passed quickly. The clean-up operation in the burned-out district continued, and Jennifer insisted on working alongside her father from early morning until they paused to rest at noon each day.

15

Even after they had cleared away all the burnt timbers and charcoal and Clinton had turned to chores around the Woodworth household, Jennifer was never idle. There were garments to be made and mended, and her hands flew as she and her mother fashioned serviceable skirts and blouses from some remnants of cloth produced by Sister Woodworth to replenish their lost wardrobe.

Then, just a few days before the scheduled departure for L'Anse, Anna Woodworth brought out another length of fabric—a fine navy silk.

"Jennifer, my dear, I've been saving this for a special occasion. Now I know it was meant for you."

"Oh, but I couldn't accept it, Sister Woodworth! You've been much too generous already!" She allowed herself, however, to caress the silky fabric, enjoying its luxurious feel beneath her fingers.

"Pshaw, child. 'Twill look much better on your lovely young frame than on this old one! Besides, even in the wilderness, you'll have need of a Sunday-go-to-meeting frock. Now, stand still and let's measure you."

The new gown lacked baleen hoops and a full skirt, which would have made it impractical indeed, but Belle set to work tatting a lace collar that could be added for a dressy occasion.

"Mama, it's beautiful," Jennifer remarked, looking over her mother's shoulder as she worked with the fine white thread.

"When we be back in Clifton, I'll make another collar of a different pattern. It will 'elp pass the time while your father's in the bal."

Clifton. Jennifer had visited the library there many times over the years, and the town had not changed much. Mining was rough, dirty work, and her parents' life would be marked by long hours and backbreaking labor. In Clifton, Belle and Clinton Crawford would occupy a mining company house. Her mother would take in a boarder or two to fill the extra rooms and bring in a few more dollars each week. They would have to start all over again. As Jennifer pondered these thoughts, an idea occurred to her.

"Mama, why don't you come with us to L'Anse? Brother

Woodworth said there's plenty of room in the Ojibway canoe, and we could share the extra bedroom at the mission house. Papa could go on to Clifton, and we could join him later."

Belle looked up from her handwork. Jennifer noticed a spark of interest in her eyes, but her mother hesitated before answering, taking time to tuck a strand of blond hair into the bun at the nape of her neck. "Work in the bal be hard enough without expecting your papa to stay alone. I ought to be there to cook and wash for him."

"He can hire someone to do those chores for him for two weeks. You want to come, I can tell!" Jennifer persisted.

The fine features that gave her mother's face a delicate beauty remained impassive. "My place be with your father."

"But when was the last time you did anything just for yourself? Twenty years ago, when you married Papa and came over from Cornwall? Mama, please do think about it. I'm sure that the Woodworths wouldn't mind, and Papa himself would be the last to object."

Belle put aside her tatting with a sigh. "You are a one, Jennifer. I guess I've no choice but to ask them about it tonight."

Jennifer threw her arms about her mother's neck. "Oh, Mama, I'm so glad you're coming!"

"I didn't say I'd be coming, mind," she said sternly. "I said we'd discuss it tonight."

"You'll go." And nothing could persuade Jennifer otherwise.

With the last-minute preparations for the trip to L'Anse completed in a feverish whirlwind of activity, Jennifer was relieved to talk quietly with her father on the night before her departure. They had drifted outside after the evening meal and walked now along the white sand of the harbor beach. In the mellow glow of the setting sun, they welcomed the cooling breeze from the lake.

"The Bentleys live on the west side of L'Anse Bay, and the Ojibways, three mile 'cross the water, on the eastern shore. If they offer to take you to the Indian village, you best go, Jennifer. The missionaries 'ave civilized the Ojibways a good deal over the past thirty years, but they not be rid of all their old ways yet."

"They seem civilized enough," Jennifer mused. "That is, the few I've seen. Two Indians came into the store this spring and, from the way they were dressed, they could have passed for white. I suppose the Ojibways at L'Anse wear buckskins, though."

"Yes, hI believe so, and right odd they'd be, tying their canoe up to the long pier 'ere, and walking Eagle River's streets dressed in fringed leather. 'Course, Indians from L'Anse never put into Eagle River by canoe. They'd walk from Hancock, up the center of the Keweena, after paddling across L'Anse Bay and through the entry to Portage Lake—just the opposite of the route ye'll be takin'."

Her mind skipped to Hancock, a town about twenty miles below Eagle River on the Keweenaw, a peninsula that extended like a crooked finger into the cold, treacherous waters of Lake Superior. Thankfully, they would not have to face the open lake waters that sometimes whipped into a frenzy strong enough to carry away Eagle River's long pier. Instead, they would travel the protected inland waterway. She wondered about the canoe they would take down the narrow inlet of Portage Lake, then into the bay, and what they would find at their destination.

It would seem strange to be away from the busy harbor town and village streets, she realized, as she walked with her father past Eagle River's odd-looking lighthouse. It was a squarish, two-story home, onto which a lookout and beacon had been added several years ago. Certainly there would be no such beckoning light at L'Anse. Nor would there be a county courthouse, stately and proud with its flag rippling high above. The thought of leaving all that was familiar behind and trusting life and limb to the Indians and their canoe suddenly caused Jennifer pangs of doubt.

As they neared the Woodworths' back door, she turned to her father. "You're absolutely certain, Papa, that these Indians can be trusted to take us safely to L'Anse? Perhaps we should take the new road, after all."

"Don't fret, daughter. Brother Woodworth told me the Ojibway canoemen proved several times they be equal to any challenge Keweenaw weather can provide."

By the following morning, as the carriage bearing the Crawford women and the Woodworths jostled over the rutted road to the little town of Hancock, Jennifer had put aside any anxiety she might have entertained. After staying overnight with some mutual friends, the little party would leave with the Indians the following morning.

Jonathan Hocking had become acquainted with the Crawfords and Woodworths while in charge of copper washing at the Cliff many years earlier. Now he and his wife, Mary, ran a millinery and fancy goods shop in Hancock. Though Jennifer had met the family when she was a very young girl, she had little recollection of the occasion.

Brother Hocking, a robust man, welcomed his guests enthusiastically. His wife, who was equally accommodating, was soon catching up with Belle on news from Eagle River and the Cliff.

Lily Ashforth, their niece, had recently emigrated from England. She was staying with them and working with Mary in the store creating stylish hats for their customers. Though somewhat plain-featured, Lily had a way with people that immediately put Jennifer at ease, and she was surprised to find herself almost bragging about her mother.

"She can sew a fine seam and tat lace collars as well." She threw her hands out in an expressive gesture. "Why, she can change the entire look of a dress by adding just a bit of her intricate handiwork at the neckline."

Lily's eyes sparkled with interest. "I *do* wish you be staying longer. I've wanted to learn lacemaking for ever so long, but you and your mother will be gone on the morrow." Lily shrugged. "Isn't that the way of it?"

"We'll be returning this way after our visit to L'Anse. Perhaps then?" Jennifer suggested.

Lily leaned forward. "Do you suppose . . . I mean, would she mind? I'd hate to impose."

"Mother would be glad to teach you—a skilled milliner. I'm all thumbs. Never could learn to tat, though heaven knows Mama was patient. But Lily, I'd love to see some of your hats. Could you show them to me?"

While the young girl went to fetch some of her creations, Jennifer noticed that the one member of the family who seemed left out of the parlor conversation was Tim Hocking, Jonathan and Mary's twelve-year-old son. The lanky lad soon disappeared down Tezcuco Street to watch the ships come and go at the docks, but he reappeared precisely at the dinner hour, with an enormous appetite.

When they arrived at the foot of Tezcuco Street the following morning, Brother Woodworth and Tim Hocking left the others in the carriage and set off in search of the Indian canoemen, who they hoped would be along the docks which lined the lakeshore.

Jennifer watched from her open carriage window as the portly minister and the slim boy walked some distance along the waterfront before disappearing from view behind the barrels of cargo ready for loading. A warm, gentle breeze carried the hiss of a steam engine as it worked the derrick loading copper onto a freighter. The pungent odor of burning wood, used to fuel lake steamers, mingled with the even stronger odor of manure from the merchants' horses. Wagons and drays jockeyed for positions along the dock, took on crates, kegs, hogsheads, chests, and casks, then slowly rolled past waterfront warehouses and up the hill into the heart of the business district.

At length the two men returned with a powerfully built young Ojibway, who wore fringed breeches but no shirt. His bronze upper torso glistened in the sun. Dark hair fell in an ebony sheet to his shoulders, except for two small braids at each side pulled to the back and fastened with a leather thong, from which a single eagle feather hung.

"Oh, my," Jennifer murmured, leaning across her mother for a better look, "what a striking man."

"The chief's son," Anna Woodworth explained. "Hawk is no

ordinary Ojibway. He studied for a year at Baldwin College in Berea, Ohio."

Hawk. How appropriate, Jennifer thought. She stepped lightly from the carriage and looked up into his face.

Her first impression had not been deceiving, for his countenance was even more impressive than his remarkable physique. His features might have been cast in copper—the broad, high cheek-bones; the angular jawline; the firm lips. Only an aquiline nose disturbed the perfect symmetry. But it was his eyes that pierced her very soul. Surprisingly, they were not the characteristic midnight black of the Indian, but a clear gray that seemed to bely his ancestry.

She placed her hand in his, and the fog in which she had been shrouded since her first glimpse of him vanished with the warmth of his touch.

"Miss Crawford, I am honored." His English was flawless, but the resonant voice was tinged with the musical cadence of his own tongue and some other language—French, perhaps.

"Oh . . . please call me Jennifer," she invited, feeling ridiculously young and inexperienced.

"Jennifer . . ."

He sounded it out, giving the "j" the soft pronunciation of the French word *bonjour,* and she thrilled to hear her name spoken as she had never heard it before.

Though his expression remained stoic, the astonishing gray eyes seemed suddenly silver, almost translucent in the bright sunlight.

The moment passed as Tim Hocking handed down the luggage and the tall Ojibway caught the bags easily, hoisting one to each broad shoulder, and turned to lead the little party to the waiting canoe.

Two Indian youths sprang lightly to their feet and greeted the Woodworths in a language that Jennifer found more charming than disturbing. Like Hawk, their skin shone like burnished copper, but beyond that, there was scant resemblance to the proud man standing before her.

Becoming aware of her surroundings at last, Jennifer found that

21

the Hockings were taking their leave, with fond embraces all around. There were promises to send news of the mission. Then it was time to board the canoe.

The craft was lean and elegant of line, but Jennifer felt a fluttering in the pit of her stomach when she noticed that the shell appeared to be constructed from the bark of a tree. And though it was large enough, she wondered how such a frail vessel could transport all of them safely to their destination.

All her old misgivings returned, and she was certain that this voyage was a mistake.

chapter
2

JENNIFER HUNG BACK as Sister Woodworth and her mother settled into the center of the canoe.

Brother Woodworth took her by her elbow and urged her forward. "It's perfectly safe, my dear," he assured her.

But she was overcome by an irrational fear and pulled free. "No . . . I–I can't. That's nothing but a . . . thin piece of bark!"

She whirled about and fled toward the base of the hill on Tezcuco Street, her heels clicking against the wooden planking of the dock.

Suddenly a firm hand shot out and grasped her arm, bringing her about.

"Where are you going?" The upturned corner of Hawk's mouth seemed to mock her.

"To L'Anse, of course," she replied indignantly. "I just prefer to travel by carriage, that's all. I'm sure one will be along presently." She tried to wrest her arm free, but he tightened his grip.

"The others are waiting. Come." Before she could stop him, Hawk had lifted her into his arms and was bearing her off.

"Put me down!" she demanded, struggling against the granite muscles that held her captive.

"I promise no harm will come to you. Trust me."

"How can I trust you? I just met you. Put me down!" She tried to wriggle free.

23

Much to her surprise, Hawk set her on the ground so quickly she nearly lost her balance.

"You are right. I cannot ask you to trust me. I will bring your bag. You will need it in the carriage." He turned and walked briskly toward the canoe.

"Hawk, wait!" she called, hurrying to catch up.

He paid no attention, returning with long strides to his boat. When she finally came alongside him, her temper flared. "Why didn't you wait? Can't you slow down? You certainly aren't very polite," she accused.

Hawk stopped so abruptly she almost ran into him. When he spun around to face her, she could see the look of consternation on his face. "*I* am not polite? You run away. You keep your friends waiting. When I offer to fetch your bag, you complain—"

"I'm sorry," she interrupted. "I didn't mean to cause all this fuss." Shrugging her shoulders, she added, "I guess . . . I'm not as brave as I thought I was. Your canoe seems . . . well . . . unsafe."

His features softened with a look of understanding. "The Woodworths have traveled many miles in my canoe," he began, his tone unexpectedly gentle. "They would not ride with me if it were unsafe."

"But the Woodworths lived among your people for many years," Jennifer reminded him. "They're accustomed to bark canoes."

"Even your mother is willing to ride with me." Hawk pointed to Belle who was already settled in.

"I know." Jennifer looked down, embarrassed by her display of cowardice. "Mother is more adventurous than I," she admitted.

A long pause followed while Jennifer struggled to accept Hawk's words, to believe that his skill and strength were adequate for the journey, but her stomach still revolted at the idea of stepping into the lightweight craft.

"It is not I alone who guides the boat—in still waters or in troubled ones—but One who lives within me. It is he who will bring you safely to L'Anse."

She looked again into the clear gray eyes, devoid of fear or guile. They mirrored the waters of the inlet, now utterly tranquil.

Taking a deep breath, she summoned her courage. "I'm ready to go with you now."

Though she spoke more confidently, she brushed a windblown strand of dark hair from her face with a trembling hand. Hawk took the small hand and drew it securely into the crook of his arm.

"The others are waiting," he said quietly. "Shall we join them?"

She nodded and moved off toward the canoe. With Hawk's long strides now measured to match hers, Jennifer felt her fears subsiding, taking comfort in the fact that, while her faith had been weakened by adversity, his was as strong as the great bird for which he had been named. She could entrust herself into his keeping.

When they reached the canoe, Hawk stepped in, then grasped her waist firmly, lifting her into the boat as easily as if she weighed no more than a hummingbird.

He took his place in the stern and, at his signal, three paddles hit the water, sending the birchbark vessel toward the center of the narrow stretch of Portage Lake with practiced skill. As the dock receded behind them, she recalled Hawk's solemn words. He was relying on more than skill or strength to bring them safely to shore. He, too, believed in the heavenly Father who would surely watch over them and keep them safe.

With silent precision, the Ojibway paddles sliced through the water. As the canoe glided over the calm surface of the lake, Jennifer began to relax a little. For the first time, she really looked at the interior of the canoe. The seat on which she was perched was not actually a seat at all, but a pile of soft fur robes. As she suspected, the canoe itself had indeed been fashioned of large strips of bark, lashed together and caulked with some kind of material she couldn't identify.

She peered at the sky. Though the sun shone brightly overhead, dark clouds had begun forming on a line to the northeast. But with the balmy July breeze on her face, there seemed no cause for concern.

Occasionally, Hawk spoke in his native tongue to his cohorts, or responded in English to Brother Woodworth's questions about the village and people at L'Anse. Most of the time, however, the Ojibways remained silent, conserving their energy for the task at hand.

Late in the afternoon, they arrived at a stretch of sand near Portage Entry. Carrying the canoe and supplies across this point would greatly shorten the distance to Keweenaw Bay, and here the passengers disembarked, following along behind the Ojibways, who hauled the bags, supplies, and the canoe itself across the sand toward the shoreline of the bay.

Jennifer felt her heels digging into the sand with each step, weighting her legs and ankles, and wondered how the three Indians could carry such a load under these conditions. Yet, their footsteps never faltered, and after a mile-long hike, they lowered their burdens onto the beach rimming the bay.

With dark clouds moving closer and meal time approaching, Hawk consulted with Gray Wolf and Red Wing. Just when Jennifer was wishing she knew enough Ojibway to understand what they were saying, Hawk spoke to his passengers in English.

"We will stop now to eat. There is a spring nearby for drinking water. Afterward we will rest, then paddle until we reach the mission." Before Jennifer could ask how many miles separated them from the mission, Hawk was off to help his companions who were spreading fur robes on the beach.

Brother Woodworth must have read the question in her mind, because his next words answered her concern. "We're about twenty miles from L'Anse now. With the wind at our backs, we could arrive in a few hours, but I'm afraid there's a storm moving in on us." He indicated the darkening sky to the north and east.

With no motion wasted, Hawk settled his passengers on the robes, brought water, then joined his companions a few yards away. Though Jennifer was most interested to know what the Ojibways had pulled from their packs to eat, she tried to curb her curiosity and bit into the sandwich her mother handed her.

Later, while Belle chatted with the Woodworths, Jennifer excused herself to stroll down the sandy beach. Weighing heavily on her mind were the events following the fire—her continuing hostility toward God, her anxiety about the future, her humiliating lack of courage exhibited for all to see! What must Hawk think of her? What must all of them be thinking?

She passed the three napping canoemen, taking care to keep her step light. It would not do to disturb them. They would need their strength to paddle twenty miles against the wind.

Jennifer approached a small point of land where the beach narrowed considerably. It would be hard to pass around it without getting her shoes wet, but since she hadn't gone far, she decided to investigate the opposite side. Lifting her skirts to a scandalous height above her ankles, she waited until a wave had receded from the shoreline, then sprinted across the wet sand.

She had nearly reached the other side when she ran full force into a rock-hard object. Hawk! The collision expelled the air from her lungs in a whoosh and threw her off balance. She felt herself falling backward as the next wave broke. With swift, sure movements, he caught her up, cradling her in solid arms and lifting her high above the water.

Angry at his intrusion on her privacy, Jennifer struggled to catch her breath as Hawk held her securely against his broad chest. "You again!" she fumed. "Can't I do anything without you carting me off like a child?"

"Should I let you fall into the water?" He threatened to let go of her when another wave broke over his feet.

She threw her arms about his neck. "No! Please don't drop me here!"

Laughing softly, Hawk carried her a few yards and deposited her on a wider stretch of sand.

Jennifer straightened her blouse and skirt. When she looked up and saw the mocking light in Hawk's eyes, her heated words tumbled out before she could stop them. "I thought you were asleep. Why did you follow me?"

"It is my duty to protect you until we reach the mission dock at L'Anse. Do you understand?"

She sighed audibly. "I suppose."

"Return now to your mother and friends," he said, his stern words matching the expression on his face. "I need rest for the journey ahead."

Jennifer opened her mouth to protest, but the sober look he fixed on her squelched further complaint.

"*Maw chon.*"

Jennifer gave him a puzzled look.

"*Maw chon*—come with me." His countenance softened as he gestured toward an opening in the thick brush rimming the beach. "I know a dry path to the other side of the point."

Jennifer followed meekly. Moments later, he stepped through the opening, disappearing in its dark shadow. Jennifer bent her head and pulled her skirt in close around her. After a few steps, she could neither see nor hear Hawk on the path ahead, and she began to panic.

"Hawk? Are you there?"

His hand found hers and held it tightly, his touch draining her fear as he led the way. Within moments the pathway brightened, and they emerged high on the beach with the point behind them. Hawk strode away, leaving her to walk alone.

Without further comment Jennifer joined her mother and the Woodworths, who were snoozing. She lay down on her fur robe and closed her eyes. Immediately, thoughts of Hawk filled her mind. She felt the warmth of his touch as he led her through the dark underbrush, her disappointment when he walked away from her once they reached the other end. *Will I ever understand him?* she wondered, before the relaxing warmth of the sun lulled her to sleep.

Later, Ojibway words spoken in the distance gently penetrated Jennifer's slumber, yet the Woodworths and her mother lay undisturbed while the Indians reloaded their canoe. Dark, thick clouds on a line to the northeast had moved closer, their ominous appearance eliciting occasional comments and gestures from the

Ojibways. A stiffened breeze whipped up whitecaps, like dabs of vanilla frosting, onto the azure waves in the bay.

Brother Woodworth stirred, his attention immediately arrested by the portentous sky. "We'd better wake the others," he suggested, calling their names softly.

Hawk approached, hunkering down to speak above the rising wind. "We must go now. The storm is moving closer."

"Are you sure we can outrun it, Hawk?" The reverend wore a worried expression. "Perhaps we should wait here until it passes."

"We should arrive at L'Anse before the storm moves onshore."

"Then we'd best hurry."

Quickly, the passengers took their places in the bottom of the vessel, and the canoemen shoved the craft off the sandy beach into the choppy waves. They paddled out some distance from shore before turning parallel to the coastline.

As they progressed southward, Jennifer noted a reddish hue alternating with white in the cliffs lining the bay, the colors forming a striped pattern.

"That's iron and calcite you see in the sandstone," Brother Woodworth explained. "The pictures they make are deceptively beautiful, for many a canoe has been destroyed along this rocky shore. There is no break in the cliffs until we reach the mission." He glanced over his shoulder at the oncoming storm.

Now that Jennifer saw the ruggedness of the shoreline, she understood brother Woodworth's suggestion to wait out the storm. There would be no possibility of beaching the canoe if the bay waters became too rough.

Suddenly, the wind switched directions, coming now out of the west. Waves which had urged them onshore now chopped at the canoe in confusion. Hawk shouted Ojibway directions to his cohorts, and the three canoemen set their paddles to the water with fresh urgency.

Time dragged by. Jennifer's mother reached for her hand, and she welcomed the comforting touch. The breeze cooled and stiffened, and Reverend Woodworth slipped his coat about his wife's shoulders to protect her from the spray that occasionally overshot the gunwale.

All the while, Jennifer worried about the distance growing between their canoe and the western shore. Across the bay, the Huron Mountains loomed along the eastern coastline, boding an even more hostile reception than the treachous sandstone cliffs to the west, yet the canoemen struggled on against the mounting waves.

An hour passed, and then another. Heavy swells rose and fell beneath them. Jennifer grew nauseous and took shallow breaths to quiet her stomach.

The braves shouted to one another, their exchanges unintelligible to her. But it was apparent that Gray Wolf and Red Wing were arguing with Hawk, gesticulating wildly. *Please, Lord, help them bring us safely through the storm,* Jennifer prayed in desperation.

The craft bobbed, directionless, as the Ojibways continued pointing at various landmarks on either shore and shouting over the roar of the wind. Suddenly, slipping sideways, the vessel tilted. Jennifer slid toward the low side of the canoe, sending the gunwale even closer to water level. Perilously close to capsizing, Hawk let out a mighty shout, digging his paddle into the water as the canoe tipped even more. His two companions followed his lead, stroking with all their strength to bring the canoe crosswise to the waves.

With her arm extended, Jennifer pressed against the low side with all the force she could muster, managing by some small miracle to brace herself. Then her mother slid against her, adding her weight to Jennifer's own. *O Lord, give me strength.* Her arm muscles burned with the effort. Gradually, the craft leveled off and the braves brought the canoe perpendicular to the swells.

Time and again, the canoe climbed the steep slope of a wave, hung precariously on the crest, then staggered in a terrifying descent to the trough below. They were being pushed from behind now, the once-northeasterly breeze having surrendered to near gale-like gusts from the west. The gray sky dimmed with the approach of evening, and eventually blackened with nightfall, chilling the winds.

Hawk spoke in English for the first time in hours. "We will not make land tonight. Lie down on the bottom. Cover yourselves as best you can. Perhaps the storm will break before dawn. Then we can set our course for the mission again."

The night dragged on. Sleep evaded Jennifer, though her mother curled close beside her and dozed from time to time. She prayed what seemed like a never-ending prayer for the Ojibways. Seven lives depended on their continued ability to keep the canoe upright in treacherous waters. The monotonous up-and-down motion of the vessel eventually rocked her into drowsiness, and Jennifer lapsed into troubled sleep.

She had no idea how long she had slept when voices disturbed her rest. Lifting her head, she discovered the first shreds of dawn backlighting the still-scudding clouds. Brother and Sister Woodworth huddled together in front of her. Beside her, Belle Crawford stirred from beneath her fur robe.

In the distance, Lake Superior raged furiously at the mouth of the Keweenaw Bay. To their right and a little behind, a dark point of land jutted from a hazy shoreline. From the gestures of the canoeman, Jennifer concluded that their conversation centered on this promontory.

"We will take shelter on the opposite side of that point." Hawk nodded, then shouted to his canoeman.

Three paddles hit the water in unison, and the trembling canoe swung into the wind. Stroke after stroke, the Ojibways fought the onrushing swells, panting and dripping with perspiration from their exertion against the headwinds of the storm.

We'll never make it! Jennifer fretted. With hands clasped so tightly together they ached, she prayed for the three on whose skill their very lives depended.

As the craft neared the promontory, the roar of pounding waves could be heard. Again and again, breakers crashed into jagged rocks at the end of the point, disintegrating into spray and foam to be washed away by the next wave. Rocky shoals surrounding the point added danger to their approach.

Jennifer was numb with fear. *Please Lord, don't let us drown.*

The canoemen steered on an angular course to the wind now, heading around the bluff, fighting to keep their distance from the deadly shallows. Great gusts from behind heaved them closer, swallowing Hawk's orders as he shouted to the canoemen in front. One swell after another pushed the canoe nearer the rugged boulders while Hawk, Gray Wolf and Red Wing stroked against a fatal destiny.

Finally, only a few yards separated them from safely clearing the last boulder. A wave rushed over the rock, obscuring it beneath several feet of water, then receded, exposing its jagged point. Only one swell cushioned them from its surface. With a supreme effort, the braves thrust their paddles into the crest of the wave—pushing, pushing, pushing. As they rode into the trough, Jennifer prayed their efforts had not been in vain. She turned to look behind her. Only inches of roiling water separated the rock from the stern of the canoe.

At last, calmer waters welcomed them on the leeward side of the promontory. Though the birchbark vessel still bobbed in the long swells, this was a smooth ride compared to the turbulent waves of the more open waters behind.

Jennifer sent up a fervent prayer of thanksgiving, wondering what other dangers might yet lie ahead. Still, they had come this far—

The canoemen rested their paddles while the craft drifted, then plied their way to the sandy beach tucked inside the cove. Pulling the canoe ashore, Hawk offered Jennifer a hand while his companions aided her mother and the Woodworths to solid ground.

Jennifer's legs, numb from hours of being folded beneath her in the canoe, gave way. Without hesitation, Hawk swung her up in his arms. Gratefully, she leaned her head against his chest.

He laid her on a dry stretch of sand, then knelt over her for a moment, a curious glint lighting his tired eyes.

"What? No scolding?" he teased.

Jennifer managed a weary smile. "How could I scold? I am truly grateful . . . but I'm surprised you could lift me at all after your battle with the waves." She began massaging her legs through the multiple layers of dress and petticoats.

Hawk dropped down beside her. "There is strength yet in my arms, but not enough to complete the journey to L'Anse. We will rest here for a few hours. When the storm lets up, we will move on."

As Hawk rose to leave, Jennifer put a restraining hand on his arm. "Hawk," she began self-consciously, "I want to thank you for bringing us this far in safety."

"I had thought you might be sorry I convinced you to ride in my canoe."

Jennifer looked into the eyes that appeared to change color as rapidly as the shifting currents of the water. An awkward silence stretched between them, and she could not think of an answer.

He turned away at last, taking the beach in a loping gait to rejoin his friends who were unloading their provisions.

Troubled, Jennifer got to her feet slowly, testing her cramped muscles before setting out to stretch her legs along the sandy shore. It appeared that the others were doing the same, and she maintained some distance from them so that she could have some time to think. Perhaps she *was* sorry she had stepped into Hawk's canoe, sorry she had encouraged her mother to come with her to L'Anse, only to expose her to such peril.

"You be all right, Jennifer?"

She turned to face Belle Crawford, noticing the fine lines of exhaustion in her face. "Yes, but you look very tired."

She smiled. "I be fine once I get to a real bed. That canoe isn't the best place to find a good night's rest. What about you? Perhaps you wish now you had not come, for the storm be with us still."

After the episode in Hancock, Jennifer was determined not to confess her shallow faith. Hawk thought her a helpless child. She must prove him wrong. "I know, but I am not as fearful as before. Oh, Mama, I guess I've grown up—at least a little—since we left home. I still don't like canoes, but I'll admit this one has served us well . . . and so have the men who brought us here."

She cast a sidelong glance in the direction of Hawk who was adding driftwood to a roaring fire, kindled by Gray Wolf and Red Wing.

"We be in good hands, it is true," her mother agreed. "Now, that fire be looking good." Belle chafed her arms vigorously. "Come. These old bones would be welcoming a little warmth."

Making their way to the campfire, the two women sank down on the sand, again protected from the damp by the plush robes. Raw hunger gnawed at Jennifer's stomach, and she looked longingly at the remaining provisions Hawk was drawing from a pack. To her surprise, the three Indians offered them generous portions, served on birchbark squares.

"Eat." Hawk handed her one of the crude plates.

Hungry as she was, Jennifer pushed it aside. "There is time enough for me to eat when we arrive at the mission. You'll need your strength."

"I have more. Eat," he ordered, "or you will weaken and grow ill." Hawk set the food beside her, then retreated to the opposite side of the fire, picked up a whole fish, and began tearing off the tender flesh with strong white teeth.

The others had been offered similar crude vessels filled with smoked fish, parched corn, and maple sugar.

"What should we do, Mama? It seems wrong taking their food."

Belle shrugged. "It appears their minds be made up to share with us."

"No doubt about it," Brother Woodworth interjected, overhearing this exchange. "They mean well, and to refuse would be the highest form of insult."

"Do eat what you are offered, my dear," urged his wife. "You'll find it tasty fare, if somewhat different from what you are accustomed to."

Jennifer bit into the smoked fish. It was delicious. The toasted flavor of the crunchy corn mixed delightfully on her tongue with the melting granules of maple sugar, and she consumed the entire meal with relish. She could see Hawk watching surreptiously, and he seemed pleased when she returned the platters, emptied of their contents.

Her hunger pangs sated, Jennifer grew drowsy, and bedded down on the soft fur robe. The rhythm of the breaking waves lulled her to sleep, and her last conscious thought was that of a tall Indian with dove-gray eyes and the aristocratic nose of the hawk.

Sometime later, Jennifer awoke. The pale sun was sinking wearily into the sea, tinging the thinning storm clouds with hints of umber and crimson. The wind had died down, but rolling waves still broke against the beach.

She brushed a hand across her eyes and scanned the shoreline, feeling something was amiss. It took her several seconds to realize— the canoe was gone!

chapter
3

THE OJIBWAYS WERE NOWHERE in sight. A few feet away, Jennifer's mother and the Woodworths huddled together by the fire.

Stretching, she moved nearer the them, extending her fingers to the flames for warmth. "Where is Hawk?" she asked lightly, attempting to conceal her anxiety.

Shading his eyes with his hand, Brother Woodworth gazed into the distance. "Hawk and his friends are scouting the river beyond the point." A tiny speck loomed larger on the horizon, and Jennifer could make out three figures, one broader and taller than the others.

The fragile craft arrived minutes later, bearing a grim-faced Hawk. His two companions beached the canoe and hurriedly loaded the provisions, instructing Brother Woodworth to cover the fire with sand.

"The wind and waves have subsided, at least for the moment," he reported. "It is safe to move on. Unfortunately, the storm blew us several miles off-course, and we will not arrive in L'Anse until long after nightfall."

The passengers took up their places in the hull, and the Ojibways shoved off the sandy beach, steering for the deeper waters of the channel.

Rounding the rocky promontory, while still a dangerous maneuver, posed less of a threat than it had when entering the cove. Once past that obstacle, they turned southward, stroking as one in silent concentration. Night fell, and with it, a darkness depriving them of all but the hazy luminescence of a cloud-streaked moon.

Hour after hour passed until the full darkness of a starless sky enveloped the birchbark vessel, shrouding its passengers. Jennifer wondered how she would endure the return journey two weeks hence. The perilous voyage had extracted its toll from them all.

From her cramped position, Anna Woodworth's reedy voice could be heard, lifted in a hymn of praise:

Praise the Savior, ye who know him!
Who can tell how much we owe Him?
Gladly let us render to Him
All we are and have.

One by one the others joined her, singing hymns until their repertoire was exhausted. Then, as before, they lapsed into a silence broken only by the rhythmic stroking of the paddles.

At last, Gray Wolf half-rose from his position in the bow, peering intently into the blackness.

"*Ickode!*"

His jubilant shout carried across the water on the remnants of a dying wind.

"Fire!" Hawk translated triumphantly.

"Guiding lights," Brother Woodworth interpreted, pointing at the coastline. "The Ojibways set signal fires along the water's edge to bring their travelers safely to shore."

Squinting into the darkness, Jennifer could barely make out a tiny flare. "There, Mama. I see it!"

"Praise be!"

Brother Woodworth spoke again. "They must have realized the wind had blown us across the bay to the east side, and set their fires accordingly. Of course, the mission lies three miles away from the Ojibway village, on the opposite shore."

Illumined by torchlight and the blazing signal fires, young boys, dressed only in breechcloths, ran along the shoreline, jabbering excitedly.

"Hawk, what are they saying?" Jennifer asked.

"We were given up for dead," he explained. "There will be great rejoicing this night."

"The Lord has been merciful," Belle murmured.

A shudder coursed through Jennifer at the thought of the near calamity, and she realized that the grief of the Ojibways for their brothers and sons would have been as keenly felt as that of her own father had she and her mother been reported lost in the storm. Suddenly she missed him very much.

Drumbeats sounded in a distinctive rhythm as the canoe glided alongside a crude dock. Gray Wolf and Red Wing leaped out, and Jennifer could see the expressions of relief and jubilance on the faces of their friends. There was much backslapping and cries of welcome, and she realized that no translation was necessary.

A discussion ensued between Hawk and a young brave—one of the villagers, who was apparently offering to relieve him on the short trip to the mission. But Hawk refused, and the birchbark vessel left the shore with only two replacements.

It was only a short while before the skilled oarsmen brought the canoe alongside the dock on the opposite shore of the bay. Candles burned in the windows of the mission house, beckoning four weary travelers.

Brother Woodworth stepped onto the dock, cupped his hands, and yelled, "Ho there! Gordon! Edith! We have arrived safely!"

The door of the house swung open, and the light spilled onto the pathway. Carrying lanterns, Brother Bentley and his wife hurried to greet them.

"Thank the good Lord!" Brother Bentley exclaimed, embracing his friend. "We feared for your lives in that fierce storm."

"Praise God, you're here!" echoed his wife.

The men steadied the canoe while Anna Woodworth, Belle Crawford, and Jennifer stepped ashore. Edith, who was a few inches shorter than Anna, hugged her friend.

"You must tell us about your journey," Gordon Bentley encouraged.

"Later, my friend. We've kept you up far too long already. But you must meet two ladies who proved to be worthy traveling companions. Mrs. Clinton Crawford—Sister Belle—and her daughter Jennifer."

Though Jennifer acknowledged the introduction with a polite smile, she was thinking of Hawk, who remained at his post in the stern of the vessel. He stood, arms crossed and feet spread wide, while the two braves shifted the cargo to their shoulders. The unloading was achieved efficiently, and when the young Ojibways disappeared up the path to the house, Jennifer found herself feeling strangely bereft. Soon Hawk would be gone and, with him, the singular aura of strength and serenity that had brought her comfort during the storm. Now she must rely once again on her own inner resources.

As the small group began their procession toward the house, Jennifer lingered behind.

In the flickering lamplight, she could not make out Hawk's features, but the proud set of his head did not betray his fatigue.

"Thank you, Hawk." The words uttered in a voice rough with exhaustion seemed pitifully inadequate. "I shall never forget you . . . what you did for me . . . for all of us."

A rare smile tugged at the corner of his sculpted mouth. "Nor shall I forget you, Jennifer." His smile faded, and he looked at her solemnly. "It is good to see this change in you."

"Change? What change?" Her face grew unusually warm, and she was grateful for the dark that masked the color invading her cheeks at his compliment.

"You are no longer afraid of my canoe." His deep voice held a hint of humor, then grew serious. "There were times when I myself doubted our safe arrival." He regarded her thoughtfully. "I hope you will not be sorry you have come."

Her mind raced back to the awkward moment on the beach in the cove. The question he had implied then had been similar. Again, Jennifer found herself unable to answer.

Behind her, Jennifer could hear Brother Woodworth thanking

the young braves. Evidently, he had returned to the dock with them to bid Hawk farewell.

"I—I must go now," she stammered. "Good night, Hawk."

As she turned to leave, she felt his eyes following her and remembered his lofty declaration. "You are my responsibility until I have delivered you safely to the mission dock." Well, now he had discharged his duty. He could return to his own people and put her out of his mind . . . as she would put him out of hers.

Leaving Brother Woodworth on the dock to send the Indians away with his blessing, Jennifer let herself into the two-story log structure, then followed the sound of voices to a common room where she slipped into a straight-backed chair.

Anna and Belle had been served tea and corncakes, and at Jennifer's entrance, Sister Bentley bustled off to the kitchen to fetch more.

"La," she clucked, "you must be hungry after your long journey. Here, my dear. Eat up. There's plenty."

She must heed her own advice, Jennifer thought, accepting the tin plate and cup from the good woman whose frame was pleasantly plump. Graying curls peeked from beneath Edith Bentley's cap, framing a round face. The kind blue eyes were a shade paler than Sister Woodworth's, and her left lid tended to droop, but her cordial manner put Jennifer immediately at ease.

"Thank you, Sister Bentley. I'm famished, but almost too tired to eat," she admitted.

Still, she bit into the corn square and, finding it deliciously moist and mealy, quickly finished it off.

"We're quite isolated here from others of our own kind," Gordon Bentley was explaining. "Edith dearly misses the times she spent with the ladies from our former parish in Detroit, so your visit will do her a world of good."

Brother Woodworth entered the room and joined his wife on a settee. He, too, was served, and conversation flowed easily for several minutes, while Jennifer's eyes grew heavy. She was nearly asleep in her chair when Sister Bentley spoke the words she longed to hear.

"What must we be thinking—keeping you from a good night's rest after all you've been through? There will be time enough for chatting and catching up. Come, now. To bed with you!"

The Woodworths were escorted to a room at the end of a hall, while Jennifer and Belle followed their hostess up a steep stairway.

Inside a generously proportioned bedroom, Edith turned back the covers of two beds lining the walls. "From here," she indicated the window positioned between the beds, "you'll be able to see the sun rise over the bay. Our table below your room looks out in the same direction, and I often enjoy a Keweenaw sunrise while sipping my morning tea."

At that moment Brother Bentley entered, setting their valises atop twin trunks positioned at the ends of the beds, then bade them a good night.

"Now, my dears," said their genial hostess, her curls bobbing, "can I get you anything more before you retire?"

"Oh, Sister Bentley, just to sink into that feather bed will be like heaven itself," sighed Belle.

"And for me, as well. You're very kind." Looking down, Jennifer eyed her disheveled appearance, the bottom of her skirt stained and torn. She did not require a mirror to know that her long dark hair was tangled and matted and filled with sand driven by the wind. Tomorrow she would welcome a bath, but for now—

Sister Bentley moved toward the door. "I can see you're tuckered out, poor dears, so I'll leave you until morning. Good night."

When Sister Bentley had closed the door behind her, Belle gave a long sigh. "Here at last. I be more than a mite tired. A real bed never looked so good." She smiled a tired smile, but Jennifer could still see a glimmer of excitement lighting her mother's eyes.

Peeling off their travel-stained clothing, they deposited the garments in a heap in the floor for laundering, and donned long nightgowns drawn from their portmanteaus. Then Belle extinguished the lamp before they climbed between the muslin sheets.

Weary beyond belief, Jennifer found herself still tossing restlessly on the stormy sea, feeling the buffeting winds and rolling swells beneath the thin bark of the canoe. Always before her was the image of the magnificent Indian who had steered their craft to a safe harbor.

"Mama?" Jennifer spoke softly into the night. "Are you still awake?"

"Yes, child . . . though I was thanking the good Lord for sparing our lives—"

"Mama, what do you think of the Ojibways?"

"All the Ojibways . . . or one in particular? You be taken with Hawk, I can tell."

"It's just that I've never known a man quite like him before. One minute, he's treating me like a troublesome child . . . the next . . . oh, I don't know . . . he's gentle and kind—"

"You needn't be ashamed of your feelings," Belle said. "We be made to enjoy the beauty of God's creation. Sometimes there be a beautiful sunrise, as Sister Bentley pointed out . . . and sometimes there be beautiful qualities in a sister or brother . . . like Hawk. Besides, Hawk be a fine specimen of a man."

Again, Jennifer felt the crimson tide flood her cheeks.

"Outside, the color of his skin be different," Belle continued. "Inside, where it counts, he be the same as you and I. He be loving the Lord, Jennifer, and that be the true test of a man." There was a long pause. "It be that quality that drew me to your papa, a poor Cornishman, unschooled as he was, and causes me to love him more today than on the day I married him."

Tears stung Jennifer's eyes as the meaning of her mother's words dawned clear. She had long suspected the inequity between her mother and father, and wondered what had attracted two such opposite people. For a moment she couldn't speak as a lump of emotion lodged itself firmly in her throat.

"Mama . . . what would I do without you?" she asked, but there was no answer. Belle Crawford had drifted into deep sleep.

Just before slumber claimed her, Jennifer savored her mother's words about Hawk. *Outside, the color of his skin be different,* she had said. *Inside, where it counts, he be the same as you and I. He be loving the Lord, Jennifer, and that be the true test of a man.*

Morning broke fair, but Jennifer and her mother rose too late to see the sun ascending over the bay. They were cheered, however, by the sight of the golden orb shining brightly, and the waters of the bay were calmer.

"Now why couldn't the weather 'ave been so fine yesterday and the day before?" Belle mused, turning away from the window to lay out her clothes for the day.

"As you've told me so many times in the past, Mama, only the Lord knows the answer to some questions," Jennifer reminded her.

Rushing to wash and dress, Jennifer and her mother joined the Woodworths and Bentleys downstairs for breakfast. Sister Bentley served large platefuls of muffins, freshly picked berries, eggs, and Jennifer ate her fill, convinced that she would never be hungry again.

Leaning back in his chair at last, Gordon Bentley regarded his old friend fondly. "Well, Brother Floyd, how about some fishing off the dock? The trout are running well this time of year, and Father Terhaust from the Catholic Mission has promised to join us later." He turned to Belle and Jennifer with an apologetic grin. "We men of the cloth may have some dispute over the finer points of theology, but when it comes to appreciating God's gifts of nature, we're cut from the same bolt."

There was a ripple of laughter at his pun, and Brother Woodworth agreed readily to the suggestion.

"Can't think of anything that would please me more. And it would give us time to discuss our mutual concerns about the mission."

After the men had gathered their fishing gear and ambled off toward the dock, the women made short work of the household tasks. Drawing water from the well out back, Edith Bentley set a large pot to boiling for laundry later in the day.

All morning, while the ladies reminisced over their chores, Jennifer was preoccupied with thoughts of the difficult journey that had brought them to this wilderness outpost. Mentally, as her hands were busy, she rehearsed the stages of the trip. It seemed months, rather than days, since she had left Eagle River, and she felt herself quite a different person from the headstrong young woman she had been. Still, there was much to learn about herself—and about Hawk.

The man fascinated her. He had faced death without flinching, more mindful of the comfort and safety of his passengers than of his own. Was this courage inherent in the Indian's traditionally stoic acceptance of fate, or was it the product of his new life in Christ? At times, he had even demonstrated a tender affection for her . . . or had she dreamed the whole thing? In any event, she must see him again, talk to him—

"Jennifer, dear, you haven't heard a thing we've been saying," Belle chided. "You be miles away."

Just three miles, Mama, Jennifer smiled to herself. And even that short distance to the Indian village, Hawk's home, now seemed interminable.

"I'm sorry, Mama. I guess I was daydreaming."

"Sister Bentley was just asking if we wished to visit the trading post. I could use a few things. It be sounding like a fine idea to me."

"John, one of our Christian Ojibway brothers, will take us," Edith Bentley explained.

"Would he take us across the bay—to the Indian village?" Jennifer blurted. "Papa spoke of it before we left, and I should very much like to see it."

Edith hesitated, the troubled look in her eyes exaggerated by her sagging left lid. "I'd feel better if we waited for another time, when our men could come with us. The Ojibways aren't accustomed to seeing unaccompanied white women in their village."

"I see," Jennifer answered, her voice quiet with disappointment.

To cover the awkward moment, Belle spoke up cheerfully. "Then the trading post it will be!"

"I'll fetch John, then," Edith said, hanging her apron on a peg before heading out the door.

Skimming the placid water of the bay was almost pleasant. With the sun shining down to caress her shoulders and lend warmth to a soft breeze, Jennifer relaxed and looked about with interest. Along the gently curving shoreline, sandstone outcroppings gave way to thick stands of white pine, aspen, and hemlock. Gulls soared overhead, piercing the air with their plaintive cries. In the light of day, Jennifer could orient herself to the bay's landmarks: the Ojibway village some three miles distant on the eastern shore, and their destination situated between and perhaps two miles to the south of it.

She listened as Sister Bentley expounded on wilderness living and the strides that had been made in the mission work during the past year. Then, nearing the shore, she began a lengthy monologue on the Crebassa family who ran the trading post.

"The Crebassas are highly respected in this area. Of their ten children, five are already grown. Peter Crebassa helped Father Baraga establish his Catholic mission here at L'Anse back in the early forties. Of course, they followed the Protestants by ten years, but the two missions have labored side by side amicably, for the most part."

Skillfully pulling the canoe alongside the dock, John held the craft steady while the ladies disembarked. Edith Bentley led the group up a trail toward a cluster of cabins, partially surrounded by the remnants of an old stockade fence. The most prominent building was a rounded log cabin, weathered by the years. This must be the post itself. Another rough-hewn structure had been recently whitewashed. Edith explained that this cabin housed the Crebassa family—Peter and Nancy and their remaining five children.

Lagging behind the others, Jennifer stooped to pick a wild daisy from the many growing along the path, adding to it some fragrant wintergreen. She allowed her mind to wander. What must it have been like twenty-five years ago, when the wilderness was yet untamed and Indians and wildlife posed daily threats to the settlers?

At that moment she heard the clear call of the whippoorwill. The sound aroused her curiosity, for she knew that bird sang only at night, unless flushed from a ground roost. Again, she heard the song and turned to see if she could spot the bird. Perhaps, inadvertently, she had stepped too near its nest.

When the sweet notes sounded for the third time, she recognized its origin. Hawk! Noiselessly, he appeared from behind a large birch.

"It was you! But how—" she began before he had closed the gap between them.

"All Ojibway boys learn the call of the whippoorwill from the time they are very young."

"You were convincing," Jennifer admitted. "Is there anything you don't do well?"

"There are certain things my culture has taught me." He shrugged aside her compliment. "One of them is to imitate the sounds of nature. Another is to stalk one's quarry without detection."

"And was I your quarry?" The impetuous question was out before she could stop the rush of words, and Hawk's gaze seemed to dwell on Jennifer's face. His gray eyes darkened, clouded perhaps by the shadows of the birches overhead, she thought. *What was he thinking? Why did he not speak?*

Flustered, she brought the bouquet she had collected to her nose, burying her face in its fragrance.

As they moved toward the trading post, Jennifer broke the profound silence. "I had hoped to visit your village today, but Sister Bentley discouraged us. She said we should wait until Brother Bentley and Brother Woodworth could accompany us."

"A wise decision," Hawk said. Before Jennifer could ask him for an explanation, he continued, "My father, the chief, has sent me to the Bentleys to invite all of you to a special feast."

Jennifer halted abruptly. Of course! She had forgotten that Hawk was the chief's son. He had probably been groomed since birth to succeed his father. She looked at Hawk again as if to size him up, but knew without taking inventory that the qualities he possessed might be expected in a man of noble birth.

"Is something wrong?" he asked, pausing with her on the path.

"No, nothing at all. I was just thinking how honored we would be to accept your father's invitation."

Hawk's silence neither confirmed nor contradicted her statement, but Jennifer was certain from the little she knew about the Indians, that few white women had been invited to feast with a chief of the Ojibway tribe.

They resumed walking, and Jennifer thought of a question she could not resist asking. "How did you know Sister Bentley was at the trading post, rather than at the mission?"

"As I paddled toward the mission, I recognized John's canoe. Often, Sister Bentley is with him wwhen he comes to trade at the post. It is a simple matter to keep track of our neighbors," Hawk explained. "I also know Brother Bentley and Brother Woodworth are fishing with Father Terhaust. Ojibways keep close watch over their village . . . and their friends." Though he didn't say so, Jennifer suspected they also kept close watch over their enemies.

As Jennifer and Hawk reached the trading post, she commented, "I still don't understand why my mother and I aren't allowed to visit your village alone. Would we be in danger there?"

"No . . . but you might feel uncomfortable. Some of my people have never seen white women except for Sister Bentley and Sister Woodworth."

"But you could escort us, Hawk," she persisted.

He moved his head from side to side, a look of amusement on his face. "Why does my village interest you so? A short while ago, you fled at the thought of stepping into my canoe."

Embarrassed, Jennifer stammered, "That . . . that was before I got to know you. I would not be afraid at all if you were there."

"It is best to wait until you can see the village in the company of other white people." His features were set, and Jennifer knew it would be useless to argue. "We live very differently from you. Some of our ways might seem . . . unusual . . . even barbaric."

Intrigued, she pressed him. "Then tell me about your people so I can be prepared." She sat down on the bench at the door of the trading post and indicated that he should sit beside her.

Ignoring her gesture, he stood towering over her. "It's not so simple." He frowned in exasperation. "I will teach you a few words of Ojibway. Then . . . perhaps . . . you will be ready to learn about our customs. Enough. I am here on business for my father." Stepping past her, he walked inside.

Jennifer followed right on his heels. By the time her eyes had grown accustomed to the dimly lit interior, Hawk had delivered his message to Sister Bentley.

"Saturday evening, then, Hawk?" she was saying.

He bowed and bade them a good day, then he stepped out the door without a backward glance.

Even in the pale light, Jennifer could read the look of delight on her mother's face and knew that it mirrored her own. Catching Belle's eye, she smiled, silently acknowledging their shared anticipation.

chapter
4

THE NEXT MORNING as Jennifer helped with the baking, her thoughts strayed often to the tall Indian on the opposite side of the bay. She was half expecting him, but as yet there had been no sign of him. More than once, she found herself in the embarrassing position of having to admit she had not been listening when one of the women sought her opinion on some subject. At those times, her mother favored her with an understanding wink, and Jennifer knew her private thoughts were not so private, after all.

Following lunch, while the others were napping, she wandered into the room where Brother Bentley did most of his studying in preparation for the Sunday sermons. Having learned of her desire to know more about the Ojibway people and their customs, he had invited her to examine his library.

Surveying the volumes lined up on the rough-hewn shelves, Jennifer pulled out a book on whose spine was hand-lettered the title, *Ojibway Dictionary*. Leafing through its pages, she discovered that the book was a compilation of hundreds of Ojibway words and phrases, along with their translations, entered by Brother Bentley himself. She began reading through the list.

Aki, earth. *Ahnede,* yes. *Equa,* woman. She skimmed down the page. *Neen-che-bah-penaindum,* I am very happy. *Ki kijewadis,* You are very kind. *Kendon jemokamon?* Do you speak English?

"This is hopeless. I can't learn the proper pronunciation without hearing the spoken language."

Frustrated, she returned the volume to the shelf and pulled out another—*Kitchi-Gami,* by Johann Georg Kohl. From the introduction, she learned that the author had spent a summer among the Lake Superior Ojibway in 1855.

In the first few pages, she made a number of startling discoveries about the women of the tribe. Disgusted, she snapped the book shut. Was this what Hawk wanted to explain to her before she visited his village?

She had respected him for his great strength and skill in bringing them safely through the storm. But if he shared the attitudes of his people toward women—

Regardless, Jennifer couldn't resist opening the book again. She read on, eagerly consuming page after page, filling her mind with facts with which to confront Hawk when she saw him again. Immersed in the text, she barely noticed the song of the whippoorwill floating through the window. Hearing it again, she laid the book aside and hurried outdoors. Perhaps she would have an opportunity to tell Hawk what she thought of Ojibway customs sooner than she had imagined!

Circling the mission house, Jennifer failed to spot Hawk until the call, *whippoorwill,* sounded again, and she saw him emerging from the woods along the path to the dock.

"*Bojo!*" he called.

She gave him a puzzled look. "*Bojo?*"

"*Bojo!*" he repeated. "It's the Ojibway greeting."

"It sounded more like *bonjour,*" she commented edgily, struggling to rein in her newfound rage.

"It's a corruption of that word. The Ojibways adopted it from French missionaries long ago," Hawk explained.

"This might be a good time for that lesson you promised me," she said, forcing a smile. "Come. We'll sit on the dock. The others are sleeping."

Jennifer preceded Hawk down the steep path to the water's edge and stepped onto the dock, perching on one of the pilings. Hawk dropped to the rough planking and swung his moccasined feet over the side.

The early afternoon sun glanced off the ripples on the bay, bathing Hawk's bronze body in its rays. Jennifer was glad his back was turned, for the sight of him filled her with a curious longing, and she almost forgot that she was angry.

Nervously she cleared her throat. "I'm not sure what you had planned, Hawk, but I have some questions for you."

"Ask them," he replied. "I shall try to answer."

"Who chops the firewood in your village?"

"The women."

"Who builds the wigwams and the lodges?"

"That is the work of women." He peered around at her, a furrow forming between his brows.

"Who plants the garden? Harvests the crops? Weaves mats and bags? Prepares the clothing? Makes the maple sugar? Cooks all the meals?" She flung her questions at him.

Hawk's expression grew solemn. "The women do all of these chores."

"Exactly!" Jennifer retorted, her anger rising.

"If you already knew, why did you ask?" he challenged.

"To make a point."

"What point? Explain carefully," he advised, his face a glowering mask.

"How can the men in your village sit by while the women do all the work?" she demanded.

"You are mistaken. The women carry out their duties. The men have theirs," Hawk countered, a spark of anger igniting in the depths of his eyes.

"Then tell me what they do besides make sport with their bows and arrows!"

Slowly he rose to his full height and leveled a look of disbelief at her. "My words will make no difference. You have made your decision concerning my people." His eyes were crystals of ice. "I thought we had forged a friendship. Perhaps I was mistaken."

He stepped to the edge of the pier and loosened the leather strap securing the canoe to its mooring.

"Wait, Hawk! Don't go!" Jennifer scrambled to her feet. "We *are* friends." She placed a placating hand on his arm.

He flicked his wrist, as if annoyed by her touch.

"Hawk, please forgive me," she begged. "I was wrong to let my emotions govern my tongue." Genuinely contrite, she added, "I want you to tell me about your people in your own way. I promise to listen and not interrupt."

He regarded her with an expression of doubt. "I question whether you can live up to such a promise."

Overwhelmed with remorse, she strengthened her argument. "I give you my word. And I think you know you can depend upon it."

Hawk searched her face, then dropped down again on the dock. For long moments, he made no reply. Jennifer waited, her heart in her throat.

"We live in two different worlds," he began, and Jennifer knew he was carefully weighing his words. "There is the white man's world, and there is the red man's world, and . . . I think . . . neither can ever completely understand the other."

He paused, looking far out past the bay. His gray eyes shimmered silver, reflecting the moving currents of the water.

"It is true that Ojibway women labor as you have mentioned, but it is a choice freely made—a service gladly given in return for the protection of their men." He spoke with an uncommon reverence for his way of life. "I know white people say Indian men are lazy. They do not understand. It is difficult for a man to keep meat in his lodge, provide skins for clothing, and protect his family from intruders. He must hunt big game even when the snow is many feet deep.

"When you come to our village, you will see other differences. Ojibways have always lived in bark-covered wigwams. Our people would not subject themselves to houses made of wood, where the walls do not breathe. And we prefer to rest our heads against the bosom of the earth rather than to sleep on feather mattresses high above the floor." He paused, his silvery eyes never blinking.

"Our people respect every living thing. It is our custom to give all objects a spirit." As if in anticipation of Jennifer's objection, he continued. "Though some Ojibways follow the teachings of Christ, many still do not, and the traditions white people call superstitions die hard. You will see charms on the cradles, or *tikinagan,* of our infants—a small pair of moccasins to ensure that the tiny Ojibway male will be fleet of foot; a bow and arrow so he will become a great hunter; a leather-covered ring to keep away illness. In generations to come, these customs will be abandoned. For now, old ways live side by side with the new."

Jennifer's eyes misted over, and Hawk turned a regal profile to her. At last, he spoke again—a gentle admonition.

"When you visit our village, observe our women and children. Decide for yourself whether or not they are content with their lot. But don't judge them by your standards. . . . This you must know, Jennifer,"—her name on his lips was like a caress—"the love of Jesus Christ lives in my heart. Because this is true, I can accept your ways . . . even if you are never able to accept mine."

There were no words to express the deep emotion of her heart. She sat in silence until the sun sank lower in the sky, never knowing just when Hawk left to retrace his watery path, back to his home and his people.

In the shadows of a birch tree beside the path, Belle Crawford wept openly, unashamed of the tears coursing down her cheeks.

Jennifer moved through the routine tasks of the next morning, subdued and contemplative. She had returned to the house after Hawk's departure the afternoon before, greatly moved by his stirring words, and unaware that her mother, too, had overheard them.

Brother Bentley's announcement at breakfast of an unexpected trip to the village brought a surprising mixture of anticipation and dread. Jennifer was not at all sure she was ready to see Hawk again this soon. She needed time to sort out the confusing implications of his words.

"Hurry, dear." Belle broke into her thoughts. "John is at the dock, waiting to take us to L'Anse. Since the Bentleys will be making sick calls, the Woodworths wanted to see their Indian friends again."

She spoke cheerfully enough, but Jennifer noticed the look of concern her mother cast in her direction, and wondered why.

The waters of the bay offered no resistance to the little craft, and soon the canoe slid neatly beside the crude pier. John stepped out, giving instructions in Ojibway to an Indian boy sitting cross-legged on the shore. Jumping to his feet, the youth sped up the bank on some urgent mission Jennifer had been unable to comprehend.

When he returned with Red Wing, she realized that it would be the young brave rather than Hawk who would act as their guide. There was more relief than disappointment in the discovery.

The party made its way to the top of the bluff. There, the forest opened to accommodate a thick cluster of bark huts. Though Hawk had tried to prepare her, Jennifer could not help feeling sorry for those who called such frail structures home. To think anyone could survive a winter in these flimsy accommodations chilled her despite the warmth of the July sun.

From her vantage point, she could see a series of trails criss-crossing the village, radiating from a long lodge situated at the edge of the forest on level ground high above the lake.

Taking one of the trails, Red Wing led the way, pointing out details of interest while Brother Woodworth interpreted.

"Walking Woman is using bark strips to weave a storage bag for wild rice." Jennifer marveled at the seamless container taking shape in the woman's skilled hands. "Her neighbor, Little Wind, is grinding corn." Little Wind, by pounding the end of a thick branch into a hollowed-out stump, reduced dried kernels to a fine meal.

Red Wing proceeded down the path, pausing to wait for Jennifer and Belle before he pointed out another woman. "Over there,

Yellow Wing is cleaning a deer hide." Next to a wigwam, a skin was spread on a log which had been braced at the foot of a stump. Sitting beside it, Yellow Wing scraped away the hair, using an iron blade set in a handle.

Everywhere Jennifer looked, the women were at work. Many of them looked up as the visitors passed, but quickly dropped their eyes. Jennifer noted the physical characteristics common among the Ojibway females—the broad, flat face; prominent features, and blue-black hair, devoid of curl. Most of them were as tall as Jennifer, a fact she found comforting, having considered herself an oddity at five feet, seven inches. But the Indian women appeared thick, their arms disproportionately slender, since they carried most of their weight through the torso. They were similarly attired in native buckskin, or tunics made of cotton and trimmed with braid or beads.

Half-naked children bloomed like a profusion of wildflowers, their pet dogs frisking about them. The game in progress seemed much like the game of tag that Jennifer had played as a child.

"Bojo! Bojo!" Jennifer called in greeting, and all but one of the small girls scattered at the sound of her voice.

"Bojo!" the child answered, then turned and ran, following her companions to a knoll a safe distance away.

"You be learning some Ojibway," Belle observed with interest, pausing to admire the plump-cheeked children.

"Only a few words," she confessed. "I thought it might be helpful when we meet the chief."

". . . or the chief's son." Belle smiled and moved on down the path where the Woodworths were deep in conversation with some elderly Ojibways.

Looking about, Jennifer noticed that all the women were busily engaged. If not at their weaving frames, they were grinding corn or crushing berries in large wooden bowls. Some, wearing cradle boards supporting sleeping infants, stirred steaming pots of pungent stew.

Intrigued by the aroma emanating from one pot, Jennifer moved closer to investigate and was rewarded with a shy smile.

The young Indian woman couldn't have been much older than Jennifer herself, but holding to the fringe of her skirt was a wide-eyed toddler and, playing with sticks nearby, another child of about three.

Searching the area, Jennifer noted the absence of all but the most elderly men. Upon closer inspection, she noticed a group of braves gathered behind one lodge. They appeared to be enjoying a game of chance, using a large wooden bowl containing several small, footed figurines. One young man took up the bowl from its hole in the ground, gave it a shake, and dropped it back into the hollow spot. When it landed, two of the figures stood upright, drawing murmured comments. Another man took the bowl and repeated the process. This time, several of the playing pieces landed on their feet, bringing a cry of delight from the lucky player.

Jennifer bit her lip, squelching the rage she felt at this frivolous activity done while wives and children toiled at chores that would keep them all clothed and fed throughout the winter.

Entering a densely wooded section of the trail, Jennifer hurried to catch up with the others, who had moved on to explore another area of the village. She failed to see the tall Indian observing her progress with interest before falling into step behind her.

Overhead, birds twittered and squirrels leaped from branch to branch, scolding the invaders of their sanctuary. The path was dappled with shifting patterns of light as determined rays of sun pierced the leafy canopy.

Suddenly, a dark shadow loomed ahead and, with a gasp, Jennifer whirled about.

"Hawk!"

"Peace, Jennifer. There is nothing to fear. It is only I."

She let out her breath, relieved. "You did give me a fright! I thought you were a bear."

"I have come to take you to my mother's lodge," he said, studying her.

"Your mother?"

"She has word you are here and wants to meet you."

"But how—"

"Have I not told you the Ojibway knows the movements of his friends at all times? Come." Decisively he stepped around her and she followed.

At a fork in the trail he motioned her to the right which opened into a small clearing. Here Jennifer found her mother and the Woodworths waiting in front of a wigwam that had been set slightly apart from the others.

At that moment a petite, dark-haired woman emerged to greet the party of visitors. A dog stayed close at her side, nuzzling her hand. The lady patted the animal, then embraced Anna and Floyd Woodworth, obviously delighted to see them again. The wolf-like dog growled low in his throat, but she silenced him with a word.

Speaking in Ojibway, Hawk brought his mother forward where Jennifer and Belle stood waiting.

"My mother, Canodens." On his tongue, the name sounded much like *Canada*.

The woman embraced Belle as if she had been an old friend. Then, turning to Jennifer, she said, "It is *honeur* to meet you, Jennifer," giving the name the soft, melodic pronunciation Hawk used. Unexpectedly, she took both Jennifer's hands in hers and brushed a kiss against each cheek.

"The honor is mine, Canodens," Jennifer murmured, thinking how very different this woman appeared from the other women of the village.

Though Canodens' complexion was dark, her wavy hair shone with reddish-brown highlights. The facial features were delicate and refined; the high cheekbones, regal rather than bold; the nose, finely sculpted. Jennifer concluded that she must be of mixed blood.

"Please come inside, out of sun," Canodens suggested.

Brother Bentley shook his head. "Thank you, but Edith and I have promised the Woodworths that they shall see Kawa."

Canodens nodded. "Hawk will guide you."

59

Jennifer followed her mother and Canodens into the low bark hut, passing through the hole which served as its door. Perhaps the others had conspired to leave them alone together. If so, she was grateful for the opportunity to get to know Hawk's mother.

Jennifer's first observation was that the bark on all sides of the lodge had been raised several inches off the ground. She understood when a cooling breeze found her. In spite of the openness, smoke from a small fire crackling beneath the smoke hole at the center penetrated the air, filling her nose with its pungent odor.

Canodens indicated woven mats on which Jennifer and her mother were to sit. The dog seemed to have his own place next to Canodens' mat, where he lay licking his paws.

From a pole near the center of the lodge hung various utensils, a sort of open Indian cupboard, Jennifer decided. Baskets, wooden bowls and spoons dangled by handles or leather thongs.

Canodens poured a beverage into small wooden bowls and offered them to Belle and Jennifer. "This is *anibishabo*, leaf-water," she explained.

Jennifer sipped the warm liquid. It reminded her of the herbal tea her mother sometimes concocted to calm her stomach.

Canodens took her place on the mat left of the doorway, sitting with one foot curled beneath her. "I pray all night during storm, when Hawk away. Thank God, you arrive safe." Her expressive face reflected her relief.

Though Canodens' simple English was inflected with a blend of French and Ojibway accents, mention of her Christian faith helped put Jennifer at ease.

Belle spoke up. "Canodens, where did you learn to speak English? And I've noticed a bit of a French accent, too."

"I learn English long ago, when little girl—at Indian boarding school, Mackinac Island. I forget most words now. *Mon Pére,* my father, he French Canadian. My mother, she Ojibway."

Jennifer couldn't resist asking, "And Hawk? He speaks such perfect English." She clapped a hand over her mouth, realizing she might have offended her hostess.

Chuckling, Canodens explained, "Miss Simpson teach Hawk. He learn much. He go college one year. When he come L'Anse again, *voila!* No accent!

"I didn't realize there was a school here," Jennifer commented.

Canodens smiled. "Mission school. Brother Bentley, he super . . . super . . . how you say?

"Supervise," Belle supplied.

"Yes. He supervise Miss Simpson."

"Does she live here, in your village?" Jennifer recalled one of the spinsters she knew in Eagle River. She couldn't imagine the woman surviving life in a wigwam, especially not in the wintertime.

"No. Miss Simpson live with LaFontes. In cabin. She not there now. She visit Detroit. Return soon. You meet." Canodens paused, smiling at her own thoughts. "When she here, Hawk much with her. He guide her. Mission make rule. She not be alone. For now, Hawk have time for you." Her gesture took in both Jennifer and her mother.

Jennifer flinched at the insinuation. It was evident that Miss Simpson had made a profound impression on Hawk. When she returned, he would take up his duties as her guide. *Why should that concern me?* she asked herself. *Hawk is not obligated to me in any way. We are simply friends.*

At that moment a young girl, whom Jennifer judged to be about thirteen, entered the wigwam, carrying a covered birchbark container. She bore the same refined features as Canodens, the same petite size, the same wavy hair falling to her waist. Though Jennifer smiled at her, the girl maintained a solemn expression.

After setting down her container, she muttered something to her mother and turned to leave, but Canodens gave a sharp command, and the girl came forward reluctantly.

"My daughter, Magidins," Canodens introduced, accenting the first syllable of the girl's name. "In your language, it mean 'Little Charlotte.'"

"Bojo," Magidins ducked her head in a gesture of acknowledgment, then quickly exited the lodge.

A troubled look clouded Canodens' features. "Magidins sad while Miss Simpson away. They good friends. They—"

Hawk's entrance brought his mother's explanation to a halt. "Ah," she said, "Hawk here now. He show you rest of village . . . and schoolhouse, *s'il vous plaît?* "

Hawk nodded.

Rising, Hawk's mother picked up the birch bark container Magidins had brought and offered it to Belle. "Take with you. Please. Maple sugar."

Jennifer rose to stand beside her mother. "You are very kind. We'll meet again soon . . . at the feast."

"I sorry," Canodens murmured. "I not see you then."

Puzzled, Jennifer asked, "Why not?"

"Hawk tell you," Canodens replied, appealing to her son with a look of distress.

He tipped his head. "The others are waiting. I will show you the school now." He urged Jennifer out the door with the gentle pressure of his hand against her back.

Outside the hut, Jennifer spoke, careful to keep her voice low. "Why won't I see your mother at the feast?"

There was a momentary flicker in the cool gray eyes, but the granite face remained impassive. "Now is not the time. I will explain later. Come. I will show you the schoolhouse now." He moved off down the trail before she could question him further.

Behind her, Jennifer could hear the Bentleys talking with her mother about Kawa. "He may be very old, but he still enjoys breeding the dogs," Brother Bentley commented.

"Just look at the pups frolicking over there." Sister Bentley pointed to a lodge a few yards away. "They're probably all from one of Kawa's spring litters."

Lost in her own thoughts, Jennifer allowed the three to pass her. Since Canodens' mention of Miss Simpson, she had been consumed with curiosity about the teacher's relationship with Hawk. *I wonder if Hawk is fond of her? Does he feel for her something more than gratitude?* Then she shrugged, putting the notion out of her mind. *How foolish of me! It's really none of my business!*

Calling to the trio ahead, Jennifer covered the distance between them just in time to enter another clearing. Here, a crude log structure crowned the crest of a promontory overlooking the bay. She estimated that they had circled back to this point some distance upshore from the dock where they had first landed.

Brother Bentley unlocked the door of the schoolhouse and beckoned them to enter. Inside, rough-hewn desks were arranged in rows facing a teacher's desk mounted on a slightly elevated platform. A stove in the center of the room obviously provided warmth for cold weather.

While the older people discussed the merits of education for the Indian children, Jennifer wandered outside.

The view from atop the fifty-foot cliff was breathtaking. For as far as the eye could see, the waters of the bay rippled in dazzling sunlight. Today there were only a few clouds, and these floated lazily in the sky-blue sea above. At her feet, ground pine, juniper, and kinnikinnick adorned the sandy loam of the bluff.

"This is an old Ojibway look-out," said Hawk, coming up soundlessly from behind her. "Over a hundred years ago, our tribe kept watch for Sioux and Fox invaders from the west."

"It's beautiful . . . and peaceful here." Jennifer felt a hot flush suffuse her cheeks and hoped that Hawk attributed her high color to the warmth of the sun and not to his own disturbing presence.

"Jennifer," he said, inspecting her closely, "it is now time to tell you why my mother cannot be at the table during the feast."

"I should think, as the chief's wife, her place would be beside her husband."

"Ojibway custom forbids." A slight frown disturbed the serene countenance.

"Why? Do women eat at separate tables? Is that it?" The idea seemed preposterous.

"That is true, but—"

"Then I'll sit beside your mother at her table," Jennifer

interrupted. "If she and the other women can't eat at your father's table, then neither will I!"

"There is more you should know," Hawk began, his lips thinning in displeasure.

She lifted a brow, waiting for him to go on.

He set his face toward the far horizon and continued. "The women will spend several hours before the feast, preparing game. They will serve the men and our honored guests. As one of the guests, you must eat at my father's table, not with my mother."

Jennifer shook her head obstinately. "No. I'll work alongside your mother to prepare the feast, and I'll eat beside her, too."

"What you are suggesting is unthinkable. Such an act would be the supreme insult to my father. Better that you did not come at all than to disgrace yourself and your people."

"Why should I be held in higher esteem than your father's wife— your own mother?" Jennifer demanded, her temper flaring. "How can I accept your people when so much is expected of the women, and so little of the men? From what I can see, there wouldn't be any feast at all if it weren't for all the work done by the women!"

"Yes?" Hawk's eyes glittered dangerously, the cool gray marble sparking with unexpected fire. "Who hunts game for the table?"

"Maybe the men stalk a few animals beforehand, but it doesn't seem like much effort compared with the hard labor of the women," she retorted. "Then to be banned from the feast table . . . it's just . . . too much to accept." She spun away in a whirl of petticoats.

Hawk's steel grip brought her about to face him. "Can't you understand? My father wishes to honor your customs by asking you to feast at his table. It's not your place to judge the way of our women."

"But they're being treated unfairly," Jennifer protested. "Why hasn't anyone told them that their living conditions are . . . are primitive? The missionaries, for example?"

For a long moment, Hawk stood rigid. In his face was a look Jennifer had never seen there. It frightened her.

"Because," he began in a voice edged with ice, "the missionaries have learned something that you have not. Change comes slowly here. Don't force your ideas on our women. It will only lead to trouble."

With that warning, he released her arm, turned on his heel, and strode away.

chapter
5

A CONFUSING JUMBLE OF EMOTIONS plagued Jennifer as she watched Hawk melt into the forest. Perhaps he was right. She was the stranger here. Yet, she thought of the young woman she had seen laboring in the hot sun over her cooking fire, three small children surrounding her. Her lot seemed harsh indeed.

Sighing deeply, Jennifer turned to retrace her steps to the schoolhouse, passing a wooded ravine. Off to her left, a riot of wild roses, daisies, and woodlilies flourished in the sunlit schoolyard. She couldn't resist picking a handful.

Looking up, she saw that Hawk had reappeared to escort them back to the village. He did not glance in her direction, but made a brief remark to Brother Bentley and started off down the trail. She followed close behind the little group, sensing the wisdom of keeping some distance between herself and the young brave.

As before, several small children lined the pathway to watch with curious brown eyes.

"*Bojo!* Hello!" She greeted one little girl, bending down to offer her a daisy. The child stepped back, seemingly ready to flee. Jennifer smiled her most encouraging smile and repeated the greeting. "*Bojo!* This is for you!"

The girl seemed both fascinated and intimidated by Jennifer's attention. Hesitantly, she inched forward until she could pluck the flower from between Jennifer's fingers, then stepped back, returning her smile. Meanwhile, the other children gathered their courage and began closing in around their peer. Jennifer offered a second flower to another of the girls. She accepted the proffered gift with an Ojibway phrase Jennifer took to mean, "Thank you." Again and again, the process was repeated until the flowers were gone.

Feeling bolder now, the first child stepped forward and pointed to herself. "Me Mani. Me Mani." Pointing to Jennifer, she asked, "You?"

Surprised at the young girl's attempt at English, she quickly answered, "Jennifer." At the young girl's puzzled expression, she repeated, more slowly this time, "Jen-ni-fer."

"Jen—" The child tried gamely to reproduce the sound.

"Jen-ni-fer," she sounded out the syllables.

With a concentration which brought wrinkles to the child's smooth brow, she tried the name again. "Jen-ni—"

Jennifer pointed to herself and nodded, "Jen-ny," approving the shortened version of her name.

"Jen-ny, Jen-ny," the little girl chanted happily. And from the bright-eyed youngsters clustered about her came the childish chorus, "Jen-ny, Jen-ny."

"Yes, that's right. Jenny." She smiled. Then, rising from her stooped position, she said, *Bojo.* I must go now."

Mani spoke over the murmurs of her friends. "Jenny . . . go?"

"Yes, but I'll return very soon." Realizing the little ones did not understand her words, she opened her arms wide in a gesture of love.

When Jennifer turned to continue along the path to the dock, she found Hawk waiting patiently for her. The children followed them to the edge of the bluff, their dogs romping among them, and watched as the party descended the slope.

Before reaching the canoe, Hawk broke the awkward silence between them. "The small ones like you. That is good." Any trace of his former anger seemed to have vanished.

"I tried to teach them my name," Jennifer chattered, pleased with his renewed attention, "but we had to compromise on an abbreviation."

To her amazement, Hawk chuckled. "Your name is difficult for us. There is no 'f' and no 'r' in the Ojibway language."

"But *you* pronounce it . . . beautifully," Jennifer pointed out.

"I worked hard when I went away to the white man's school. It is not pleasant to be the object of ridicule."

Jennifer felt a stab of sympathy for the dark-skinned stranger who had braved an alien world to help his people.

Hawk helped her into the canoe, and she took a seat on a pile of furs in the stern of the boat. Behind her, Hawk positioned himself for the return trip, explaining that John wished to visit longer with his relatives in the village. Her mother, the Woodworths, and Mrs. Bentley were already comfortably ensconced in the center of the canoe, while Brother Bentley took up the paddle at the front. Though Jennifer could only turn halfway around for fear of tipping the canoe, she could see the many small faces crowding the edge of the bluff to see them off, and she gave them a final jaunty wave.

With the canoe well out into the bay, Jennifer ventured a comment to Hawk over her shoulder. "Your mother said you spend most of your time as a guide to Miss Simpson when she is in L'Anse. I hope I shall have a chance to meet her."

"You will meet her . . . soon."

Jennifer yearned to see the expression on Hawk's face as he spoke. Perhaps she could read in his eyes what was not revealed in his voice. But she remained fixed in her position, her face toward the bow. *Why does this trouble me so?* she pondered. *What difference does it make what Hawk may feel for this woman? I've known him for only a few days*—And her heart answered, *Long enough to feel. . . . Long enough to know.*

She was jolted to consciousness by the sound of birchbark sliding against the pilings of the dock. The trip across the bay had passed more quickly than usual.

Springing lightly to the planking, Hawk assisted the women, then fell behind as they proceeded up the bank toward the mission house trail. Jennifer thought it strange that he did not take the lead as he usually did, but at the doorstep, his reason was made clear.

Drawing her mother aside, Hawk asked, "Sister Crawford, may I speak with you?"

A look of surprise on her face, Belle nodded, then stepped aside to let the Woodworths and Bentleys pass.

Feeling awkward, Jennifer excused herself. "I'll go in and help Sister Bentley with supper."

She reached for the latch of the door, but Hawk restrained her with a touch. "Please. Don't go. You should hear what I have to say."

Taking shape in her mind were memories of their discussions— her fiery barrage of questions about the plight of the women, his thoughtful answers; her refusal to accept Ojibway tradition, his calm defense of them; her angry threat to express her disapproval; his stern warning. . . . How humiliating if he were to tell her mother! Perhaps he would even ask Belle to caution Jennifer about her attitude in order to avoid problems at the feast!

Lifting her eyes to Hawk's in a silent plea, Jennifer thought he had never seemed more remote. Tall and majestic, his Indian heritage was supremely evident, with only the pale eyes betraying his link with the white race.

He squared his shoulders, broadening his bare chest. "Sister Crawford," he began, "when I went away to the white man's school, I learned much about your customs. I learned that, if a gentleman wished to spend time with a young lady, he asked permission of her parents. So I ask you now. May I call on Jennifer during your stay at L'Anse?"

Jennifer had to stifle a giggle. The idea of this noble man humbling himself in respect for a ridiculous custom was almost as humorous as it was gallant.

Belle smiled as she regarded the young man before her. Her face was alight with pleasure. "Hawk, you are a one," she said fondly. "You have proven to be our friend many times over. Of course, you have my permission. The question is, do you have Jennifer's?" She turned to go inside, laying her hand on her daughter's shoulder for an instant as she passed.

Suddenly, Jennifer was alone with Hawk, her mind reeling with a thousand thoughts. *This is no ordinary Indian. I've never known anyone quite like him. But we're worlds apart. And why would he want to call on me after all I've said today?*

"Do I have your permission, Jennifer?" His voice flowed like honey, rich and golden.

In an effort to lighten the atmosphere, she shrugged. "It seems you already have—called on me, that is—yesterday. Remember? Or did you come only to prove how very different we are?"

Uncharacteristically, Hawk shifted his weight, burying the toe of his moccasin in some loose soil. "I would have asked yesterday, but your mother was napping. Besides, it was just as well that I waited until now." He lifted his head and pierced her heart with his penetrating gaze. "Perhaps something of great importance passed between us."

There was deep meaning hidden in his words, and Jennifer found herself staring into those incredible eyes, now taking on the hue of forest green. She was unable to do more than nod mutely.

Instantly he was off, his lithe body taking the trail at a graceful lope. She watched him untether his canoe and take up the paddle, sending the craft skimming across the shining waters, as straight as the flight of an arrow.

He must care about me, she thought, *but why? Nothing can ever come of our friendship once I leave L'Anse.*

Smiling to herself, Jennifer resolved to enjoy Hawk's company while she could. These few days of adventure would be forgotten soon enough once she left the mission. But for now, the trip was serving its purpose well. Since she had laid eyes on this remarkable man, she had barely given the devastating fire a thought.

Jennifer sat alone on the dock, watching the sun set. Floating in the evening air from the common room, she could hear the voices of her mother and their friends reminiscing about their youth.

It was dark by the time Jennifer made her way inside and up the stairs to the room she shared with her mother. Moments later, Belle appeared, attempting to hide a yawn behind a slender hand.

"'Tis been a long day, Jennifer," she said. "And an eventful one, I'll wager." She cast a knowing look at her daughter.

Jennifer did not respond immediately, but sat on the edge of her bed in her nightgown, still weighing what had taken place between herself and Hawk.

"Mama," she said at last, "what were you thinking when Hawk asked permission to see me? The look on your face was so strange. You seemed lost in another world."

Belle, who had been brushing her long blond hair, laid aside the brush. "I be thinking of myself when I be your age, and your father paid me court. So full of adventure, he was, with his talk of sailing across the Atlantic to live in the Keweenaw. That trip and this one seem much alike."

Jennifer narrowed her dark eyes, studying her mother intently. "You must have loved Papa very much to risk so much for him . . . leaving Cornwall to live in a strange land."

"That I did," Belle reflected. "I look at you and see myself as I was then . . . so young and strong and full of questions about what life be having in store. It takes courage, that it does, to strike out into the unknown."

Jennifer made a wry face. "It seems I was short on courage the day Hawk had to coax me into his canoe." The two women chuckled. After a time, Jennifer continued. "Mama, you're much braver than I. You didn't even hesitate that day."

Her mother shrugged. "But, Jennifer, you saved the three of us from the fire."

"Our lives were at stake. I had no choice. To make a conscious decision to leave home is a different matter."

"You chose to come to L'Anse," Belle reminded her.

"But I wasn't looking for adventure. I was running away. I thought this would be a safe place to escape from memories of the fire," she confessed. "Of course, I hadn't counted on the storm."

"Still, you came through just fine, and I be proud of you. Now, it's time for sleep. Brave or not, I be planning to store up memories to take home to Clifton," Belle said, plumping her feather pillow. "Tomorrow, I be exploring these trails while the Woodworths and the Bentleys be making calls. Will you be seeing Hawk?"

"I don't know, Mama. He didn't say. I'm still learning how to interpret the things he *doesn't* say."

Pulling back the covers, Belle slipped between the sheets. "He'll be here," she said confidently, extinguishing the light on the stand beside the bed. "Sweet dreams."

"Sweet dreams, Mama." But Jennifer lay awake long into the night, thinking of the gulf that separated her from Hawk—a gulf far greater than the waters of L'Anse Bay.

" 'It is said that the yell of the poor bear, when crushed beneath this merciless weight, is frequently heartrending, and very like the cry of a suffering man.' " Jennifer closed the book, *Kitchi-Gami*, and laid it aside. Kohl's description of the bear trap used by the Ojibway was fascinating, but not enough to claim her complete attention.

For two hours she had read, hoping to pass the time until Hawk appeared. Still, he had not told her when to expect him. Indians apparently had no concept of time. It was all so frustrating.

She worried about her mother, too, alone in the woods. Though Belle had assured her daughter she would not stray from the trails, Jennifer wondered what could have kept her mother's interest since well before lunch. She shook her head as she recalled her mother's departing words.

"Now don't you give a thought about me today. My sandwich be in my pocket. I'll be back when my feet give out." She had kissed her daughter's cheek and wagged her finger. "And give Hawk my greeting when you see him."

Jennifer paced back and forth across the small room, wondering whether she should go looking for her mother, or wait in the hope that Hawk would soon arrive to go with her. The Woodworths and Bentleys had taken the canoe to make their visits, so she couldn't ask their advice, nor could she paddle to the Ojibway village to seek Hawk's aid.

Suppose her mother had gotten hurt, and couldn't walk? Suppose she had stumbled into . . . Jennifer gasped at her own thoughts . . . an Ojibway bear trap? She could be crushed beneath the weight of a rock-laden log!

The possibility galvanized her into action. Taking pen and paper in hand, she dashed off a note, saying she had gone looking for her mother, included the time—three o'clock—then wedged the note between the door and its frame.

The trail behind the mission house led her first past the neighboring Catholic Mission, then southward in the general direction of the trading post. The path between the trees seemed well traveled, the soil having been worn away until it was recessed by several inches. She set a rapid pace, pulling her skirts close about her and ducking beneath the overhanging tree branches along the way.

Always on the lookout, she worried that her mother might have struck off from this main trail at some point to venture into the forest and had become so lost she might never find her way back. Belle was an avid student of nature. The sighting of lady's tresses preparing to bloom, or the "see-bit, see-bit" song of a Nashville warbler could have beckoned her mother astray. With only her instinct to guide her, Jennifer stayed with the trail, her legs soon feeling the strain of her pace, and her heart thumping faster and louder with the effort.

"Mama! Mama!" she hollered, then paused to wait for a response. The forest answered only with an eerie silence.

Eventually, the trail intersected with a less well-traveled path. *Dear Lord, which way should I go now?* The narrower trail seemed just the sort of path her mother would have chosen. She decided to follow it.

Curving around a dense stand of trees and cutting past several outcroppings of rock, she could barely distinguish its direction at times. But the moment she took her eyes off her feet to get her bearings, she stubbed her toe on one of the many stones littering the trail.

When she came to a granite boulder, she paused to rest, drawing her knees beneath her chin. From her perch, she observed her surroundings, catching a glimpse of the blue bay through an opening in the branches. Evidently, the trail followed a course near the shoreline. Gulls called to one another, their cries magnified by the open water and carried to her on a gentle breeze. Remembering the beach at Eagle River, a lump formed in Jennifer's throat.

She listened for a few minutes, massaging her feet through the thin leather of her shoes. Very faintly, she detected the cry of some other bird blending with that of the gulls. She tucked a strand of long, dark hair behind one ear to listen.

"Elll . . . elll . . ."

The cry was almost human. Jennifer was tempted to leave the difficult trail and cut through the woods toward the shoreline to see if she could spot the bird responsible for the haunting call, but she was afraid to leave the path, poorly marked as it was. She waited, hoping to hear the call again.

"Elll . . . elll . . ."

There it was again. Disturbed by the sound, Jennifer slid from the boulder and tried to fix its location in her mind. Recalling something Hawk had said in one of their conversations, she dislodged several small rocks from the ground nearby and balanced them in the crags of the granite boulder and on its summit. Finding a fallen branch, she broke off a sturdy twig, stripped it bare, and scratched an arrow in the thin soil, pointing in the direction she would head. She laid it on the dirt along with two smaller twigs to form a stick arrow.

Pushing her way past prickly hemlock boughs, she struck off toward the bay. Needles scratched her hands and face and tangled with her hair, tugging painfully at her scalp. Stopping to free several knotted strands, she heard the call again, this time, more distinctly.

"Help me! Somebody, please help!"

It had to be her mother's voice! Jennifer fumbled with the

stubborn pine branch, finally forfeiting some of her hair by pulling the twig free with a sharp yank.

She cupped her hands to her mouth and filled her lungs with air. "Mama, where are you?"

"Over here! Near the water! Help!"

The response drew Jennifer toward the bay, and to her left. She fought her way through the underbrush growing at the edge of the forest, beating back the shin-tangle tearing at her skirt. At last, she stood atop the sandstone cliff overlooking the bay, and searched for signs of life along the rugged shore to the west.

"Here! Over here!"

Spotting a white speck against the jagged, red sandstone, Jennifer hurried across an opening to the area. Belle had fallen about halfway down the treacherous bluff and had lodged against a scrub white cedar, its bent trunk growing out and up from the face of the cliff. Somehow she had managed to pull herself up over its trunk, wrapping her arms and legs tightly about the tree.

"I'm coming, Mama! Hold on!"

Dense underbrush lay ahead. Jennifer picked her way along the precipice, grabbing balsam branches to steady herself as she fought for footing in the thickets at the edge of the cliff. Prickly limbs caught fast in the lace edging of her cuff. She jerked her wrist free, leaving a scrap of white lace behind. Hand over hand, she struggled on, hugging the thorny scrub that clawed at her delicate skin. Steeling herself against the pain of her scratches, she dug in her toes and sidestepped her way toward her mother. Eventually, the edge of the cliff opened up and Jennifer ran across a bare stretch of ground.

"Careful!" Belle warned.

Surveying the distance between herself and her mother, Jennifer discovered that the next stretch of bluff was even more thickly overgrown than the last. If she could make her way past it, she would be directly above her mother.

Gritting her teeth, she plunged her hands into the brambles, feeling blindly with her foot for her next toehold. Kicking against the ground cover, she wedged her right foot in, then brought her left foot alongside it. Replacing one foot with the other, she progressed slowly.

"Get help!" her mother shouted. "You can't make it!"

Jennifer's heart pounded furiously, but fear for her mother's life drove her on. "Lord, please help me," she prayed.

Palms damp with sweat, she forced her way along the cliff, step after step, handful after handful of scratchy needles. Suddenly, her toes slipped off the ledge. She felt herself falling and tightened her grip on the prickly boughs. Sharp needles ground into her flesh as the branches bent with her weight, lowering her over the side.

Attempting to gain a toehold, she kicked against the face of the cliff, but the soft rock crumbled and fell away beneath her. She tried to pull herself up, but her aching arms lacked the strength. Inch by inch, she felt her hands slipping down the pine boughs.

chapter
6

ONE MOMENT JENNIFER WAS SLIDING into space, the next, her position was reversed. Someone had grasped her firmly by the wrists and was hauling her up, to the top and over the edge of the cliff.

Jennifer opened her eyes and looked into the face of her rescuer. Hawk!

"My mother—"

"I know. Hurry." He held her close as they made their way toward Belle.

The strength of Hawk's embrace fortified Jennifer, though her knees trembled under the impact of their dilemma. Within moments, they were standing a few feet from her mother.

Below the top of the bluff, just out of reach, a ridge was sculpted into the face of the cliff. Beneath this ridge was the tree bearing Belle Crawford's slim form.

"Hawk, hurry!" Belle pleaded, struggling to keep her balance on the scrub pine.

"Hold on!'" Hawk's voice was steadying, and Jennifer found herself somewhat reassured.

She panicked, however, when she discovered that he had disappeared into the thick brambles, returning with a length of grapevine. Inspecting the vine, he grunted his dissatisfaction and quickly discarded it. Dropping to one knee, Hawk drew his knife from its sheath and began ripping his buckskin breeches from knee to ankle. When he had torn about a dozen lengths, he knotted them together to form a long rope.

The brave tied one end of the rope around his waist, made a large loop in the opposite end, and lowered it to Belle. "Put the loop under your arms!"

Belle let go of the tree and grabbed the rope, working it over her head and beneath her arms.

"I will pull you up now. Brace your feet against the cliff and walk up the side. Trust your weight to the rope."

Hawk backed away from the edge of the cliff into the brambles.

As Belle worked her way toward the ridge, Jennifer warned frantically, "Easy, Hawk! Go slow! She's almost to the—" Just then, her mother lost her footing. Jennifer gasped. "Don't let go!" she begged. Her mother dangled against the cliff. At the other end of the rope, Jennifer could hear bushes snapping and knew Hawk had fallen.

"Mama slipped!" A fresh wave of fear overwhelmed her.

Instantly Hawk was on his feet, pulling the rope taut.

Her mother approached the ridge for the second time. Jennifer prayed fervently. "Please, Lord! Help her!"

With a groan, Belle mounted the ridge.

Jennifer watched the makeshift rope as it slid past, spotting a loose knot several inches below the top of the cliff. Flinging herself to the ground, she lay face down and took hold of the buckskin thong below the weakened area. Straining to take the pressure off the knot, she hung on for dear life.

Slowly . . . oh, so slowly . . . Belle progressed toward her daughter, their hands two feet apart on the rope . . . a foot apart . . . mere inches . . .

Suddenly the knot gave way, searing the flesh as it slipped through Jennifer's fingers. Desperate, she tightened her grip on the shortened leather.

Behind her, she heard Hawk crash into the thicket. Below, her mother struggled to find a toehold in the cliff. Now bearing Belle's full weight, Jennifer felt herself being tugged relentlessly toward the edge.

"Hawk!" Jennifer cried, half-sobbing in frustration. "Help!"

The next moments were a blur. She dug her toes into the ground, praying they would catch a root . . . a rock . . . anything! Faster and faster she slid across the surface of the bluff.

She heard the sound of Hawk's body crashing through the underbrush, felt his hands on her ankles, drawing her away from the edge. She could feel the tender skin scraping against the rough ground.

Working his way forward, Hawk added his strength to the fragment of rope still holding Belle and pulled, hand over hand. Jennifer watched in profound relief as her mother's head appeared at the top of the cliff. Belle eased herself over the edge to safety, collapsing in an exhausted heap.

When she could catch her breath, Belle reached for Jennifer, and the two women clung together, sobbing hysterically.

"Jennifer . . . oh Jennifer!" She brushed her daughter's tear-stained cheek. "I thought—"

"Hush, Mama," Jennifer soothed. "We're safe now."

When they released each other, Hawk squatted beside them. "Sister Crawford, are you all right?"

Belle looked into the young brave's face. "Thanks be . . . thanks be," she took a long breath, "to the good Lord . . . and to you. She closed her eyes wearily. "I be needing . . . to rest."

"You will soon be resting in your own bed, Sister Crawford." Turning to Jennifer, he examined her scratches with a practiced hand. "And you, Jennifer. I will help you cleanse your wounds when we return to the mission."

Jennifer looked into his eyes, reading a wealth of emotion there. She smiled weakly, noticing for the first time his disheveled appearance and the oozing scratches on his now bare legs, and a flood of tenderness rushed over her. "And I will tend yours," she said softly.

He leaned back on his haunches, one hand shielding his eyes as

JENNY OF L'ANSE BAY

he noted the location of the sun in the sky. "We should start back soon. The Bentleys and Woodworths will worry."

Gently lifting Jennifer to her feet, Hawk bent to help Belle. Together, they supported her on the walk back.

"How did you find us?" Belle asked, when at last her strength returned.

"Sister Bentley told me Jennifer had gone looking for you. I set out to find her. I found a stick arrow beside a boulder . . . and this." From a pouch hanging at his waist, he produced a bit of white lace and handed it to Jennifer.

She recognized it immediately. "How did you manage to see such a small thing?"

He did not reply at once. Finally, he said, "It was a part of you." His simple explanation filled Jennifer with a tingling warmth.

Without warning, Hawk halted abruptly, signaling the women to follow suit. "There, to the left—an Ojibway bear trap." He pointed to the cleverly disguised device and left the path to examine it, kneeling some distance away.

Jennifer gasped. "One of those horrible contraptions with logs and rocks heavy enough to crush a bear's back?"

"How did you know about the *l'assommeur?*"

"I read about it in a book. Now I can see for myself that everything that was written about it is true. A person could be killed as easily as a bear!"

A mocking smile curved his mouth as he looked back at her. "So *that's* how you've been learning about Ojibway customs."

Annoyed, Jennifer retorted, "Yes, from a book written by a man named Kohl. What could possibly be wrong with that?"

"Nothing. Mr. Kohl writes well, but he writes as the white man sees, not as the Ojibway sees." Hawk sprang to his feet with the quiet grace of a cat's leap.

This elegant movement, along with Hawk's words, reminded Jennifer that in spite of his one-quarter white blood and his ability to speak near-perfect English, Hawk was first of all an Indian.

As Hawk continued to lead them through the forest, stopping

occasionally so Belle could rest, Jennifer realized that she and her mother had taken a circuitous path. Hawk's trail was shorter and straighter, bringing them to the mission house in half the time.

The Bentleys and Woodworths welcomed them with sighs of relief and profuse words of gratitude to Hawk. Edith Bentley set a kettle to boil for herb tea, and mixed the ingredients for a poultice to apply to cuts and bruises. Meanwhile, they insisted that Belle rest in the best chair, and Anna Woodworth fetched pillows and a shawl for her lap.

"I'm sorry to be the cause of worry," Belle said, holding Jennifer's hand as her daughter rested at her feet. "I be so taken with the birds, I didn't pay attention to my feet and, before I knew it, the edge of the bluff gave way. Thanks be to the good Lord—and to Hawk here—everything turned out well."

All eyes turned to the handsome brave, who stood by, waiting to be sure his charges were well cared for before taking his leave.

"La, Hawk!" Sister Bentley cried. "Just look at you! However did you shred your trousers? And you need something on those cuts, son!"

The Indian looked down, and Jennifer sensed his embarrassment. "It is nothing. We needed a rope for Sister Crawford—"

Deftly Jennifer changed the subject. "I'll draw some more water for the poultice. Hawk, will you help me?"

He was at her side in an instant, leading the way to the well outside the back door. Drawing a bucket of fresh water, Hawk took the cloth from her hand and dipped it into the bucket. "We must care for your wounds, too," he said, squeezing the water from the towel and dabbing at the bleeding cuts on her right arm. Carefully, he blotted away smudges of dirt. His touch was so delicate that she felt no pain from his ministrations.

When he had repeated the process with her left arm, he allowed her to sponge off the worst of his own scratches. Then, he took the towel from her and dropped it into the bucket to soak. Facing Jennifer, he lifted her chin and looked deep into her eyes. "I could not easily forgive myself if you had been badly hurt today. You should not go wandering off," he scolded tenderly.

She stepped away, tossing her head in defiance. "It was Mama who went wandering off! I only went to find her. I would never have left the cabin if I hadn't read about those awful bear traps. I was afraid she had stumbled into one and gotten hurt. As it turns out, she might have!"

"I understand," Hawk sighed. "You blame my people for your troubles. It is ever so."

"That's not exactly what I mean—"

"Tomorrow," he stated firmly, "I will take you to my village. You will spend the day with my mother in preparation for the feast. You offered your help. We will accept it, and you will find out more about our ways."

"Good!" she interjected, but her comment went unnoticed.

"By the time you're done, you will know Ojibway women are not unhappy with their lives."

Jennifer awoke at sunrise the following morning and, except for some stiff muscles, was no worse for her experience at the cliff. Belle, too, was recovering quickly, though her arm was wrenched, and it would be necessary to carry it in a sling for a day or two.

Anticipating the prospect of a day in Hawk's village, Jennifer dressed quickly in a simple white blouse and black skirt.

But when he saw her, he shook his head. "Those clothes will not do. They are much too fine for the work you will do this day."

"The fire destroyed all my clothes but one dress, and that was ruined when I helped my father clean up the rubble. I had to do quite a bit of sewing, so everything I brought with me on this trip is new."

"Never mind. My mother will have something for you to wear."

Jennifer let out a peal of laughter. "You flatter me! Your mother is so tiny. I'd never fit into her things."

He kept his gray eyes fixed on hers, never dropping them to pursue the ripe womanly curves of her body. "Have you forgotten that Indian garments are loose-fitting? You will find them most comfortable."

"Perhaps you're right," she conceded. "Then shall we go? I'm eager to begin my day."

Handing Jennifer a paddle and instructing her to move forward to the bow, Hawk gave her a quick lesson in canoeing and soon she was helping to propel the light craft across the bay. And though her sore muscles protested the new demands made on them, she was determined not to utter a single word of complaint.

Instead, she turned her thoughts to the pleasant scene—blue sky dotted by white puffs, and a warm breeze that lifted the heavy dark hair from her neck.

Beaching the canoe, Hawk helped Jennifer ashore, then led the way to his mother's wigwam. Again, the children swarmed like honeybees to a flower, buzzing among themselves in Ojibway. Occasionally, there was a shy *Bojo*, and she returned the greeting gladly.

Canodens welcomed Jennifer with a hug, kissing each cheek. Magidins, who had been sitting near the fire, left without a word. Jennifer sensed disapproval in her frown, and wondered why the young girl had seemed to dislike her on sight.

Even the red-tinged, wolf-like dog stood up and let out a low growl, his coarse hair bristling. Canodens scolded him and sent him outside.

Then she stood back and eyed Jennifer from head to foot before unrolling a cloth bundle on her mat. Inside were a dress of coarse broadcloth, leggings of the same fabric, a black silk neckerchief, and a pair of moccasins.

"Wear these, *s'il vous plait.*" Canodens pushed the garments into Jennifer's hands, appealing to her with an expression that made up for her limited knowledge of English.

Tentatively, Jennifer accepted the clothing and Canodens slipped out of the lodge, leaving her alone to change. How different the broadcloth breeches felt from the ruffled petticoats she was used to wearing. The moccasins were soft on her feet, but thin compared to her hard-soled shoes.

Hawk's mother reappeared just as Jennifer was slipping on the loose tunic. "We pick berries. Put in *makuk*. Like this." Canodens showed how to tie the bark container to her waist.

Jennifer followed her example, tying one of the containers to her own sash.

Picking up a small ax and some larger, white bark *makuks,* Canodens gestured toward the door.

Jennifer followed Canodens out of the lodge and down the path into the woods. Older girls, with their mothers, traveled the same path, carrying their white bark containers. Magidins went too, walking several feet ahead of them with another girl of about her age.

They soon came to a thicket of blueberries, where a covey of pinewarblers were feeding. The birds took flight in a cloud of beating wings, and everyone went to work filling the little *makuks* at their waists. Canodens introduced Jennifer to the woman picking beside her. Sope stood taller than Jennifer, a broad-faced, large-boned woman. Since she couldn't speak English, she talked to Jennifer in Ojibway, relying on Canodens to translate.

At first, the questions were of a general nature: Had Jennifer been frightened during the storm? How long would she be staying? How did she like the Indian village at L'Anse? Then, she asked a question Canodens must have felt was inappropriate, for, instead of translating, Hawk's mother said something to Sope in Ojibway, bringing the conversation to an end. Jennifer caught only two words—the name of the village teacher, *Laura Simpson.*

Canodens left the blueberry thicket to chop at the taller branches of a nearby cherry tree, making the fruit easier to pick. Magidins moved closer, taking her mother's place beside Jennifer in the blueberry patch.

In sketchy English, she said, "Miss Simpson good teacher. She love Hawk. They marry soon. Feast honor her return. Hawk tell you?"

"No ... he hasn't," Jennifer replied, taken aback by the information.

With quiet contempt, Magidins hissed, "Go home, white girl! Hawk never love you!"

The girl moved away, leaving Jennifer dumbfounded.

chapter

7

TROUBLED BY MAGIDINS' OVERT HATRED, Jennifer wondered how the girl had drawn such conclusions about her. Perhaps there was more to Hawk's relationship with Laura Simpson than his position as her guide. But if their relationship was a romantic one, Jennifer wondered why he had asked permission to call on her.

The obvious answer seemed to be that Hawk was biding his time until Miss Simpson returned. Jennifer was a convenient, safe diversion for the few days she would be visiting. The idea was infuriating!

At a nearby cherry tree, Magidins looked up from time to time, watching Jennifer through slitted dark eyes. She carried on a conversation with her friend in Ojibway, pausing to giggle hilariously. Jennifer could only imagine what she must be saying about her.

Canodens had moved on to another tree with her ax. Jennifer emptied the blueberries from her makuk and joined Magidins. The young girl's conversation stopped abruptly. As Jennifer began filling her makuk with the bright red fruit, she spoke to Hawk's sister.

"Thank you for telling me about Hawk and Miss Simpson. Now I understand." She smiled sweetly, counting on her soft words and pleasant expression to convey her message, then moved on to work near Canodens.

But, inside, she was seething.

As she picked cherries, Jennifer tried to convince herself that the news was of no consequence. The warmth that had welled in her only yesterday could easily be attributed to gratitude. After all, Hawk had saved her life . . . and her mother's! Any other lingering attraction could be the result of natural curiosity about his culture and his willingness to share Ojibway life with her during her visit.

If Jennifer's reception from Magidins had been cold, the genuine welcome she felt from the women of Hawk's village was compensation enough. After a morning of berry picking, the women returned to the village, and for several hours, Jennifer helped Canodens clean and cook fish.

There were many more varieties than Jennifer had ever seen before, and she learned the Indian names, carefully repeating them after Canodens: suckers, trout, salmon-trout or *siskawet,* whitefish or *atikameg,* and sturgeon. There were also small perch, sunfish, and herring.

There was also more than one method of cooking the fish. Some were cleaned, then placed between the sections of the spit, over an open fire. Other fish were impaled whole on a stick stuck into the ground and angled over the fire. As the fish cooked, it was turned to expose all sides. Jennifer learned afterward how to split the succulent meat and season it with maple sugar.

Some of the fish were boiled in a cauldron. The heads of suckers were a special favorite cooked this way, Canodens explained. Several fish were partly dried, the skin and bones removed, and the flesh spread on clean birch bark to dry some more. Then, it was rubbed with the hands until soft and fine, and mixed with new sugar. Jennifer helped Canodens store this confection in makuks. As she did, Canodens explained with a combination of her broken English and hand gestures that the food was eaten with a spoon and considered a great treat.

Later, Canodens took Jennifer to Sope's wigwam, where the woman was preparing turtle. Some were boiling in a pot. Others were roasting over a fire. She had thrust one end of a linden stick into the mouth of one turtle to give it a sweet flavor. As the stick burned, the smoke imparted an incense that would ensure a tasty dish.

To Jennifer's dismay, she learned that other delicacies enjoyed during the cold winter weather were the nose of the elk, the tail of the beaver, and the paws of the bear!

As the two women returned to Canodens' lodge, they passed a woman peeling the quills from a porcupine that had been inflated.

"We use quills, make pretty," Canodens explained, pointing to her moccasins decorated with dyed quills. With some difficulty, she explained that porcupines were also eaten, but only half-cooked. Jennifer's stomach writhed in protest, but she concealed any expression of distaste.

Working side by side with Canodens outside her lodge, Jennifer observed how to mash and dry berries for winter storage.

They worked together for some time in companionable silence. Feeling the heat from the hot sun and the cooking fires, Jennifer had long since bound her flowing hair with her black neckerchief, and from the back, she could have passed for any of the young Indian maidens in the tribe.

"Hawk tell me you want eat with me at feast," Canodens wore a look of concern. Her French accent became more pronounced as she continued in an apologetic tone. "This not *possible*. At feast, it ver' *important* you eat with chief. Understand?"

"Yes, of course," Jennifer hastened to assure her, though she didn't understand at all.

The worry lines disappeared from Canodens' forehead. "Good," she replied, her mouth easing into a smile.

As the sun dipped toward the west, Hawk returned for Jennifer, waiting outside his mother's lodge as she changed into her own clothes again. Magidins' words about Hawk and Laura Simpson had returned to haunt her, and she was dreading this encounter with him.

Emerging from the lodge, she thanked Canodens for sharing her day.

"You come again, Jennifer," Hawk's mother said, "I must teach you how cook bird. How cook deer. Bear and rabbit, too."

"It's kind of you to invite me," Jennifer responded. Under the circumstances, however, she thought it unlikely that she would accept the invitation.

As she walked with Hawk down the path to the canoe, he asked, "Are you tired from your work today?"

"No more so than when I helped Papa clean up the rubble from the fire, and certainly not as dirty."

"Did you find contentment among the women of my village?"

"Ye-e-s, but I can't explain why," Jennifer countered. "For all the work they do, the least of their rewards should be the privilege of sitting at the feast table."

Hawk stopped and turned to her, a shadow of annoyance crossing his face. "You can't change our custom. Not in time for the feast, at least."

"So I learned. Your mother explained the best she could how important it is for me to sit at your father's table." With a note of resignation in her voice, she added, "Out of respect for you and your parents, I'll do as you ask, but I won't like knowing I've been given a privilege the women of your village can't enjoy. Nor do I understand why such a custom exists."

"For now . . . it is enough that you try." They resumed the long walk down the slope until Hawk again broke the silence. "Did you talk with any of the other women?"

"Yes, Sope spoke with me . . . with your mother's help, of course. Sope seemed more interested in me than the others."

He nodded. "Magidins and her daughter, Ajawac, are together often."

"Who?" Jennifer asked, the name sounding strange to her ear.

"Ajawac," Hawk repeated. Jennifer listened carefully this time, noticing that the accent fell on the first syllable. "Mother has heard the two girls talking about you."

"So I was right," Jennifer murmured under her breath, recalling their hilarious laughter under the cherry tree.

Approaching the canoe, Hawk held it firm with his foot while Jennifer stepped in and took her place in the bow. Neither spoke as they began paddling across the bay to the mission.

After a long silence, Hawk observed, "You are very quiet. Perhaps you are more tired than you thought."

She did not turn, but responded over her shoulder. "No. Not tired. Disappointed, perhaps, that your sister dislikes me."

"Magidins has few friends, and you are a stranger to her. It will take time for her to accept you."

Jennifer couldn't brush off Magidins' feelings about her so lightly, nor did she wish to discuss Hawk's sister with him just now. They completed the trip in silence.

Reaching the dock, Hawk lingered, compelling Jennifer not to return to the house before they had talked.

"Something bothers you. Am I right?" he asked as they settled onto the rough planking. He leaned toward her, reaching out to brush a strand of damp hair from her face.

Jennifer was tempted to cover his hand with her own, to hold on to this moment that had evoked such a surge of tenderness in her. Instead, she pushed his hand away and bit the inside of her lip, hoping the pain would blot out the warmth she was feeling for him.

Hawk waited patiently. "What troubles you? Perhaps you have changed your mind about the feast, now that you have seen Ojibway food."

"No . . . I haven't changed my mind . . . about the feast." She could not look at him, could not bear the gentle compassion she would find in his face. Yet, what kind of man was this who could court two women? Stirred by the anger of his deception, she thrust out her chin. "But I wonder if it would be wise for me to be present. Your sister said the feast will be in Miss Simpson's honor. Somehow, Magidins has the impression I'm trying to come between the two of you."

Hawk's jaw flexed in anger. "The feast is in *your* honor—yours and the Woodworths. Magidins knows . . . I will speak with her."

"No, Hawk!" Jennifer cut in quickly. "Please don't. I should never have mentioned it. Magidins will know I told you, and she'll dislike me even more."

"Magidins must learn not to interfere." Hawk's profile, turned to her now, seemed chiseled in granite, and she knew nothing she might say would persuade him otherwise.

"Then speak to her if you must," she sighed, "but, in either case, it will make no difference."

She rose to her feet. Hawk was beside her instantly, his hands gentle on her shoulders. The raven head bent toward hers, targeting on her soft lips, but an adroit sidestep removed her from his embrace.

Presenting her back to him, she said in a tone laced with steel. "There is something I must know. Is it customary in your world for a man who is to be married to show . . . favor . . . to another woman?"

"What!" Hawk's sharp question slashed the air.

Facing him again, Jennifer repeated, "Your sister told me that you and Miss Simpson will be married soon."

Hawk's face was an inscrutable mask. Studying her for an endless moment, he remained silent. Then he paced restlessly, pausing at last before the piling where Jennifer had sunk to brace her suddenly trembling knees.

"The teacher will not marry . . . and I have not yet chosen *any* woman to share my wigwam. I hope you choose to believe me rather than my meddlesome sister, but whatever your decision, I speak the truth."

Jennifer was bewildered. "I'm not certain what to believe. You and your mother have both spoken so highly of Miss Simpson. And when Magidins . . . I just assumed the teacher meant a great deal to you."

A troubled look registered briefly on Hawk's strong features. "That I will not deny. She loves my people, and they return her love. For three years she has lived among us. She knows our language, our customs, and accepts us as we are." He gazed into the far distance. "And what is between the teacher and me should not be shared with another." Jennifer's breath caught in her throat and she ducked her head, feeling like an intruder. Yet she strained to catch the next soft words. "This I will tell you. There is great respect, mutual concern for our people, yes, even affection. But the teacher will never marry. Her mission is her life. She is my friend. That is all."

The silence lengthened. To speak now would be to violate a sacred trust. Hawk had confided in her, had opened his heart. Such sharing was rare among Indians, Jennifer knew, for they prided themselves on the stoic acceptance of their destiny. Perhaps it was Hawk's belief in Jesus Christ that had softened his heart and made him vulnerable to her. She was warmed by the thought, and hot tears crowded her eyes.

"But you and I, Jennifer, are *more* than friends. Is it not so?"

Through a mist of emotion, she looked into his face. "How . . . can you possibly know what is in my heart?"

"You have not spoken . . . but your eyes do not conceal the truth."

His soft declaration flooded Jennifer's cheeks with burning color, and she brought up both hands to cool them. "I'm very grateful to you for saving my life, of course . . . but beyond that—"

"We care much for each other."

"You put words in my mouth," she argued feebly.

He arched a brow. "It is useless to deny what I can see for myself."

She took a shallow breath. "All right. We care for each other, but I'll admit to nothing more. We've faced death and danger together. Such things can charge the emotions. In a few days, I'll be gone, and soon after, we'll forget—"

He held her gaze in a timeless moment. "And does one forget so easily the sunrise of the heart?"

At his words, Jennifer rose swiftly. "It's growing late," she murmured, noting the long shadows cast by the tall pines at the water's edge. "I must go. The others will be wondering where I am."

And without a backward glance, she fled to the sanctuary of the mission house.

The following morning, a storm that had been brewing over the broad Superior waters moved onshore. Gale force winds whipped the waves into a frenzy of foam on L'Anse Bay while Jennifer watched from the mission house window.

Despite her best intentions, thoughts of the tall Indian teased her mercilessly, and her mind churned with the intensity of the white-capped walls of water that came crashing against the shoreline. His words of the evening before returned again and again. "And can one so easily forget the sunrise of the heart?" When she saw Hawk again, she would be sure to ask him just what he had meant.

By evening, the bay was no calmer. Somewhere, behind banks of ominous, dark clouds, the sun set over the choppy swells.

All through the night, and again during the next day, the foul weather showed no signs of abating. By nightfall, Jennifer had prayed a hundred times for the return of fair weather—and Hawk. But when she went up to bed, the fierce roar of the wind and the thunderous surf provided an unwelcome lullaby.

On the third morning, Jennifer awakened later than usual. All was quiet, and the floor of her bedroom was dappled with light streaming through the window. Drawing aside the muslin curtain, Jennifer viewed the day. It was well into the ninth hour, she guessed by the position of the sun over the now tranquil bay. Undulating swells mirrored the brightness of the sun and rolled in meekly to lap at the beach. Though the debris littering the grounds bore mute testimony to the violence of the past three days, there was nothing left of the savage wind except a gentle breeze. The rain-washed sky showed bright blue between billows of startling white clouds.

Jennifer dressed quickly, ate a hurried breakfast, and joined the others who were cleaning up after the storm. Reassured to learn that there had been only minimal damage to the living quarters, Jennifer set about to stack broken limbs and twigs for firewood.

By early afternoon, beads of sweat dotted her upper lip, and she swiped a grimy hand across her damp forehead. The sleeves of her once white blouse had been rolled above her elbows, and she had secured her tumbling curls with a piece of string she had found. Stretching, she massaged a painful catch in her back with one hand, and shielded her eyes with the other, scanning the far horizon, but there was no sign of a tall Indian in a birchbark canoe.

In a reflective mood, Jennifer washed her hair and brushed it dry. Then she took out the lacy collar and cuffs her mother had made and sewed them onto her navy blue dress. In spite of Magidins' dire predictions, she would attend the feast with her head held high.

"I be sorry to leave," Belle said, entering their bedroom. "There be some good people here."

Jennifer looked up from her valise where she had been searching for a ribbon to match her blue dress. "And what do you think of Hawk, Mama?"

The older woman did not answer right away, but reached into the portmanteau, coming up with a length of blue satin which she handed her daughter. "There be about him the noble bearing and strength of the red man," she said, "and the manners of the white man, but he be different from both. I think he be loving the Lord with all his heart, so he will not be giving it lightly to another. The woman he chooses for his wife will have the love of a good man."

Jennifer gave a short laugh, hoping to dispel the sudden tension in the room. "No doubt some Ojibway maiden has already caught his eye—if not his heart."

A soft tap came at the door and Belle opened it to find Sister Bentley standing there. "Come in. We be nearly ready."

"There is something I must tell you before the feast." There was a furrow of concern on the woman's brow.

Slanting her daughter a reassuring look, Belle inclined her head toward the only chair in the room and sank down on the bed opposite their guest. Jennifer made short work of her hair and stood poised at the wardrobe, waiting expectantly.

She had observed that the droop of Sister Bentley's left eyelid was more pronounced under strain, and tonight it was almost closed, though her right eye was wide, revealing the delicate blue of her iris. "I don't know how much you may have been told about the customs of the Ojibways, but—"

"I know we'll have fish and porcupine," Jennifer interjected with a merry laugh, hoping to set the woman's mind at ease.

Sister Bentley nodded. "There are certain *other* creatures the Ojibway are fond of serving as well," she said, biting her lower lip, "creatures one wouldn't think of eating under normal circumstances. Nevertheless, whatever is served, you mustn't look shocked, or the chief will be greatly offended. It is most important that we, who have come to bring the message of Christ's love, pay him the respect due any host. Do you understand?" At their sober nods, she continued, "The Ojibways' eating utensils are crude, and each guest is expected to provide his own table service, so I'll be carrying along enough for each of you."

"Thank you, Sister Bentley," Belle said. "You be most kind and thoughtful to prepare us. We'll try to abide by your instructions."

When the woman had gone, Belle turned a quizzical look on her daughter. "Now what do you suppose she be getting at, Jennifer? Did you learn something you forgot to tell me while you were at the village?"

Shaking her head, Jennifer replied, "I'm as puzzled as you are." With a slight shrug, she added, "But we'll find out soon enough."

When an Ojibway canoe approached the mission house dock a short while later, Jennifer's heart fluttered at the prospect of seeing Hawk once again, but her anticipation turned to concern when she realized Red Wing had come alone.

chapter
8

THE MYSTERY OF HAWK'S WHEREABOUTS was soon resolved. As Red Wing leapt onto the dock in a single fluid stride, he muttered a few words in Ojibway to Brother Bentley. Jennifer caught only one of them . . . *Hawk*.

Moments later, the reverend interpreted: "Hawk left this morning with Gray Wolf to bring Miss Simpson from Houghton. They would have fetched her two days ago, but the storm delayed their trip. They won't be back until tomorrow." Fixing his gaze on Jennifer, he added, "Hawk sent a message. He's sorry to miss the feast."

Suddenly Jennifer's enthusiasm for the outing vanished.

Belle put a steadying arm about her daughter. "Never mind. We won't be letting a disappointment cloud our enjoyment of this evening."

She *was* disappointed. Jennifer felt the sharp pang of it—a loss of something—or someone—she did not even possess. Not trusting her voice, she thrust out a determined chin and, lifting her skirts, she stepped into the canoe and settled herself gingerly beside her mother. At least, not seeing Hawk meant that her encounter with the mysterious Laura Simpson was also postponed. She could take some comfort in that.

The light craft bobbed over gentle swells as Red Wing, assisted by the two men, propelled them over the bay. When at last they drew alongside the Ojibway dock, a cluster of villagers stood waiting to greet them. As if on cue, the group parted, and the chief stepped forward.

Even without the full ceremonial regalia, Jennifer would have recognized him anywhere. He was wearing an intricately beaded headband, embellished with the tail feathers of an eagle, and a dark shirt, embroidered with bright colors in a Jacobean design. Around his neck hung a large silver medallion suspended on a wide, flat necklace woven of bright glass beads. At his waist dangled a beaded pouch. His leather breeches bore a stripe of dyed porcupine quills down each side, and on his feet were beaded moccasins.

Still, it was not his dazzling attire that struck Jennifer, but the remarkable resemblance to his son. This could be Hawk himself at some future time—the raven hair silvered at the temples, his tall stature unbowed by the years.

The voice, when he spoke, was rich and deep, and Jennifer closed her eyes for a moment, imagining that it was Hawk uttering those words of welcome. Feeling a nudge from her mother, she opened her eyes to find Brother Bentley making the introductions to "Kitchiogema." When her name was called, she followed the lead of the other ladies and made a shallow curtsey.

The chief spoke again, raising his hands in a gesture more eloquent than words. "Welcome, my friends," translated Brother Bentley. "Let our feast begin."

There was a low undertone as the Ojibway braves murmured their approval. "Ho, ho. Ho, ho."

The chief led the way up the slope toward the council lodge. Across the village, Jennifer could see cooking fires burning in deep trenches, tended by native women, some of whom she recognized from the day before. The gamey smell of roasting meat wafted through the air.

At the council house, a procession of women carried in wooden platters laden with the results of their labors. Curious, Jennifer stepped nearer. Her stomach turned when she recognized a roasted dog in its coat of singed hair. Its eyes, still in their sockets, bulged with a look of terror and pain. She was certain it was the same dog she had seen at Canodens' lodge.

Bile rose in Jennifer's throat. How could the woman cook her pet dog?

She bolted into the woods a few yards away. Leaning against a tree, she lost the contents of her stomach on the bed of needles beneath.

Within moments, her mother was at her side. "Jennifer, what be the matter?"

"I'm all right now, Mama." She straightened, bracing her sore midriff with one hand.

"What happened? You be fine one minute, and the next, as pale as milk."

"I can't stay here another minute. We must try to leave as quickly as possible."

By this time the two other white women had taken note of their absence and had found them beneath the tree.

Anna Woodworth was clearly concerned. "Is someone ill?"

"Please ask Red Wing to take me back." Jennifer struggled for control. "It is better I leave now than to bring disgrace on you. I can't possibly eat . . . *dog!*"

Revulsed by the memory of the unsavory dish she had spotted, Jennifer made a move as if to leave, but Sister Woodworth placed a restraining hand on her arm. "Please reconsider, my dear. Your presence would be sorely missed."

Sister Bentley clucked her tongue softly, her head moving from side to side. "Dear me. I was afraid of this. I tried to warn you, but I'm afraid I should have been more explicit. You have a right to be distressed, Jennifer, even shocked. But try to see it their way. White people raise pigs and cows and chickens and think nothing of killing and eating them. The Ojibway feels that way about dogs."

"But the dog I saw was the same one Canodens keeps for a pet," Jennifer insisted, feeling queasy again.

"No, no, dear. You're mistaken," insisted Edith Bentley. "Canodens would never allow anything to happen to her pet. The dog you saw is one raised for food."

"Regardless, I wouldn't be able to eat a single bite . . . not with a dog staring at me from the tabletop. I'm going to ask Red Wing to take me back." She must make him understand. Her use of the language was limited, but she could always resort to hand gestures.

"Wait, Jennifer." Sister Bentley's tone was more commanding than pleading. "I'm afraid you have no choice. Your action would be judged a serious breach of the relationship we have labored so long to establish here. Your leaving would set our work back. I'm afraid we must all brace ourselves and behave as normally as possible."

Jennifer cringed. Perhaps the worst was yet to come. Magidins was right. She did not belong here.

"Jennifer?" Her mother's voice was soothing. "You be right to be upset if the dog were Canodens' pet, but now that we know it's not, can't you just pretend it be like one of the chickens I roast for Sunday dinner?"

Suddenly the humor of the situation struck her, and she looked at Belle with new appreciation. This woman had endured the same hardships she herself had experienced since beginning their journey to L'Anse—the storm, the tumble over the cliff . . . Yet she seemed quite willing to accept yet another trial without flinching. There was a serenity in her mother's face that she had never noticed. Suddenly Jennifer felt ashamed, and her heart told her she must stay.

Squaring her shoulders, she smoothed her dress. "You're right, Mama. We mustn't keep our new friends waiting."

In front of the lodge, a crackling fire burned brightly, attended by young boys. Sparks rose in the dusky sky as they fed the flames with fresh chunks of wood, and the incense of cedar filled the air.

Brother Bentley seemed relieved when the women reappeared. "The chief is inside, overseeing the last-minute preparations," he said. "He's sent a messenger to the pit fires to tell the women the feast will begin." Pointing to a semi-circle in front, he added, "His people plan to entertain us with dances here, after the feast."

Soon, all was ready, and the chief emerged from the council lodge to bid his guests enter. Down the center of the room ran a narrow table consisting of rough-hewn planks, and on both sides, a crude bench for the guests. Jennifer found herself seated to the right of the chief, with Belle on his left. A single fire burned at the far end of the lodge. Behind this, an impressive display of robes covered an elevated platform.

Shortly after the Bentleys and Woodworths joined them, men from the village entered and began filling in the remaining places. "Heads of households," Brother Bentley explained.

As the room filled, Jennifer dared to look about, hoping her stomach would not betray her. To her left were baskets woven in bright designs of blue, red, and green and filled with parched corn. Some wooden bowls held maple sugar crushed to bite-size lumps. Others contained the fish and sugar delicacy Canodens had shown her a few days before.

On the table several varieties of fish were easily identifiable— boiled whitefish, smoked salmon, and fried sunfish and perch. Thankfully, there were no half-cooked porcupines. But, looking to the right, Jennifer spotted the dog she had seen earlier and quickly averted her eyes.

The feast took on a pagan atmosphere as the native men filed into the room. Their upper torsos glistened with a fresh application of bear grease, adding new pungency to the smoky lodge air. At their throats hung bear-claw necklaces, and eagle feathers adorned their long, straight hair. Weird shadows cast by the flickering firelight seemed to dance across the walls of the lodge. Jennifer felt the chasm between herself and Hawk widening ever deeper. For though he himself was a Christian now, this was the culture out of which he came. These were his people.

When the parched corn and maple sugar were passed, she spooned a little of each onto her birchbark plate, then passed them along to the Bentleys. She swallowed hard as the chief removed his hunting knife from the sheath at his waist. Anticipating his next move, she looked in the other direction as he began carving the main course. When she looked at her plate again, she saw that she had been served a large slab of the bloody flesh. Waves of nausea assailed her, and she had to force her thoughts elsewhere lest she scream out in horror.

Just at the moment she would surely have fainted in spite of all she could do, Brother Bentley leaned toward her and whispered, "Slip the food you don't want into your napkin, but be certain no one sees you. Before we leave the table, I'll take it from you."

Jennifer nodded, watching as the chief served Belle. She recognized the stricken expression her mother had almost succeeded in hiding behind a stiff smile. Brother Woodworth whispered to Belle, and Jennifer assumed he was making a similar offer.

When all the guests had been served, the chief cut a sizable portion for himself and began chewing. The tribesmen followed his example, making loud smacking noises, followed by grunts of satisfaction.

Cutting her meat into large pieces, she waited for an opportunity to dispose of it in her napkin. When the chief turned to chat with her mother, she hid the meat in the folds of cloth on her lap.

Thus preoccupied, Jennifer almost missed the conversation between Belle and the chief, as Brother Bentley interpreted. "The children of my village must learn your language," he was saying. "They must understand the customs of the white man. It is the way of the future. Ojibway roots run deep in this land, but our branches bend before a new wind. White people will come in greater numbers to live beside us. We must be prepared. That is why I sent Hawk to the white man's school. Now he will help his own people."

Jennifer could see her mother's delight in the chief's words. "You be wise, Kitchiogema. We must learn from each other. Thank you for welcoming my daughter and me to your village."

When the chief turned a penetrating gaze on her, Jennifer felt herself growing warm. Perhaps her thoughts were more transparent than she knew. She smiled politely and busied herself with her food, grateful that he made no attempt to engage her in conversation.

Gradually, the meat and fish were consumed, the corn baskets and sugar bowls emptied, and the dinner guests escorted from the lodge. In the milling about, Jennifer managed to dispose of the dog meat in her napkin without detection.

Outside, a doleful drumbeat told some ancient tale, signaling the beginning of a ritual dance. It was unlike anything Jennifer had ever seen, and she looked on in fascination as the chief led her small group toward the place of honor.

The women and children, who had consumed their meal while tending the fire pits, now gathered, joining in the strange chants that punctuated the movements of the dance.

At the chief's uplifted hand, the drum stopped. He spoke in a commanding tone, announcing the dance of the hunt, and the beat of the drum resumed at an increased tempo.

From the far end of the circle, a young brave, clad only in breechcloth and moccasins, entered the shadowy edge of firelight. His grease-slickened body caught up the rhythm of the drum as he moved around the circle, pausing from time to time to look for footprints of the game he was stalking. Suddenly, he beckoned to a group of his friends, dancers who were awaiting their cue, and they ran to join him. With dramatic portrayal, they moved cautiously toward their invisible quarry. Taking aim, they let fly imaginary arrows, then rushed forward, finishing off the deer with their hunting knives. The leader then returned home in triumph, carrying the fallen game across his shoulders.

The crowd sent up a roar of approval.

The drums took up yet another beat, and chaotic dancing began. This time, the older men, women, and even children participated. Jennifer was relieved to see Canodens among the group, her wolf-like dog waiting patiently nearby.

At length, the chief again raised his hand. The drumbeats faded and the dancers drifted away from the fire. With Brother Bentley's assistance, he offered his benediction to the evening's celebration. The genuine respect he accorded his white guests sent a current of warmth deep into Jennifer's heart.

She was still savoring the feeling when, shortly after, she stepped into the canoe to begin the journey home. In spite of its uncertain beginning, the outing was destined to become a precious memory.

Jennifer swung her legs over the dock and allowed her feet to dangle, almost tempted to slip off her high-topped shoes and plunge her toes into the deliciously cool water. But etiquette dictated that no proper lady should show her ankles, let alone appear in public without her shoes and stockings! How much more sensible the clothing worn by the Indian women, she mused—shapeless garments of fringed deerskin or coarse woven fabric that permitted the air to circulate freely. She had noticed the difference the day she had helped Canodens prepare for the feast. When the women were not barefoot, they wore soft, supple moccasins that gloved the foot comfortably and allowed the wearer to move noiselessly over the forest floor.

She knew instinctively, therefore, that no Indian approached her now, for the loose planking vibrated with the thud of each booted footstep. Looking up, she smiled to see her mother holding her skirts high to avoid snagging them on the rough timbers.

"Ah, Jennifer, I thought I might be finding you here on this hot day." Belle sighed and tucked a few wisps of straying blond hair into the neat bun at the back of her head. "'Tis a real scorcher."

"That it is—until the sun sets at least. Then I expect we'll welcome a fire."

The woman settled herself beside Jennifer, and they lapsed into a comfortable silence born of years of intimacy.

There was little air stirring today, and the pale waters of the bay were glassy smooth, ruffled here and there by an occasional playful breeze or the arching flight of a silvery fish. Only when the northwest wind swept down from the heavens to disturb the tranquil waters would the mirror-like surface froth with whitecaps, the greater depths taking on the hue of sapphire.

"Your thoughts be far away, daughter."

"I'm thinking about the feast last night—"

"And Hawk? Was he in your thoughts?"

"Yes . . . only because the Ojibways are his people, and I will never understand their ways." She frowned.

Jennifer recalled Brother Bentley's words when she and her mother had first arrived. He and his wife had been away from others "of their own kind" for a long time, and missed the companionship and encouragement of members of their former parish in Detroit—like the Woodwards. Hawk was not 'of her own kind," no matter how much education he had received. The glaring differences between them had never been more pronounced than at the feast.

And how did Laura Simpson fare here? Jennifer wondered. No doubt that young woman possessed a ruggedness of character that thrived on adversity. Perhaps she had even learned to relish eating dog!

"You be sorry to leave here, and he to see you go." Belle's quiet comment had the effect of a thunderbolt.

Startled by her mother's perception, Jennifer gasped. "How can you know, Mama—about my feelings or his? Besides, when Hawk returns, Miss Simpson will have need of him again."

"Perhaps—" Belle said enigmatically, getting to her feet. "The afternoon be slipping away, and I want to pick berries for our supper. Will you be coming with me?"

Jennifer searched the horizon once more, still nurturing a secret hope. If only she could catch sight of the golden sunset reflecting off flashing paddles as Hawk's canoe skimmed the waters of the bay. If only she could see him, talk with him—

"Not just now. I'll catch up with you later."

Belle nodded and started up the slope to pick up the trail worn smooth by the silent footsteps of a century of native Americans.

"Mama!" Jennifer called after her. "Whatever you do, don't veer from the main path."

There was a hearty laugh. "Never fear! I'll not be taking any risks today—not with my rescuer away!"

Jennifer had nearly given up hope of seeing Hawk when she spotted his canoe gliding into the dock. He was alone. A fluttery feeling came over her as he leapt lightly to the pier, kneeling to secure the light craft by a leather thong.

The angle of the late afternoon sun heightened the burnished copper of his skin, and when he rose and faced her, his gray eyes caught her brown ones and held them. He was strangely silent, the inscrutable mask of his face failing to conceal the taut lines of tension. An odd current flowed between them and he reached for her, pulling her into his arms, as if needing the security her nearness could bring.

"Hawk, what is it? What's wrong?"

He did not reply, but cradled her head against his great chest. She yielded pliantly, listening to the strong rhythm of his heart, scarcely breathing lest the moment end.

"I must see Reverend Bentley," he said at last, releasing her reluctantly.

"He's working on his sermon, I believe. He asked not to be disturbed."

Without a word of explanation, Hawk started for the mission house.

Something was amiss, Jennifer thought, or he would not interrupt the minister's meditation.

Following at a distance, she watched as he entered the house, then sank down on the slab step of the porch. Inside, the voices of the two men could be heard, muffled by the chinked logs of the lodge. Their conversation was urgent, intense, and at times Jennifer could almost make out their words.

She rose and walked a few steps from the building. It would not do to be found eavesdropping, however innocently. Clearly, something was dreadfully wrong.

When Belle appeared in the clearing with her basket of berries, Jennifer was relieved to see her. "Hawk's back," she explained. "He's talking with Brother Bentley."

At her mother's uplifted brow, Jennifer hurried on. "It seemed to be a matter of grave importance."

Belle's expression sobered instantly. "I pray nothing went wrong in Houghton. Did he speak of Miss Simpson or Gray Wolf?"

At that moment the reverend cracked the door. "Sister Belle, are you there? I would have a word with you, if you please."

"Of course." As she passed by, Belle gave Jennifer's shoulder a little squeeze.

The air of mystery was almost palpable now. Jennifer paced restlessly, struggling alternately with anxiety and resentment. What were they keeping from her?

At length she was summoned to the common room where Sister Woodworth was already seated, calmly sipping tea.

"Sit down, dear," Sister Bentley invited and poured a cup for Jennifer before seating herself in a straight-backed chair beside the fire.

"Well, Jennifer, it appears the stormy weather has left us for a while." She stirred a lump of maple sugar into her tea. "There was some crop damage, though, which may mean a lean winter for the Ojibways. Of course, there will be plenty of fish and game. And, fortunately, the young braves are great hunters."

Since no comment seemed to be required, Jennifer forced the steaming liquid past the lump in her throat. Her thoughts roiled. This idle chit-chat was obviously devised to take her mind from the storm brewing behind Brother Bentley's closed door.

Sister Woodworth took up some needlework. At this point Jennifer's composure shattered. Why, they might as well be sitting in their parlor back home!

"Would someone please tell me what has happened?"

Before either of the ladies could answer, the door creaked open and Brother Bentley himself stepped out. Jennifer started so violently that the contents of her cup splashed down the front of her dress.

"My dear," he said gently, beckoning to her, "we must talk."

Swiping at the damp spot on her skirt, she rose and accompanied the reverend into a small room, where his few books and a weathered Bible lay open at his desk.

Catching Belle's eye, Jennifer was only slightly reassured by a stiff smile. She perched on the crude chair Hawk drew up for her.

Without preamble Brother Bentley began. "I'm afraid we have received some very bad news today."

Jennifer darted a glance at Hawk, but the implacable mask was still carefully in place.

"Miss Simpson will not be able to resume her duties as teacher for the village children. The ship on which she had booked passage to return to us, the *Lady Superior,* sank during the storm." He swallowed, then continued. "There were no survivors."

"No—" Jennifer's voice was barely audible. Suddenly, she felt the horror of being swept into the cold waters of Lake Superior, helpless against the force of the *Kitchi-Gami,* the Big Sea Waters. She turned to look at Hawk. "I'm so sorry. I know how much she meant to you. . . ." facing Brother Bentley again, she added, "to all of you."

"It is a great loss, of course." He paused and cleared his throat. "We are left, not only with our grief, but with the need to find a suitable replacement. The children are making significant progress in the English language, and it is important that they continue to pursue their studies. . . . Hawk has made an excellent suggestion in which the rest of us concur."

There was not a sound in the room as the reverend got to his feet and, with his hands clasped behind him, turned to look out the window. "If you are willing, we are asking you to assume the post of mission teacher for the next year."

chapter
9

JENNIFER SAT IN STUNNED SILENCE.

Eight years at the Eagle River School had not prepared her for such a formidable responsibility, though she had devoured every book she could get her hands on, reading many of the four hundred volumes in the library at nearby Clifton.

Even if her formal education proved adequate, there was the Ojibway culture to consider. Their way of life seemed increasingly alien to her. She wasn't sure she was made of stern enough stuff to endure a winter in this remote wilderness.

Then there was Hawk. Would it not be easier to walk away from him in a few days rather than to risk the pain of his scorn—or worse yet—his pity, if she failed?

Jennifer cast a troubled look at her mother. Belle was solemn, and shook her head. "If you choose to stay, your father and I would be proud. But we cannot make such a decision for you."

"But I—I don't know if I'm qualified—"

Hawk had not moved. He stood proudly erect, his arms folded over his chest. His countenance gave no hint of what he might be thinking. Did he wish her to stay?

"You!" she cried as a new thought dawned. "Hawk, *you* are the ideal replacement. You are better prepared, know your own people, the language—"

An uplifted hand halted the rush of words. "No." The word was uttered with finality. "After many hours of prayer, God has given me this answer. Ojibway children must understand the white man's world. They will learn best from one who has lived long in that world." His stern demeanor softened. "Always, while I was on my knees, your face was before me."

Deeply touched by Hawk's answer and shaken by its meaning, Jennifer again turned to Brother Bentley. "I'll need time to think."

He nodded. "Of course. Talk it over with your mother. But I'll need your answer by tomorrow night."

He and Brother Woodworth left the room. She expected Hawk to follow, but he lingered on.

Her mother laid the palm of her hand against her cheek. "Pray about it, dear. The Lord will guide you to do the right thing." But before Jennifer could ask her opinion of what that "right thing" might be, Belle was gone.

The young Ojibway took the chair beside her and leaned forward. "If you stay, I will guide you and translate for you. I will protect you with my life." He rose to leave. "I pray God will help you decide."

She started to reach out to him. There were so many questions she wanted to ask him, but it was as if something were holding her back.

Jennifer remained in the room alone. Once again her life had been turned upside down. First, there had been the fire and the dark days that followed. She had blamed God for allowing the disaster, feeling that she and her parents were being punished for no reason. Now, when she had managed to gain some measure of peace, she felt all off balance again.

Had she been dreading the day when she would leave L'Anse and see no more of Hawk and his people, or looking forward to it because she was afraid of losing her heart here? Perhaps it was a little of each.

She stood and moved to the window where she could see the watery expanse of the bay, fringed by lengthening shadows. The late afternoon sun glistened on the water. She watched as a pigeon hawk rose from a stand of white pine, found an updraft, and soared heavenward.

"Dear Lord," she prayed, "are you telling me something I am too blind to see? Is it possible that you allowed the fire to destroy our home so I would visit L'Anse just at this time? Is this where you want me to serve you? I am so weak, Lord. So frightened . . . If I am to teach, I have much yet to learn—"

Preoccupied, Jennifer toyed with her supper. She heard little of the table conversation that flowed around her, so lost was she in her own thoughts.

Afterward, while helping to put away the tin plates, she found herself opening the wrong cupboard door at least three times. Still distracted, she picked up a cup to wipe it dry, but Belle took the towel from her hand.

"We'll finish up here. Why don't you take a walk to clear your mind. We'll never be finding anything in the morning as long as you're 'helping!' "

Jennifer gave her mother a grateful hug and stepped out onto the front porch. In the west, the red ball of the sun was edging toward the water, splashing the sky with streaks of pink and orange. Back in Clifton, her father would be coming up from the mine, heading home now.

Oh, Papa, I wish you were here so I could talk to you. Just when I need you most, we're miles apart.

She started along the path that led south past the Catholic Mission. As she walked, it seemed that she could hear her father's words. *You are no longer a child, Jennifer. You must make your own decisions, with the help of the heavenly Father. But remember this—in order to hear his voice, you must stay close to him.*

"I've drifted so far away from him," Jennifer said aloud into the silence of the dense forest. "Somehow I've let things come between us." Stepping off the path, she knelt beneath an oak tree.

"Dear Lord, please forgive me. I've been wandering from your way," she confessed, "miserable in this wilderness I created for

113

myself. I've been blaming you for the things that have gone wrong, when all the time you have been with us—protecting us, giving us strength, showing us the way out. Maybe it took the fire—losing the *things* I considered important—to show me that you are all I really need."

She walked on, hearing the soft night sounds as the dusk deepened, feeling a slow release of hidden resentments. "If this is your plan for me, Lord, show me clearly."

Turning toward the mission house again, Jennifer thought of the obstacles ahead if she were to stay, not the least of which would be the Indian children's acceptance of her. They had loved their former teacher, and no one could expect to take Laura's place. But, Jennifer wondered, would they open their hearts wide enough to let her in?

And what about Magidins? The young girl had lost not only a beloved teacher but a close friend. *Only the wisdom of God can tell me how to bridge such an awful chasm.*

Could Hawk be right in thinking God wanted her to assume such an overwhelming responsibility? Perhaps it would be best for someone else to take the position, someone dedicated to a missionary's role in life. Maybe, by accepting Brother Bentley's offer, she would actually be robbing a more suitable missionary teacher of the opportunity to serve the Lord.

As she neared the mission house door, she was thankful she could take another day to decide. Stepping over the threshold seemed to symbolize the next phase of her life. Whether she stayed in L'Anse or went with her mother to live at Clifton, she would be stepping out on faith into an uncertain future. She would simply have to trust the Lord.

Jennifer awoke the following morning, refreshed and confident that she would be able, with the Lord's help, to come to the right conclusion about the teaching post.

Hawk called at the mission house soon after breakfast and found her at a small table in the common room, reading passages from Psalms. Belle sat across from her, tatting a bit of lace.

"Jennifer, Sister Crawford, I have come to take you to the LaFontes,'" he said. To Jennifer, he explained, "If you teach at L'Anse, you will live with them."

"Is it right to intrude at this time?" Belle asked anxiously. "They must still be grieving the loss of poor Miss Simpson."

Hawk was adamant. "Jennifer must meet Angelique. Then she can decide whether to stay.'"

Jennifer closed her Bible and set it aside. "You're right, of course. They might not want me there. Then the answer is simple. I'll return with Mama to Clifton."

"Do not expect an easy answer." Hawk gave her a level look. "Angelique will like you."

As Jennifer and Hawk paddled toward the cabin, he supplied some details about the family.

"Angelique was raised in a convent in Quebec. She is full-blooded Ojibway, an orphan. Her husband, Pierre, brought her to L'Anse twenty years ago. He is French-Canadian—a trapper and fisher, and also he makes furniture. They have no children. If you stay, Jennifer, Angelique will treat you as a daughter."

The trip from the mission house to the LaFonte home was over before Jennifer had time to ask the multitude of questions racing through her mind.

While Hawk tied up the canoe to a birch tree overhanging the water's edge, Jennifer and Belle walked toward the small cabin nestled in a stand of pines. At that moment a tall, slender woman stepped onto the front porch and waved.

Even from this distance, Jennifer could see that the woman was not wearing the typical Indian garb she had grown accustomed to seeing, but was dressed in a skirt, blouse, and white apron. Were it not for her bronze skin and jet-black hair pulled back to expose the broad forehead of the Ojibway, Angelique would have looked just like any other settler's wife.

When they came face to face, Jennifer found that the Indian woman's stature topped her own impressive height, and the hand she extended in welcome pressed hers with equal warmth.

"I hope our visit is not ill-timed." Belle voiced her concern.

"Nevair," the tall Indian insisted, her Ojibway dialect heavily accented with French. "Angelique glad to see you." She looked Jennifer over appraisingly. "Jenni . . . Jenni . . . My English no good," she gestured in exasperation.

"Then just call me Jenny," Jennifer suggested, remembering the difficulty experienced by the Indian children in L'Anse.

Angelique's countenance brightened. "Jenny. Easy." She caressed the name with the soft "j" used by Hawk and his mother. Smiling at Belle, Angelique said, "Come inside. Both of you. I show Jenny her room."

The woman opened the door, including Hawk with a gesture of her head. But he had spread his legs in the stance of a long wait. "I will wait outside. After they have seen your home, I will show them the trail to the village."

Belle and Jennifer followed Angelique through the common room into a small adjoining bedroom. There, a pine four-poster bed claimed most of the space, with a matching dresser along one wall. Opposite that was a stone fireplace, closed off for the summer by a board painted with gay woodland flowers. Muslin curtains trimmed with red braid were tied back at the single window, which looked out on the forest. Covering the floor was a braided rag rug of bright reds, blues and greens.

Jennifer pressed her hand against the slightly worn crazy quilt covering the bed. A stiff cornhusk mattress resisted her touch.

"In winter, I give you feather bed," Angelique told her. "Weather here cold, but no worry. Feather bed keep you warm. Every morning, I build fire."

Fingering the smooth knob atop one of the posters, Jennifer commented, "This is a cozy room."

"Ah, cozy. I like better than 'small'." The woman smiled, though there was a certain melancholy lurking beneath her words. Stepping up to the window, she pointed. "See path to village? Hawk come each morning, take you to school."

"Yes, I see it," Jennifer commented, craning her neck in the direction of Angelique's finger. "Look, Mama, it's a path much like the one at the mission house."

Belle joined her daughter at the window. "Hmm. I hope you've learned a lesson from your mama and won't be letting the birdcalls lure you into the woods." Jennifer's voice blended with her mother's in a peal of laughter, much to Angelique's puzzlement.

"It's a long story," Jennifer explained. "Mercifully, we can laugh now. Ask Hawk to tell you someday."

"I will. I like stories." She moved toward the door. "Come. I show you where you take meals."

Jennifer and her mother followed Angelique to the common room where one wall accommodated a large fireplace. Before it stood a small pine table finished with so many coats of varnish it shone like glass.

"In winter, I keep fire here," Angelique told them. "You stay, I cook *atikameg*, whitefish, for breakfast."

Jennifer was unable to stifle a groan, followed by a shudder of revulsion.

"Jenny no like fish?"

"I like fish very much, but not for breakfast," she moaned.

The Ojibway woman smiled. "Angelique forget. Others not eat fish every meal like LaFontes. I wonder why Angelique and Pierre no grow fins!"

Jennifer forced a smile, but turned away lest her expression betray her true feelings. Belle rescued the conversation.

"Tell us about this beautiful . . . bag, is it? Mrs. LaFonte," she asked, stooping to caress the furry object.

"Laura make," Angelique said proudly. "She plenty smart, that one."

While Angelique described the process of constructing a sewing bag from four deer hooves, Jennifer let her eyes roam over the rest of the room. Several carved wooden pipes, probably Pierre's, lined the fireplace. By the front window stood a pine rocking chair polished to a warm glow. Opposite this was an armed chair draped with rabbit fur blankets.

This was the room where Laura Simpson had spent much of her time, perhaps here at the table, marking papers in the evenings, or reading . . . or drinking herb tea with Angelique. And in her spare time, she had created lovely gifts for her friends. Jennifer shook her head, wondering how she could possibly live up to such a tradition.

"You stay, then?" Angelique was asking her, having come to the end of her lengthy lesson on native bag-making. "You live with Angelique and Pierre?"

Jennifer glanced at her mother.

Belle offered a tentative smile. "It be up to you, dear."

Turning to Angelique, she explained, "It's an important decision. There's so much to think about—"

Angelique put a finger to her lips, then spoke quietly. "Hawk wishes you stay. He tell me so."

Uncertain how to respond, Jennifer cast her eyes downward.

"Do not be sad, Jenny. I remember twenty year ago. Pierre bring me here . . . to strange place." Laying a gentle hand on Jennifer's shoulder, she added, "Angelique pray for you. Everything be all right."

Looking up, Jennifer found the Ojibway woman's eyes moist with tears. Perhaps she was remembering when she was new to L'Anse. It must have been difficult for her, having been brought up in a large city with white children for her friends. Unlike the other Ojibways, she had lived in an orphanage in Quebec, not in this wilderness. The thought was comforting.

"Thank you," Jennifer breathed. "I need your prayers."

Belle stepped toward the door. "Your home is lovely, Angelique, but we must be going."

"Then I say good-by, and God bless. Remember—" She grasped Jennifer's hand— "Pierre away much . . . now Laura gone . . . Angelique ver' lonely. You come back. Please?"

The liquid dark eyes melted Jennifer's heart, and she gave the woman an impulsive hug.

When Jennifer and Belle made their farewells to Angelique and stepped outside the door, Hawk was standing where they had left him. "We'll walk to the village." He indicated the path Jennifer had seen from the bedroom window. "Come back later for the canoe."

Off at a brisk pace, they followed the trail past hemlocks and oaks, around a rocky promontory looking out over the bay, then into thick woods once more before entering the Ojibway village.

Minutes later, they stood outside the council lodge on the flat grassy area where the dancers had performed after the feast.

"My father is inside." Hawk inclined his head toward the bark-covered structure. "I will tell him you are here. He wishes to speak with you." He disappeared into the dim interior, leaving Jennifer to wait with Belle for his return.

At that moment she caught a flash of black fire. It was Magidins, her dark eyes blazing.

Addressing Jennifer, she spoke with contempt. "Go home, white woman! You not walk in Miss Simpson's moccasins. She good teacher. She care about me. She care about all Ojibway. You not stay here long!" she prophesied. "Magidins see to that!" And in a whirl of deerskin fringe, she was gone.

Stunned, Jennifer could not speak, but turned to her mother in bewilderment.

chapter
10

BELLE PLACED A SUPPORTIVE ARM about Jennifer's shoulders. "Magidins be angry she's lost a good friend. She didn't mean what she said."

"I'm not so sure, Mama. Do you remember when I came to the village to go berry-picking with Canodens?"

Belle nodded.

"Even then Magidins resented me. She thought Hawk would actually marry Laura Simpson someday, wanted him to. I think she feared I would get in the way. Maybe she even blames me for Laura's death."

"Give the young girl time to get over her loss, dear. She'll come around."

"I wish I could be sure of that." Jennifer looked doubtful. Magidins' undeserved fury stung more than she cared to admit.

Moments later, Hawk returned with his father, translating the chief's words.

"Our village is very sad. We have lost a dear friend. But we must think about the future. Our children need a teacher." Turning to Jennifer, he continued. "Please help us. Stay at L'Anse. Teach our children. We will be forever grateful."

Still unsure of her answer, Jennifer responded evasively, swallowing past the lump in her throat. "If it be God's will, I shall stay."

Hawk quickly translated her words, and the chief nodded in understanding.

As they turned down the path to leave, Jennifer thought of Magidins. The chief's sincere invitation could not remove the flaming arrow that had lodged in her heart with his daughter's pronouncement.

"How can I remain in L'Anse when your sister hates me so?" Jennifer's question, hurled into the atmosphere, erupted after their return to the mission.

The Bentleys had persuaded Hawk to take the noon meal with them, and the women had shooed both of them out of the house afterward, saying that things would be in a sorry state the day three women couldn't clean up a little mess of dishes.

Now Jennifer sat with Hawk on the pier, watching the dragonflies skimming over the bay. All day, her encounter with Magidins had simmered in the back of her mind, waiting until now to explode from her lips. It was the last hurdle she faced in making her decision to take Laura Simpson's teaching post.

The question hung between them, but the answer was not his to give. He could say only what he felt. "L'Anse will not be the same for me if you go."

Jennifer had thought she wanted to hear these words. Instead, she was more confused than ever.

"There will be trouble if I stay. Magidins made that clear to me today when we were waiting for you outside the council lodge," she sighed.

"Are you afraid of my sister? A thirteen-year-old girl? Magidins will come to like you. You will see."

"You make it sound so simple. It's not simple. Magidins is going through a difficult time."

With conviction, Hawk stated. "You are strong, Jennifer. And you have the Lord in your heart. They will see him in you, and they will love you. My people need you."

Without another word, Hawk stepped into the stern of his canoe, cast off the line, and paddled away.

As Jennifer watched him go, she couldn't help thinking what her life would be like if she left L'Anse and returned to Clifton with her mother. Already, she could hear the bells ringing every eight hours for change of shifts at the mine. The rowdy miners, trying to forget their grim lot, would drink and carouse into the night. Bitter feuds between the Cornish and Irish immigrants often broke out, ending in injuries. There would be boarders to wash and cook for. And one day would blend into the next. The work seemed dull compared with the challenges she was certain to face at L'Anse.

She made her way up the sloping bank toward the mission house. Maybe Brother Woodworth could recommend some Bible passages that would help her make her decision. She must give Brother Bentley her answer tonight, and the day was more than half over.

Brother Woodworth sat in Brother Bentley's desk chair, his Bible open in front of him. "In Isaiah 50, verses 4-7, we read:"

The Lord God hath given me the tongue of the learned, that I should know how to speak a word in season to him that is weary: he wakeneth morning by morning, he wakeneth mine ear to hear as the learned.

The Lord God hath opened mine ear, and I was not rebellious, neither turned away back.

I gave my back to the smiters, and my cheeks to them that plucked off the hair: I hid not my face from shame and spitting.

For the Lord God will help me; therefore shall I not be confounded: therefore have I set my face like a flint, and I know that I shall not be ashamed.

Brother Woodworth glanced up from his Bible, peering at her over his spectacles. "Those are the passages Brother Bentley once told me he found most helpful when deciding to accept the call to be a missionary. Maybe there is something for you, Jennifer."

"I'm not sure. . . . Brother Bentley came here to serve. I came to forget."

"Perhaps God was closing a door behind you. If not for the fire, you wouldn't have come to L'Anse in the first place." He rose and, clasping his hands behind his back, began to pace the confines of the small room.

"When Hawk came here yesterday to tell Brother Bentley and me what had happened and to suggest you be offered the teaching post, I had no doubt God approved the plan. You've been raised in a God-fearing family, you get along well with the Ojibway children, and you've come to know some of their customs." He paused to regard her with a smile. "It helps that you and Hawk are friends, since he would be your guide and interpret for you while you're here."

Jennifer thought of the day they had met on the dock in Hancock, and Hawk had borne her, protesting, toward his canoe. "Yes. We have made our peace since that first encounter," she admitted. Her thoughts turning to a more serious matter, she said, "Still, Brother Woodworth, many of the Indian ways are strange to me. I'm not sure I can ever accept them."

He nodded, a look of empathy in his eyes. "That will come in time. Years before the Bentleys came to take our place, Anna and I had our own obstacles to overcome. The Lord will help you. Trust him. He has already provided you an understanding friend in Hawk."

In all that had happened, she felt God's hand strongest in leading her to Hawk. Knowing the tall Indian had awakened in her a desire to know the Lord better, to follow him as Hawk followed him—in complete trust. At times, there were other feelings too fleeting to define—feelings that filled her with a warmth she had never known.

Brother Woodworth moved to the desk and closed his Bible. "Jennifer, Brother Bentley and I believe God has sent you here to serve him, but the final decision is yours. I'll be praying for you." He buttoned his jacket as he made his way to the door, stretching it taut over his ample girth.

"Thank you, Brother Woodworth," she murmured. "Your advice is most appreciated."

When the good man had left, she closed her eyes. She thought about her childhood and her Grandma Jen. The wise, sweet woman had shown serene faith in every circumstance, including her last days of suffering and death. Grandma Jen's influence had profoundly affected Jennifer, and a fresh wave of grief assailed her, to be replaced by happier memories.

Grandma Jen had been the first to tell her about God's love, about Jesus, his Son, and how he had been sent so all who believed on him could be saved to live with him eternally. Jennifer remembered the moment when she had begun to understand God's plan of salvation. How wonderful, how reassuring to know she would never have to fear death, but would have a place in heaven reserved for her when her life on earth was over.

The faces of the Ojibway children flashed to mind, their keen, dark eyes filled with wonder and curiosity. Some were too young to know Jesus. Others, who had accepted him as their Savior, would find it difficult to stay close to him in the face of ridicule from other members of their family. It was these who would need an example of Christian love, someone who could demonstrate a life of faith in the midst of trials. Well, she knew something about trials, all right. And with Hawk's strong faith—

As for Magidins, she considered the words from Isaiah that Brother Woodworth had read: "I gave my back to the smiters. . . ." She would weather the young girl's rebellion. She would turn not only her back, but the other cheek, as well.

Suddenly, she knew what she must do. There was no longer any question that all roads had led her to this moment of decision. She would stay in L'Anse.

The large, golden ball rose above the eastern horizon to illuminate clear skies and play off tiny ripples of L'Anse Bay. Belle folded her dressing gown and laid it in the portmanteau, then closed the bag.

"Are you sure you have everything, Mama?" Jennifer began another search of the room, opening and closing dresser drawers, looking in the wardrobe, peering under the bed.

"You've asked me three times, daughter! Everything I brought to L'Anse be right here." She patted the leather bag. Eying the makuk of maple sugar Canodens had given her, she added, "Plus a few things I've picked up along the way."

A knock sounded on the door and Belle opened it to Brother Bentley. "May I take your bag down, Sister Crawford?"

"I be ready."

Brother Bentley carried out the valise, then Jennifer closed the door behind him. Turning to her mother, she noted a sudden flicker of apprehension on Belle's face, mirroring her own rising feeling of uncertainty. How would she endure the long year without her mother's counsel, her friendship?

Watching the tall blond woman walk across the room to gaze out the window for the last time, Jennifer memorized the details of her mother's appearance—the straight back, the proud set of her blond head with the knot at the nape of her neck brushing the tatted lace trim of her collar, the dark blue skirt, gathered at the waist and falling in soft folds over her rounded hips. As much as she loved her mother, her father loved her, too, and needed her with him. She could envision the joyous reunion in Clifton and hugged this thought to herself, against the lonely days ahead.

Her mother turned from the window. "I must be going down now, Jennifer. It is time." The words were spoken quietly.

At the sight of her mother's tear-filled eyes, Jennifer rose from the bed and threw her arms around her. "I'll miss you so much," she said, burrowing her head in Belle's shoulder. She felt comforted by the familiar scent of lilac. "Give Papa my love and tell him I'll write."

"I will," her mother promised, holding her tightly before stepping back. She pulled a white lace handkerchief from her pocket and dabbed at the corners of her eyes. "We be thinking of you, praying for you." Forcing the corners of her mouth upward, Belle added, "Time will go fast, and before you know it, the year be over."

"I wonder if I can last a whole year!" Jennifer cried, giving way to a fresh torrent of tears.

Belle lay a cool palm against her daughter's cheek. "The Lord be with you. Never forget that." She bent to pick up the makuk, but Jennifer stooped quickly and retrieved it, carrying it down the stairs behind her mother.

By the time the two women had reached the dock, Hawk had arrived in a second canoe. Since Jennifer had accepted the teaching position, Hawk would not leave Ojibway territory except to escort her. Another Ojibway brave, Amongs, or "Little Wasp," had been chosen by the chief to assist Gray Wolf and Red Wing in returning Belle and the Woodworths to Hancock.

Before Belle Crawford stepped off the dock, she fixed a piercing gaze on Hawk. "Take good care of her. She be precious to me."

"And to me," Hawk agreed solemnly. "You need have no fear for her safety, Sister Crawford."

Jennifer kissed her mother's cheek one last time and when she had settled into the canoe, handed her the makuk.

Brother and Sister Woodworth were already seated and bade Jennifer and the Bentleys a tearful farewell as the craft eased away from the dock.

Jennifer's throat was tight with emotion. As if sensing her need, Hawk stepped up beside her, lending her confidence to face the parting.

They stood for an eternity, it seemed, watching the canoe become a tiny speck on the western horizon. Finally, Jennifer could no longer see the waving hands, could no longer distinguish one passenger from another. Then the speck disappeared from view, carrying with it the final pages of the past.

Lifting her chin in a gesture of determination, she turned to Hawk. "Will you take me to Angelique's now? I might as well start getting used to my new home."

Jennifer's' clothing hung in the wardrobe. Her comb and brush had been placed on the dresser top, and her toiletries in the top drawer. Mentally she composed a list of items she would need in the coming months.

Before her mother left, the chief had suggested that Belle prepare a trunk for Jennifer and send it to Hancock. Then, when the Indians made their annual fall excursion to the harbor town, they could pick it up and bring it to L'Anse. Since they would be using their Montreal canoe, a large vessel nearly forty feet long, there would be plenty of room for the bulky trunk.

The list complete, Jennifer drew out a piece of paper and began to write:

July 30, 1867

Dearest Papa,

I miss you more than you could know. Your guidance would have been a comfort when I was trying to decide whether I should take the teaching post here.

Every night, I pray for your safety in the mine. Please be careful. It is a dangerous business.

I wish you could meet Hawk. He is the most remarkable gentleman I have ever known (except for you, of course)! As long as he is my guide, you needn't worry. He will accompany me wherever I go.

Hawk's father, *Kitchiogema,* or Great Chief, is concerned about the ability of the Ojibway children to understand the language and customs of the white people. He supports the efforts of the mission school teachers and urges parents to have their children attend school regularly.

Hawk's mother, Canodens (diminutive for Charlotte), promised to teach me more of the Ojibway women's work. School will not start here until the first week in November, so there will be plenty of time for me to learn Indian crafts. There will also be wild rice to gather and store in the storage pits near the village. Seed corn, seed potatoes, and maple sugar are kept there also.

Please give Mother the enclosed list of goods to put in my trunk.

I pray God will keep you safe until the year is over and I can see you once again.

Affectionately, Jennifer.

July faded into August, and August into the lazy days of September. Canodens taught Jennifer how to prepare for winter by putting away provisions and tanning hides for the heavier clothing they would need for the cold weather.

Her ability to speak Ojibway improved gradually as she daily heard it spoken around her. It was a complex language, but Jennifer was determined to master it, even though she would have to abide by the rules of the Mission Board when school started, speaking only English in the classroom.

Magidins kept her distance, spending most of her time working alongside Sope's daughter, Ajawac. Jennifer always spoke pleasantly to the young girls, but seldom did they return her greeting. Hawk's sister kept herself aloof from her family, as well, preferring to drift about in a world of her own. She was still obviously mourning the death of Laura Simpson, Jennifer suspected, and hadn't yet forgiven her for accepting the former teacher's post.

Taking inventory of the teaching materials available to her, Jennifer found a few textbooks and reference books locked in the bookcase at the schoolhouse, but supplies were minimal. She longed for the books she had used as a student in Eagle River. These, of course, had been destroyed in the fire. There were not even slate boards and slate pencils for the students, only a large blackboard at the front of the room for the teacher's use. Something must be done.

Belle had written to say she was enjoying the Clifton church, renewing acquaintances with people she had known before they had moved away, though she missed Brother and Sister Woodworth and the Eagle River townsfolk. Jennifer wrote back, suggesting that her mother ask some of the young adults in her new church if they would be willing to donate their used schoolbooks, slate boards, and pencils to the missionary school, and to include them in the trunk she was preparing.

As time drew near for the school term to begin, Jennifer made a visit to each family in the village. The Bentleys had impressed on her the importance of winning the parents' favor in order to ensure good attendance at school, and Hawk set about to teach her some appropriate remarks to put the parents at ease with her.

The conversation always began with Jennifer's question, *"Kendon jemokamon?"* (Do you speak English?) to which the Ojibway parent would frequently answer, *"Kawin nin jananashin"* (I don't speak English) or *"Pangi, pangi"* (Little, little).

Jennifer would then proceed with the Ojibway sentences on which she had practiced so diligently. "I want to learn Ojibway. It's a beautiful language. You must help me."

This simple entreaty often unleashed verbose offers to help, delivered so quickly in the native tongue that even Hawk, highly skilled in both languages, had difficulty keeping up with the translation.

In response, Jennifer would say, *"Ki kijewadis"* (You are very kind).

In this manner, she earned respect and admiration from the Ojibway families.

Early one morning during the last week of October, an urgent knock sounded at Jennifer's bedroom door. Angelique had appeared earlier to stoke the fire in her fireplace, so Jennifer was awake, though she had not yet dressed. She quickly pulled her wrapper around her, wondering who could be there. Certainly Angelique would have identified herself.

Jennifer hurried toward the door, thankful for the rag rug separating her bare feet from the cold plank floor.

A second time, there was a pounding on the door, and then Jennifer recognized Hawk's voice.

"Open, Jennifer!"

chapter
11

WHEN JENNIFER SWUNG THE DOOR OPEN, she stood face-to-face with Gray Wolf. He was holding onto one end of a huge trunk, while Red Wing carried the other. Jennifer stepped aside to let them enter.

"*Nin mamoi-awa!*" she cried when she saw the trunk. "Thank you! Put it here." She indicated a place at the end of her bed.

The two braves lowered the trunk into position, setting it down without the slightest thump, then disappeared without a word.

Hawk stood in the doorway, the trace of a smile curving his lips.

"It's here. I can't believe it's finally here!" She knelt to unfasten the leather straps across the top, but found them bound too tightly.

"Is there no greeting for me?"

"I'm sorry. Good morning, Hawk." She barely looked up from the uncooperative buckles. Hawk dropped to one knee, loosening them with ease.

"Ah. Trunk come," Angelique said upon entering the room, her eyes alight with pleasure. "Jenny happy now."

"Help me, Angelique! Let's see what Mama has sent!" Jennifer lifted the heavy lid, riffling through the layers of paper packing.

Hawk headed toward the door. "I'll return for you in one hour— to take you to the schoolhouse."

"Yes, Hawk. I'll be ready." But she took scant notice of his departure.

Removing a letter from the top layer, she laid it aside to read later, then held up a two-piece brown wool outfit. "Look, Angelique! Indian breeches and a tunic. Mama knew these would be more useful on the trail than a dress."

"Put on breeches, braid hair, people think you Ojibway!" Angelique remarked with a sparkle in her eye.

Jennifer laughed. Carefully unfolding a package wrapped in tissue, she discovered two delicate ecru lace collars. She held them out to Angelique.

"Mama made these, too."

"Your mother ver' clever lady." Angelique handled the lace with a delicate touch, examining the fine work before handing the collars back to Jennifer.

"I know," she sighed. "I feel so useless sometimes. I could never do such intricate detail. Mama tried to teach me once, but she finally gave up. I was all thumbs!"

"All . . . thumbs?" Angelique held up her ten fingers, turning them this way and that, an expression of bewilderment in her ebony eyes.

Jennifer smiled, squelching an almost irresistible urge to burst into uproarious laughter. "No, Angelique. I mean I am clumsy . . . awkward." Catching sight through the open door of the attractive deerhide bag Laura had made, she sighed heavily. "I could never make anything like that, for instance."

Angelique touched Jennifer's arm in understanding. "You clumsy make lace, Indian bag, mebbe. When school start, you make fine teacher. You see."

"Oh, I hope you're right, Angelique. I hope you're right."

Turning again to the trunk, Jennifer lifted out two knitted shawls—one in brown, and one in a pale shade of blue. She flung the brown one around herself. It was of heavy yarn, large enough to cover her head as well as her shoulders. She put it aside and tried on the blue shawl. This one was of a more delicate fiber, just right for a cool spring morning. She gathered her hair with one hand, then let it fall in a dark tumble over the soft wrap.

"Turn around," Angelique said. *"Joli,* pretty. Wait 'til Hawk see," she teased.

Beneath the shawls were undergarments: a knee-length cotton chemise edged with her mother's fine eyelet embroidery; white cotton drawers with tiny decorative tucks; and two pairs of warm black woolen stockings. Jennifer transferred them directly to the drawers of her dresser.

She beamed when she held up the next item, a long woolen coat. "Mama made certain I wouldn't be cold this winter," she said, trying it on over her wrapper. It fit perfectly. She hung it on a peg on the wall and knelt beside the trunk again.

Another large piece of brown paper concealed the remaining contents. As Jennifer peeled it back, she gasped.

Angelique bent closer. "Books?"

Jennifer lifted a Webster spelling book from the trunk, then a slightly worn McGuffey reader. In addition, there were two more readers and an arithmetic book. "I wonder how she ever managed to find all these. Remarkable, considering the cost of books, and the tradition of passing them on to younger children in the family until the books are falling apart with age."

Angelique opened one of the beginning readers. Lines furrowed her forehead. She looked up, a hint of sadness in her expression. Her head moved slowly from side to side.

"What are you thinking, Angelique?"

"These books fine for white children, mebbe. Ojibways not understand."

Jennifer took the book from her hand and read aloud the simple words and sentences on the first page. Looking up at Angelique, she asked, "Not even this first reader?"

Angelique solemnly shook her head. "When school start, you see."

"I thought Miss Simpson had made good progress with the children's English lessons."

"Some." She shrugged. "Still, they not read good. They not write good. I know. I went school one day last spring. I help Miss

Simpson. These books too hard. Mebbe older ones understand. Magidins, *peutetre,* perhaps."

Jennifer slowly closed the book and ran her hand over the cover. She began to think the challenge ahead was greater than she had anticipated.

"Do not worry, Jenny. You do fine," Angelique reassured her. Looking in the trunk, she said, "Come see, under books."

Jennifer reached far into the trunk and produced a slate board. Taking a closer look, she realized that four more had been packed beneath the books. "Well, Angelique, the children will learn something this year, or my mother's efforts will be in vain."

Angelique smiled. "They learn. I believe." Rising to her feet, she said, "I make breakfast. Hawk be here soon. You dress."

But the moment Angelique had left the room, Jennifer settled herself on her bed to read the long letter from her mother.

October 25th, 1867

Dearest Jennifer,

I hope you be happy and well. We be fine.

When the congregation at Clifton learned you needed supplies at your mission school at L'Anse, many be eager to help. Some brought books their children no longer needed. Others gave me money toward slate boards and slate pencils.

Please, don't be too disappointed I haven't sent another dress. The tunic and leggings seemed more fitting. They will serve for everyday wear. With the new collars, you can change the look of your navy blue dress several times.

I have two boarders now. Both be recent arrivals from Cornwall. One has relatives in Glasgow, where your papa's great-grandfather lived before moving to Cornwall.

I hope Hawk and his family be well. How is Magidins? I pray for her.

Your Papa be very tired when he comes home from the bal, but he enjoys his work. He has shared the Gospel with several of his crew members, and many be converted.

I be praying all will go well for you at school. The first day always be the hardest.

Lovingly, Mama & Papa

At the bottom of the letter, Jennifer's father had written a postscript in his own hand. Though many Cornish miners could neither read nor write, having forsaken an education to start work in a mine at a young age, he had acquired his modest skills by attending night school in Cornwall.

P.S. Dearest dauter, I think and pray about you every day. Mother spoke well of your gide, Hawk. I am glad he be a good man, and you get on well. Please forgive me not writing a hole letter. I am not much good at it. Let us no how school goes your 1st week. Love, Papa.

Jennifer laid the letter on her dresser, a sudden wave of homesickness engulfing her. She missed her parents, especially Papa, whom she had not seen in several months now.

As she reached for the tunic and breeches, she thrust these feelings from her, determined to dwell on happier thoughts. The excitement she had felt upon seeing the trunk again bubbled up within, and she hummed as she dressed herself in the new outfit her mother had sent. Slipping her feet into the soft moccasins Canodens had made and given to her, she began to sense a feeling of well-being that was new to her.

Using the small mirror over her dresser, she parted her long, dark hair down the middle and plaited it into twin braids, tying the ends with leather thongs.

Entering the common room where Angelique was setting the breakfast table in front of the fireplace, Jennifer pivoted about for the older woman's approval.

"Jenny!" Angelique's eyes were wide. "Not look like you. Look like ver' pretty Indian maiden."

"Do you think Hawk will like it?"

"He like."

Hiding a blush of pleasure, Jennifer reached for the tin plates to set the table. From the fireplace, she took down two mugs. Hawk would not eat his breakfast with them, but he favored the hot tea Angelique brewed of mint leaves and fir branches.

She heard the cabin door open and knew he had come back, so

turned to face him as he entered the common room. He paused, a sharp intake of breath betraying his surprise.

"Is this . . . a gift from your mother?"

Jennifer nodded.

He stepped forward and slowly walked around her, taking in the moccasins, the dark woolen breeches, the tunic. She could not quite read the expression in his gray eyes as they came to rest on her dark hair. "You have braided your hair." He touched the soft plait with a tentative finger. "You are an Ojibway woman." It sounded like the ultimate compliment.

Flustered under his scrutiny, Jennifer attempted to inject a note of humor. "I just hope the children are as convinced as you seem to be. I haven't passed their test yet."

Hawk sat, and she took a place across from him at the small table. Angelique brought fresh bread and a jar of preserves, followed by a steaming pot of herb tea.

To Jennifer's surprise, Angelique returned with another mug for herself. Her hostess was not in the habit of sipping tea with Hawk and Jennifer, preferring to arise at dawn to prepare breakfast for her husband before he left to check his traps and nets.

There were few necessities Angelique and Pierre could not provide for themselves from the surrounding wilderness, but these Pierre obtained by offering furs and fish in barter at the Crebassas' trading post, or in the nearest white settlement. Should his traps prove empty or some special need arise, Pierre applied his hand to furniture-making, a skill he had practiced in Montreal. The results of his labors, a delicately-carved rocking chair or handsomely finished chest of drawers, sold quickly and at a premium to wealthy copper mine owners.

"Jenny, tell Hawk about schoolbooks," Angelique urged.

Hawk was still staring at Jennifer, fixing his gray gaze on every detail of her new image, and she was grateful to shift the focus of attention elsewhere.

"Well, in addition to my new winter clothes, Mama sent books and slates. I'd like to take them by the schoolhouse after breakfast, if you'll help me."

He nodded his agreement, never dropping his eyes from her face, framed by the silken braids over either shoulder.

"Hawk—" Angelique leveled her dark eyes on him—"I say today we clean school. *Oui?*"

Jennifer gave Angelique a puzzled look. "I can sweep out the room, dust the bookshelves, and put things in order myself. I thought that was part of the job."

Angelique shook her head. "Canodens and Sope help me."

Glancing at Hawk, Jennifer was about to protest further when his look stopped her. "The mission board makes assignments. You teach. The women clean. Angelique, today is a fine day for cleaning."

Following breakfast, Angelique got out three woven sacks and helped Jennifer pack the school supplies. Autumn was in full evidence as they walked the LaFontes' narrow trail. A crisp breeze caught Jennifer full in the face, and she huddled into her shawl as she followed Hawk and Angelique up a hill and down a gentle slope to the junction with the main path to the village.

Recent winds had already stripped the trees of many of their colorful leaves, but the burnt red of the oaks and rich gold of the birches provided flashes of color amid the deep green hemlocks and stark maples. Jennifer was glad for the warmth of her new woolen clothing as she rustled through the leaves filling the path.

Hawk set his usual brisk pace, so Jennifer concentrated on keeping up, following the path as it veered away from an outcropping of rock, wound around a large tree or past an occasional clearing where an Ojibway family had established a wigwam and planted patches of maize, potatoes, and squash.

The blue waters of the bay were occasionally visible through a web of bare branches. Eventually, the path transversed a lookout point, offering full view of the rippled Keweenaw waters and the two mission houses on the west shore. Overhead, geese honked as they flew southward in their "v" formation. Hawk paused. On past trips to the village with Jennifer, he had learned her appreciation for such rituals of nature, and waited until the flock had disappeared before resuming his pace.

In the village, they stopped at Canodens' and Sope's lodges to ask their help before continuing their trek to the schoolhouse.

When they arrived, Hawk unlocked the door and the women stepped inside, recoiling at the musty odor. Propping the door with a rock, Hawk opened the windows, admitting the fresh breeze.

"I will go now," Hawk said, his gaze lingering on Jennifer. "My father has summoned me to meet with him. When you are done, I will know it and will return for you."

Angelique wasted no time in tackling the grime of the past months. With a cornshuck broom, she swept the floor, then, drawing water from a well in the schoolyard, she added strong lye soap and attacked the desks. The stove with its heavy coating of soot could wait.

Jennifer found a rag and wiped off her desk and chair, then dusted the bookcase. In the distance she heard voices, and looked up through the open door to see Canodens and Sope entering the schoolyard, carrying more buckets, brushes, and soap. Tagging along reluctantly were Magidins and Ajawac. Jennifer was surprised to see Hawk's sister. The girl had barely spoken a word to her since her threat to cause trouble if Jennifer accepted the teaching post.

Sope pointed to Jennifer's costume. "Pretty."

"*Nin mamoi-awa*," Jennifer replied, thanking her in her native tongue.

Sope then fell in beside Angelique, who was now polishing the coal-oil lamps. In the rear, as far from the others as they could get, Magidins and Ajawac murmured in their musical dialect. From the dark expressions on their faces, however, their comments were not the usual pleasantries, Jennifer thought.

At last Canodens left her own work and approached Jennifer's desk, where she was still removing one of the many layers of dirt.

"When you finish, Magidins and Ajawac will . . . how you say?" She made a circular motion as if polishing the desk top.

"I'll do it," Jennifer told her quickly, not wishing to press her prospective students into service so soon.

Canodens leaned close to Jennifer. "Please . . . let girls help you. They do for Miss Simpson. They do for you."

She glanced up at the girls. Jennifer had an uneasy feeling they were discussing her again. She wondered whether Magidins were here against her will. If so, Jennifer could not imagine that polishing the desk had been her idea. Yet, perhaps such a chore was a badge of distinction among the other students. It couldn't hurt to grant permission.

Jennifer shrugged. "All right, then. If they wish it."

When the supplies were arranged to her satisfaction, she walked to the back of the room where the two girls were giving a perfunctory swipe to the smaller desks.

"I am finished at my desk." Jennifer spoke in English, gesturing toward the piece of furniture.

Magidins did not look up. Ajawac responded with a puzzled smile. Jennifer assumed the younger girl had not understood. Having learned sufficient Ojibway to translate, she repeated her statement and immediately turned her attention to the blackboard.

Before she had finished writing her name and the date of the first school day on the board, Ajawac was at her desk with scrub brush, water, and soap. Jennifer looked toward the back, where Magidins remained, concentrating her energies on a single spot. Was this the girl's tacit protest against Miss Simpson's replacement?

Jennifer continued her work at the board, putting up common Ojibway words with their English equivalents, along with some simple arithmetic problems. She was aware when Magidins left her work and came to stand in front of the bookcase, but did not acknowledge the girl's presence. For quite some time, Magidins stared at the volumes, then pulled out the spelling text Belle had sent. When Jennifer approached Hawk's sister, the young girl quickly closed the book and replaced it on the shelf.

"Take the book home with you." She held the book out to her. Head held high, Magidins ignored her offer and walked away.

139

"Magidins!" Canodens spoke sharply, but her daughter did not hesitate in her escape through the door. Canodens hurried after her. Though she returned shortly afterward, apologizing for Magidins' rude behavior, Jennifer couldn't help feeling hurt.

When Jennifer completed her work at the blackboard, she noticed that Ajawac had finished polishing her desk and was washing one of the front row seats. Jennifer ran her hand over the smooth desk top in which she could now see her own reflection. "*Oneegishin,* It is good. *Nin mamoi-awa,* Thank you."

Ajawac beamed. "It is good. Thank you," the girl repeated, as if reviewing the English words. "You welcome, Miss Jenny."

Jennifer pointed to the bookcase. "Ajawac, would you like to take a book home with you?"

The young girl responded with a puzzled frown. Jennifer took her by the hand and led her to the bookcase. Removing an old English-Ojibway grammar book, one of several left by Miss Simpson, Jennifer placed it in Ajawac's hands.

"Take this home. Study. Bring to school Monday." Jennifer spoke in English, simplifying as much as possible.

Ajawac eyed the spelling text Magidins had been looking at earlier and quickly exchanged books. "Ajawac take home, study, bring to school Monday," she promised. The troubled frown replaced by a beaming smile, she hurried toward the door.

"Ajawac! Wait!" Jennifer called out. She started to follow Sope's daughter, but Hawk, who had reappeared an instant before, caught her by the elbow as she passed the cast-iron stove.

"Let her go," he advised.

"But the spelling text is too hard for her."

"It's not too hard for Magidins," Hawk observed. "Ajawac looks up to Magidins. She wants to gain my sister's favor. She knew Magidins wanted the spelling book. Now, Ajawac will offer it to her."

Jennifer narrowed her eyes, wondering just how long Hawk had been observing the little scene. "But they could have both taken a book, if they wished." Remembering what Angelique had told her earlier about the children's ability to understand only the simplest reader, she said, "Ajawac might like the first McGuffey reader."

Hawk glanced toward Sope.

Jennifer took his subtle hint and slipped the reader from the shelf, then approached the woman, suggesting in Ojibway that she take it to her daughter.

Sope accepted the book with a broad smile, nodding her thanks.

The morning hours passed quickly. By noontime, the room sparkled. Each desk had been waxed to a shine. The floor planks were bleached clean by the lye soap used by Canodens and Sope. Hawk, who had disappeared once again into the mysterious domain of the men, had sent a young boy to clean and test the woodstove, and a cheery fire took the chill out of the air. Newly-washed windowpanes gave a clear view of the bluff and bay beyond.

Caught back at each window were red and white checkered curtains, laundered and rehung by Angelique. They added a colorful, cozy touch to the natural pine walls.

While Canodens and Sope gathered their cleaning supplies together and prepared to leave, Jennifer thanked them for their help. When they had gone, she went to Angelique, who was fussing with one of her gingham curtains.

"I think I can face the first day of school now," she confessed. "You have made my job easier. The room looks lovely!"

"Merci," Angelique said. "I go home now. Make dinner."

Jennifer's eyes swept the immaculate room, coming to rest on Hawk's tall figure waiting by the door.

"If Hawk will permit me, I'd like to stay awhile longer, just to be sure I'm ready for the children when they come."

Angelique nodded, slung her woven bag over her shoulder, and left.

Jennifer sat behind her desk and looked out over the room. She envisioned each row of desks filled with students, older brothers and sisters sitting beside younger siblings. Hawk came forward to stand over her.

"You think deep thoughts," he observed.

"I'm thinking about Monday," she confided. "I thought the children were more adept at English, but if Ajawac is any example, I can see I was wrong. It's too bad Magidins dislikes me so. She could be a great help. Instead, I sense she'll try to make things difficult. I wish I knew how to get through to her. I'm afraid she'll ruin school for the rest of the children."

"Perhaps not. There has been much arguing between my mother and my sister. Magidins must attend school until next year, when she is fourteen. But she resists. Still, she is only a child—and an Ojibway. She must obey."

A sudden chill coursed through Jennifer. "She may be required to attend, but if she comes against her will, she can sow seeds of discontent among the others. . . . I have a feeling I may come to school on Monday, after all the work that has been done today, only to find that I am not prepared, after all."

"Do not fret. I will personally come early on the first day to start the fire. While the room is warming, I will return for you at the LaFontes'."

Damping the fire, Hawk noted the good supply of firewood neatly stacked in readiness for the following week. "Come," he said to Jennifer. "Angelique will have your meal waiting. Think no more of the first school day. All will be well."

Jennifer rose slowly from her desk. "That is my prayer, Hawk," she said with a long sigh.

Still, as they walked down the path through the schoolyard, she could not resist taking one last look at the little building on the bluff. In the bright October sunlight, the schoolhouse seemed a peaceful haven. She hoped that, come Monday, she would still view it that way.

The first day of school dawned cold and clear. Jennifer was ready long before Hawk arrived at the LaFontes' to escort her to the village.

Angelique tried to assure Jennifer all would go well, though it was evident from the way she scurried in and out of her young boarder's bedroom that Jennifer was not the only one suffering from nervousness.

Jennifer had dressed in her woolen tunic and breeches and heavy wool coat. Draped over her shoulders was the brown shawl which would serve as a scarf for both her head and neck, sealing out the bitter wind that had whipped the bay waters into little white caps. She stood by her sunny window, watching for signs of Hawk on the trail.

When Angelique entered her room, she turned to face her.

"I pray for you, Jenny. No worries. Now, here is lunch—plenty much—make you strong." She handed Jennifer a *makuk,* slipping the handle over her arm.

The weight of the container hung heavy on Jennifer's wrist. "What did you put in here? Lake Superior sandstone?" she teased as she lifted the bark lid for a peek.

"Sandstone? No! Biscuits!" Hands on hips, the Ojibway woman glared in mock anger, then burst out laughing.

After the first awkward days, when each had guardedly appraised the other, this kind of word play had eased many a tense moment. Today, as she faced the first day of her teaching duties, Jennifer was especially grateful for the little ritual.

"I make extra biscuits and smoked fish. Enough for you and Hawk." She pointed out the window. "He come now." Angelique hurried to open the back door.

Jennifer tucked the corners of her wool shawl beneath her coat collar, then pulled on the fur-lined doeskin gloves Angelique's husband, Pierre, had given her and stepped into the back hallway.

Dressed for colder weather, Hawk wore long buckskin breeches, heavy blanket moccasins inside leather ones, and a thick wool blanket draped over his left shoulder. Into the hem of his blanket had been sewn the outline of a hawk, identifying the garment as his own.

"Take good care, my Jenny," Angelique whispered. She stepped forward and kissed Jennifer on each cheek.

143

When they stepped out the door, a cutting wind whipped around the corner of the cabin.

"The breeze off the bay is cold, but the schoolhouse will be warm." Hawk took the *makuk* from her and moved swiftly down the trail.

Jennifer took one and a half steps to each of Hawk's strides. Her stomach twinged uneasily, and she was eager for the school day to begin. Once she made contact with her students, she was certain to feel more confident.

As they came to the lookout, Jennifer noticed the rays of the sun bouncing off the frothy waves of the bay. Along the narrow Indian trail, its beams filtered through bare branches, shedding dim light on the decaying carpet of fallen leaves. The fresh cold air invigorated her, cleansed her, braced her for the hours ahead. With her cheeks stinging and her nose thoroughly chilled, she looked forward to warming herself at the school stove.

At last they arrived at the village and continued across to the line of trees separating it from the schoolhouse. Eying the treetops, Hawk slowed his pace. Jennifer looked up also, thinking he had spotted a bird, and scanned the row of hemlocks.

Suddenly, he took off at a fast trot. Jennifer hurried after him. When the school came into view, she thought it odd that the windows, freshly washed on Saturday, seemed dark. Only a thin trail of smoke issued from the chimney. Perhaps the fire in the stove had gone out.

Hawk set the *makuk* aside and ran to the door. Jennifer followed close behind.

"Stay back!" he warned, flinging open the door.

Out billowed clouds of black smoke. Hawk coughed and stepped back, shielding his face with his blanket.

Terror struck Jennifer's heart.

Fire!

chapter

12

ALL THE HORRID, NIGHTMARISH MEMORIES of the fire in Eagle River flooded over Jennifer.

In moments, the initial cloud of black smoke had thinned, and Hawk started into the building.

"No, Hawk! Don't go in there!" Jennifer ran after him, certain that if he disappeared into the schoolhouse, she would never see him alive again.

He hesitated near the doorstep. She clutched his forearm with both hands and tried to pull him away from the door, but he stood, unmoving.

"It is smoke, not fire. I think the damper on the stove is closed. No harm will come to me," he assured her, peeling her fingers from his arm. "Stand back, away from the smoke."

Jennifer's pulse raced as the image of the flames of the Eagle River fire raged in her mind. "Lord, protect Hawk," she prayed.

She heard the sound of wood against wood as the windows were raised. More smoke poured from the building, and Angelique's once-bright red and white checked curtains, now dingy with a coating of soot, fluttered out the open window. Jennifer's stomach turned at the sight.

Shortly, Hawk emerged from the building. "Someone closed the flue." His jawline tensed with anger. "The room is full of soot. You cannot hold school here today."

"Who could possibly have done such a thing?" she gasped.

"We can only guess. I left the door unlocked after I started the fire. Some students arrive early, and I saw no reason to lock them out. I did not believe my sister would do this—" The scowl on his face was frightening in its intensity.

"How do you know it was Magidins? She resents me, it's true, but surely she wouldn't—"

"I am certain it was she. I will talk with her, make her confess."

"No, Hawk. Don't pressure her. It will only make matters worse."

"My sister must be punished!" His cool gray eyes flashed with unexpected fire.

"Hawk, was Magidins coming to school today? You mentioned an argument between Magidins and your mother. Maybe she wasn't coming at all."

"No. She would not openly defy my mother's word. Too, she had changed. She seemed happy about this day. Now I know the reason. She was planning . . . *this!*" His gesture of disgust took in the ruined curtains, the soot-covered desks, the smoked walls. "I will take you to the LaFontes' cabin, then the women will clean the schoolhouse."

Jennifer stood firm, her chin thrust forward. "No, Hawk. This time, I can't let them do the work. It is because of me that their hard labor must be done over. I'm staying."

"Then I stay, too. The work will go faster." His simple declaration brought a rush of warmth that took Jennifer by surprise.

Upon closer inspection, Jennifer found the place to be in far worse condition than it had first appeared. Everything was covered with a layer of black film, including all the books her mother had sent. Before she removed her coat, she cleaned a peg and a section of the wall behind it to protect her new garment from the soot.

As the children arrived, she explained what had happened. Some returned with bark containers of water, soap, and brushes to help with the cleaning, but there was no sign of Magidins and Ajawac.

At lunchtime, Jennifer dismissed the few children who remained,

146

set the biscuits and smoked fish on the stove to warm, then drew up a chair at her desk to eat with Hawk.

"We're almost through," Jennifer observed. "The room will be ready for school tomorrow, except for the curtains. I'll take them to Angelique's and wash them myself."

Hawk strode across the room to an area still black with film. "Magidins will not do this again," he said sullenly. "I will see to that."

"Don't be too hard on your sister," Jennifer warned. "It will only make matters worse for me."

With his back still turned to her, he spoke quietly. "This is my fault," he confessed. "When I was young, the mission teacher was a stern man. Mr. Quigly asked difficult questions, then scolded the students when they answered incorrectly. His tongue was sharp.

"He believed in the Bible verse, 'Spare the rod and spoil the child.' His rod was in constant use.

"I studied hard, as did my sister, so we were able to answer his questions." Jennifer could see the taut muscles of his back beneath the Ojibway blanket. "For some time, we were the only ones who escaped punishment.

"Then one day, Mr. Quigly asked questions that were not in our lessons." There was an unbelievable quiver in the deep voice, and Jennifer strained to hear his words. "He struck us many times. When we went home, our hands were bruised and swollen."

Jennifer closed her eyes, recoiling from the imagined pain of a rod whacking against sensitive knuckles. The man was a monster! How could he have been allowed to hold such a position of trust . . . and in the name of Christ? She was incensed, but kept quiet.

Hawk continued. "I was eleven years old, Magidins, five. I could not forgive the cruelty of a man who would strike an innocent child. The next morning, I came to the schoolhouse early. I broke his rod into pieces, threw them into the stove, and closed the damper. When he arrived, the room looked as it did this morning.

"So, you see, I am responsible for this act of disgrace," he said, turning to face her, his silver eyes glittering. "Magidins learned her trick from me long ago . . . before Jesus Christ came to live in me . . . before I learned that his way is a way of peace. . . . But Magidins does not know this yet. She was wrong."

"I'm sure she doesn't believe she is wrong. She was only showing her loyalty to Laura Simpson," Jennifer ventured in a hushed voice.

"After I speak with her . . . she will understand."

They spent the next hours in quiet contemplation, working side by side. There was no need for words. And only when the room was restored to shining order did they leave, locking the schoolhouse door carefully behind them.

"Magidins would not admit she closed the damper," Hawk said the next morning on the way to the school. "In fact, she was angry when I accused her."

"Then maybe she was telling the truth," Jennifer mused. "Maybe she didn't do it, after all."

"I am certain she did it." His bronze features were set.

"But perhaps someone else—"

Hawk shook his head. "No. It was Magidins. I have gone over it in my mind many times. All of the other children were eager to start school. Even Ajawac. Only Magidins had reason to make trouble for you."

"Ajawac and Magidins seem to be very good friends," Jennifer observed.

"Their friendship is new. It began after Miss Simpson left L'Anse for Detroit. Until then, Magidins spent little time with Ajawac."

Jennifer was thoughtful, considering this new information. "Then I am glad she has Ajawac now."

With Hawk standing by, Jennifer registered each child. Some had only an Ojibway name, difficult to understand and spell. Others also had a Christian name. Without Hawk's assistance, she thought, it would have been impossible from the beginning.

When her registration list was complete, Jennifer opened class with a reading from the Bible in English. Observing the whispered

Ojibway words of question, the puzzled looks on small dark faces, she knew that the formal prose of King James had compounded the problem. She must think of some way to make these special moments meaningful each day.

Laying the Bible atop her desk, she glanced over the roomful of bright-eyed youngsters. All ages and sizes, they waited expectantly for her first instructions. She breathed a prayer for guidance.

Spotting Magidins and Ajawac at a shared desk at the back of the room, she called their names. When they hesitantly came forward, she beamed an encouraging smile and handed them the grammar books to distribute among the other students, hoping to elevate them in the eyes of their classmates. Ajawac seemed genuinely happy to cooperate. But Magidins' help was given grudgingly and, Jennifer was certain, only because Hawk was still present, standing with folded arms at the door.

Jennifer made no mention of the previous day's incident. Those who had helped with the cleaning had already been thanked, and there seemed no reason to dwell on the unhappy event.

When the school day ended, Jennifer was exhausted. A great deal of energy was required to explain even the simplest directions, and the response of her students was evoked only with considerable effort. Again, a difference in the two races was clearly evident. The Indian children were shy and reserved, making their participation much more difficult to obtain. Jennifer had seen this characteristic in Hawk many times. He did not share freely, and the few times he had openly confided in her now came back to her as special treasures to be guarded.

On the way back to the LaFontes', Jennifer mentioned her difficulty.

"Ojibway children are taught early to be quiet, so their enemies will not hear them. Sometimes, when you spoke to a child," he said, recalling the day's activities, "you thought he did not understand. This is not always true. The small ones have learned to think long before answering."

"I'll try to remember to give them more time," Jennifer said, grateful for the insight, but feeling the distance widening between herself and her new charges. "I feel so inadequate, so restricted, not being allowed to speak any Ojibway in the classroom!" she blurted. "How did Miss Simpson manage?"

There was a long pause as Hawk measured his words. "She asked a student who knew both languages to translate."

Jennifer sighed. "Magidins could be a great help to me, if only she would. I'm afraid, without you there, she won't cooperate at all."

"I am satisfied that you will find a way."

At the moment, such a blessing seemed beyond Jennifer's comprehension.

That evening, she gave thought to the situation with Magidins and Ajawac. Perhaps a first step would be to separate the girls, yet she hesitated to take such a drastic measure. Since the class consisted of a variety of ages and abilities, much of the instruction had to be given either individually or in small groups. There was no doubt in Jennifer's mind that Ajawac would progress more rapidly without the constant distraction of her friend.

In the days ahead, Jennifer discovered that Ajawac had not given the spelling text to Magidins, after all. Though it was far too advanced for her, she carried it to and from school each day. And, to Jennifer's amazement, when she assigned Ajawac a page in the grammar book and a few words from the spelling text, the girl came fully prepared the following day.

Magidins, however, was another matter. It was painfully evident that the young girl reported to the schoolhouse only because she had no other choice. She spoke as little as possible during their instruction time, and her answers to Jennifer's questions frequently consisted of the words, "I do not know." Even with the simplest sentences, she made mistakes, intentional mistakes, Jennifer was sure. The minutes spent with the difficult girl were distressing, but Jennifer was determined to reach her.

As the days and weeks passed, Ajawac was consistently prepared for her lessons, eager to show her improving ability in English and to tackle new spelling words and grammar assignments. Jennifer began to rely on her for simple translations when younger students faltered.

As Ajawac bloomed, Magidins became more and more withdrawn. Finally, Jennifer dropped the verbal part of Magidins' instruction altogether, assigning her lessons to be written out in grammar and arithmetic. Though Hawk's sister no longer participated in question-and-answer periods or in oral recitations, she *did* complete her written lessons each day. These seldom required correction.

Ajawac's desire to please Jennifer seemed to cause a widening gap in her friendship with Hawk's sister. And one day, they stopped sharing a desk. Ajawac had taken her usual place in the back of the room, having arrived early as was her custom. Magidins, who came at the last minute, slipped into a different seat, one which had previously been unoccupied. When Ajawac encouraged Magidins to join her, Hawk's obstinate sister refused.

It saddened Jennifer that Ajawac, who was a year younger than Magidins and not as bright, was suffering for having become her helper, but there seemed nothing she could do about it. If the friendship were to survive, the young girls would have to work out their own problems.

The students who really delighted Jennifer were the small girls. Mani was the most responsive, and her circle of friends instinctively followed her leadership. Unlike Magidins, her influence on her peers was positive, and these first-year students made rapid strides with their English.

Time passed quickly. November days were often dark and drear, with heavy gray clouds obscuring a colorless sun. Jennifer's trips to the schoolhouse were made in early morning darkness.

One frosty day, when the sky was clear and the air still, the sun made a rare appearance. It eased above the horizon in a blaze of red, dancing off glazed branches and weeds, making the pathway to the village appear encrusted with diamonds and rubies. When Jennifer and Hawk reached the lookout, they paused while she beheld the jeweled scene with breathless wonder.

When late November winds grew brisk and cold, Pierre LaFonte insisted that Jennifer ride his small horse to the village. At such times, Hawk led the mount down the trail, often through a dusting of powdery snow.

One evening in early December, the cold Lake Superior winds howled past the LaFontes' snug cabin for hours, dropping a thick blanket of snow on the house and surrounding woods.

"The snow, she is ever'where," observed Pierre who had risen from his chair beside a roaring fire and was peering through a small round circle he had cleared on the frosty window "The horse, he no' make it to the village, for sure."

"But how will I get there?" Jennifer looked up from her book, alarmed at the implication.

"Hawk have way. You see," Angelique comforted, a gleam in her eye.

"Will he teach me how to walk on snowshoes?" Jennifer had seen Pierre's snowshoes in the back entryway, and the thought had crossed her mind earlier. Staying upright in deep snow took skill, she knew.

"*Demain,* tomorrow, you see," was all Angelique would say.

Jennifer tossed all night, fearing she would be late for school if she had to learn how to walk on snowshoes first. She was out of bed, had stoked her fire, and was dressed before Angelique came to her room.

"What? Dressed already!" Angelique exclaimed.

"I couldn't sleep. I want to be ready the moment Hawk arrives. It will probably take extra time to get to school in the snow, and I wouldn't want to be late."

"Do not worry, Jen-ni. Hawk get you there plenty fast."

As Jennifer straightened her room, she heard the tinkle of bells and looked out her window. To her astonishment, two bell-collared dogs approached on the woodland trail. The bushy-tailed, wolf-like creatures barked good-naturedly, pulling beind them a most unusual conveyance. It was a long, low, boxy affair, the front of which tapered into an upward curve. At the rear, Hawk occupied a small driver's platform. The vehicle skimmed the snow on narrow runners, coming to a halt outside the back door.

After breakfast, Hawk bundled Jennifer into the sledge, wrapping her in a great bearskin robe. Angelique deposited a warmed stone in her hands and warned her not to expose them to the air, or she would risk frostbite.

At the crack of Hawk's whip, the dogs dashed down the trail, the sledge gliding smoothly over the three-foot layer of white. The dogs yelped with excitement. Hawk ran alongside to guide the animals, or rode behind Jennifer. Though the icy air chilled her exposed cheeks, she felt as if she were flying!

That day the children came to school on snowshoes, shaking them off and stacking them in the vestibule before the start of class. During recess, they again donned their leather and wooden footgear and went outside to slide effortlessly over the snowy schoolyard, while Jennifer plodded through the heavy drifts with cumbersome boots. More than once, she eyed the snowshoes enviously.

During the afternoon, the children began making little gifts to be used as decorations for a Christmas tree and later given to members of their families. Weeks earlier, Jennifer had asked them to bring bits of birchbark and buckskin, lengths of leather thong, scraps of broadcloth and calico. To the children's collection, Jennifer added pieces of bright red felt Angelique had obtained at Crebassa's trading post and some lengths of ribbon Pierre had bartered for at the white settlements.

With so many of the children still dependent upon her for guidance, Jennifer was exhausted after an hour and a half. Today, even the more capable students seemed unable to make simple decisions for themselves, and were no help at all with the younger ones. Jennifer was relieved when there was only an hour left before time for dismissal, and they could put aside their slates and crafts, and rehearse Christmas carols.

Traditionally, beginning with the first missionaries to the Ojibways, the mission teacher was responsible for preparing a special program to be presented a few days before Christmas. Not only was this occasion used to demonstrate the children's newly acquired skills, but as an opportunity to proclaim the birth of Christ to unbelieving parents. With that responsibility in mind, Jennifer had carefully selected the carols the children would sing.

The first was her own particular favorite, "Silent Night," which she taught in Ojibway, using a translation made by Father Baraga, a well-loved priest who had once served at the Catholic Mission in L'Anse. Even though the words were in their native tongue, the children seemed unable to remember them, and their singing sounded flat, more like a chant than a hymn. It was with a sigh of relief that Jennifer rang the dismissal bell at the end of the school day.

As the last child left the building, she sat facing a roomful of desks, strewn with futile attempts to create gaudy birds, miniature canoes, and oddly dressed cornhusk dolls. Coupled with her earlier frustration in helping the children make decorations for the tree, Jennifer felt defeated. Even the yelping of the sledge dogs signaling Hawk's arrival did not move her from her chair. Instead, she stared out the window, watching her young students glide toward the village on their snowshoes, an activity so natural it seemed they were born to it.

Stepping inside the door, Hawk brushed new-fallen snow from his fur cap and blanket. His mouth turned up at the corners as he paused to look at the children's crafts.

Jennifer rose from her desk with a sigh. "I plod through the snow in my clumsy boots, but the children move with ease and grace on their snowshoes. If they could only do half as well at their gift-making tomorrow." She picked up two canoe-shaped pieces of birch bark from a nearby desk. "A gift for Mani's brother, I suppose."

Hawk took the canoe from Jennifer's hand and laid it aside. "Tell me. What gift would please *you* for Christmas?"

Jennifer moved toward the back of the room. "To win Magidins' confidence, to share the story of the infant Jesus, to see it make a difference in the students. The mission rule requires me to read a verse from the Bible and say a prayer every morning, but sometimes I think I should spend the time trying to improve their English. I seem to be failing at everything I try to do."

"You are planting seeds. Leave the harvest to God," Hawk suggested.

"I suppose you're right." Jennifer pulled on her heavy coat and wrapped the brown shawl tightly about her head. "I'm ready to go home and curl up by Angelique's fire. Perhaps tomorrow will be a better day."

As time for the Christmas program drew near, Jennifer felt heartened by the children's efforts. They had managed to memorize two Christmas songs and had completed their gifts, hanging them on the tree Hawk had brought in from the woods and placed in the corner of the room. It was a beautiful, full hemlock with plenty of branches for the dozens of ribbons, dolls, moccasins and pine cone bric-a-brac. There were strings of popcorn and cranberries as well, a touch of the familiar that made Jennifer long for home.

Throughout the endless rehearsals and Christmas preparations, Ajawac was pleasant and helpful, while Magidins all but refused to participate. Jennifer tried not to let the sullen girl's attitude affect her own, but her heart often ached for Hawk's sister. Magidins had lost her friend, shut Ajawac out, and become a silent, brooding island in the back of the classroom. Each night, Jennifer prayed for a way to break through Magidins' invisible barrier, but it seemed to grow thicker with time, as did the ice on L'Anse Bay.

A few days before the Christmas program, Angelique helped Jennifer bake cookies. Her personal Christmas gift to each child would be a gingerbread man. Angelique helped her decorate each one with dabs of colored frosting and pieces of broken nuts, gathered from the woods in the fall.

Night fell crisp and clear over the Ojibway village on the evening of the Christmas presentation. Bright stars blinked on as parents and children made their way through newfallen snow to file into the tiny log schoolhouse.

Parents listened attentively as students stood before them to sing. A capella voices—slightly off-key—told the story of the first Christmas Eve in song.

Afterward, little ones hastened to claim their handiwork from the tree and distribute gifts to appreciative parents. When the fir stood bare, save all but the paper star on top, Jennifer moved around the room, handing each child a cookie from her box. There were exclamations of delight from all the students . . . until she came to Magidins.

Her black eyes sparking, Hawk's sister put her hands behind her, refusing Jennifer's gift. Embarrassed and hurt by this intentional slight, Jennifer placed the cookie on the desk in front of Magidins and moved on to the next child. Apparently, Magidins intended to nurse her resentment, not even setting it aside for a single evening.

Compared to other such special events that Jennifer could recall from her past life in both Clifton and Eagle River, the atmosphere in the room seemed subdued. Christmas had always been a time of intense excitement and anticipation, and there was a general air of gaiety during the season that found expression in loving deeds. There had been whispered secrets and shopping expeditions and the sound of music and rejoicing in the little church back home.

Tonight, the faces of the parents were solemn, and now that the program was over, the children themselves had sobered, leaving off the childish giggles and excited chatter she had come to expect from them. Quietly, they donned their wraps and hurried out the door, murmuring their farewells.

Jennifer, too, was eager to end the evening, eager to find some joy yet in this most blessed of all seasons. With Hawk waiting for her at the door, she fought a swelling ache in her throat and the threat of tears that stung her eyes.

Straightening her desk, she walked toward the back of the room, where her coat hung on a peg. As she did so, she noticed Ajawac standing uncertainly at the rear.

"Ajawac! Why are you still here?"

"I want give you this." Removing a package from her desk, the young girl handed it to Jennifer with a shy smile. "Merry Christmas, Miss Jenny."

chapter

13

HESITANTLY, JENNIFER ACCEPTED THE PARCEL. "How thoughtful of you, Ajawac, but I have nothing for you.'"

"You already give me . . . these," she reminded Jennifer, holding up the speller and the grammar text she had received the day before school started. "Open now," she urged, indicating her gift to her teacher.

Jennifer removed the string and peeled the paper away. Inside were two pure white doeskin moccasins lined with white rabbit's fur. The toes were beaded with an intricate design of red, blue and green. Jennifer removed her heavy shoes and slipped her weary feet into the soft fur.

"These are beautiful, Ajawac, and so warm! I shall treasure them always because they came from you."

Ajawac's dark eyes were glowing like twin stars when she left the schoolhouse.

At the young girl's departure, Hawk came forward to help Jennifer straighten the room. A few scraps of paper littered the floor, and she bent to retrieve one of them, her gaze falling on Magidins' desk. Her heart plummeted. There lay the gingerbread man, now broken in pieces.

"I was hoping the Christmas preparations would soften your sister's heart," she told Hawk, "that somehow the story of Christ's birth would get through to her, but I can see I was wrong." Sadly, she gathered up the crumbs.

"We must keep praying for her. It is all we can do."

So far, she mused, all her prayers for Magidins appeared to be futile. The girl stubbornly resisted all overtures of friendship.

All the way home, as Hawk urged the dogs on, Jennifer contemplated the problem. This short break from the regular routine would do both her and Magidins good, she decided. And perhaps the new year would bring a more hopeful outlook.

Hawk brought the sledge to a stop outside the cabin door. A fine, powdery snow was falling, resembling a crystal curtain in the lamplight. Lanterns in each of the windows beckoned Jennifer to the warmth inside.

"In two days it will be Christmas," Hawk observed, helping Jennifer out of the sledge. "I will come to you." Removing a glove, he pressed a finger against the corner of her mouth, forcing it upward. "Then, I want to see smiles."

"I'll try," Jennifer promised, her lips curving almost against her will. "Good night, Hawk."

She stepped inside out of the cold, and Angelique rushed to help her off with her heavy coat.

"How was Christmas program? Parents like?"

"I think so." Jennifer said wearily.

"And did children like gingerbread men?"

Jennifer nodded. Anxious to change the subject, she held up the package Ajawac had given her. "I was not expecting this."

Angelique exclaimed over the white moccasins, then offered Jennifer a mug of hot cocoa. She sipped the sweet drink in silence, and retired to her room.

Angelique had already lit a fire in the fireplace, and the room felt especially cozy. Jennifer removed her tunic and leggings and pulled a warm, soft flannel gown over her head. From her top dresser drawer, she took out the ruffled nightcap her mother had recently sent.

Beneath it was a birchbark box, decorated with porcupine quills.

She ran her fingers over the delicate design. This would be her Christmas gift to Hawk. Patiently, Angelique had taught her how to craft the quill box, and Jennifer was pleased with the results of her handiwork.

As she sank into the downy softness of the feather bed, Jennifer wondered what gift Hawk would bring her. He had mentioned he was preparing a useful item, but she couldn't think what it might be. Still turning over in her mind the events of the evening, she drifted into a dreamless sleep.

Jennifer spent the following morning in the kitchen with Angelique, helping bake breads sweetened with dried fruits. During the afternoon, she rekindled the fire in her room, demanding privacy to wrap her gifts for Angelique and Pierre—lacy, flowered handherchiefs her mother had sent her for Angelique, and new woolen socks for Pierre. She wrapped them in the brown paper she had decorated a few days earlier. Angelique had given her a raw potato and chrome yellow dye, and with them, Jennifer had stamped a star pattern onto the drab wrap, turning it into a festive covering.

Before the first light of dawn on Christmas morning, the delicious aroma of maple syrup wafted to her through the crack beneath her bedroom door. When she reached the kitchen, she found Angelique baking maple syrup pie, a French-Canadian recipe she had brought with her from Quebec.

Breakfast was a small feast, served later than usual. When they had finished eating, Jennifer helped wash dishes and put the kitchen in order. Then Angelique ushered her into the common room, where Pierre sat smoking his pipe.

"It is time for gifts," she announced, her eyes twinkling. "Pierre, bring Jenny's present, *s'il vous plait*. Jenny, close eyes until I say open."

Jenny obeyed, listening as Pierre's moccasined feet crossed the plank floor to the bedroom he shared with Angelique at the opposite end of the cabin. Moments later, his footsteps returned, slower now, and with a scuffing sound, until she heard the gentle thud of something being set on the floor.

"Now, Jenny, look."

She blinked open her eyes, gasping with surprise at the sight they beheld. Before her stood a rocker, decoratively carved and glowing with the warmth of highly polished pine, obviously Pierre's handiwork. Covering its back and seat were crazy-quilt cushions of Angelique's design.

"Oh, my," she breathed, stunned by the generosity of their gift. "It's too much—"

"Ah, ah!" Angelique wagged her finger. "Jenny come home tired after school. Must have place to rest." She pulled Jennifer over to the chair. "Sit."

Jennifer dared not argue. She eased herself down onto the thickly-padded seat, leaned against the back, and gave a push with her foot. The wooden floor creaked softly as she rocked. "It's perfect, absolutely perfect." She rose to plant a kiss on Angelique's cheek, and another on Pierre's. "Thank you both so much. Now, it's time for *your* gifts." She hurried to her room to fetch the two tiny parcels which now seemed wholly inadequate.

"Merry Christmas, Angelique, Pierre." She handed each a package.

Angelique opened her gift first. Her mouth formed an "o" as she held up the delicately tatted handkerchiefs, one at a time, and laid them out on the table to admire. "So ver' pretty. Your mother make?"

Jennifer nodded.

"When I use, I remember this Christmas, and you, Jenny. Tomorrow, I write your mother. Thank her." She squeezed Jennifer on the shoulders.

"Now, I open," Pierre said, quickly unfolding the paper covering his gift. Fingering the thick woolen socks, he asked Jennifer, "You make?"

"Yes. I hope they fit."

He kicked off his moccasins and pulled them on. *"Parfait. J'aime*

162

beaucoup. Perfect. I like ver' much." He worked his moccasins on over them and walked about the common room to test them further, then disappeared into the kitchen. When he returned he was carrying the maple syrup pie. "Mmm. *Le dessert*. So good, he smell, I could eat all."

"Oh, no!" Angelique protested, taking it from him and setting it on the table. "You sit by fire. I get knife. Cut you nice piece." She had just started toward the kitchen when Hawk entered the cabin.

Pierre greeted him heartily. *"Joyeaux Noel*. You come in time for maple syrup pie."

"Then I have come at a good time." Hawk flung off his heavy wraps, his gray eyes searching the room for Jennifer. "I bring greetings to all of you in the name of the One who was born on this day."

Noting that he had come empty-handed, Jennifer covered her disappointment with a cheerful smile. "Merry Christmas, Hawk. I have a little something for you in my room."

Drawing the box from her drawer, she fingered the quill design she had labored over for so many hours, determined that it should be perfect for Hawk. Had Laura Simpson ever presented him with a handmade gift, Jennifer felt sure it would have been flawless in every detail. Sighing, she turned and left the room, holding the little box behind her.

Hawk was warming himself at the fireplace, the angular planes of his face relaxed in an expression of satisfaction. Beside him was propped a pair of handsome new snowshoes.

"For you," he said, gesturing toward the wood-and-leather gear. A look of pride flashed through his smoky eyes, and Jennifer knew that he had been equally concerned that she approve the gift he had made for her.

The snowshoes were adorned with a black thunderbird set against a red background on the forepart, and black webbing on the mid- and rear-sections, complemented by yarn fringes. The crafts-manship was superb, and she all but forgot about the quill box. Hastily setting it on the table, she knelt to examine the wood frame of the snowshoes, tracing with her finger the curve where it bent toward the heel.

"Hawk! You could not have pleased me more!" She looked up at him, her dark eyes shining with pleasure. "I must try them at once!"

"There is time after pie," Pierre suggested. "Besides, do you forget your gift to Hawk?" He inclined his head toward the box on the table.

"Oh, of course!" Jennifer exclaimed, picking up the quill box and handing it to Hawk.

He turned it over and over in his hands, smoothing the wood, tracing the intricate design of the hawk on its cover. On the bottom, he located her initials, JMC. For a breathless moment, Jennifer thought he would not speak.

At last he lifted his head, a spark of amber light reflecting in the depths of his eyes. "It is fine work, a place to keep one's greatest treasures . . . earthly treasures. Here," and he held the box against his chest, "in my heart, I hold those things that cannot be made with hands." The look she read in his expression sent a warm tide pulsing to her cheeks.

Angelique entered just at that moment, bearing a tray laden with the mouth-watering slices of pie, and Jennifer hurried to help her set them out while Hawk and Pierre stoked the fire.

As they gathered around the table, Jennifer thought of her parents, who would be sitting down to Christmas dinner with their boarders about now. She wondered if this holy day would bless them as abundantly as it had her, and prayed it might be so.

Later, Jennifer dressed warmly and followed Hawk as he carried her snowshoes outside and laid them on the snow. He helped her into the buckskin thongs that secured the foot to the apparatus, then slipped into his own snowshoes.

"Slide one foot past the other," he explained, demonstrating with grace. It looked simple enough.

Arms out to the side for balance, Jennifer gingerly placed her left foot forward, then attempted to bring her right foot toward the other, snagging the front snowshoe in the process. Without warning, she found herself lying flat on her back in the snow.

Throwing back his head, Hawk let out a hearty laugh, his deep voice resounding through the snowy woods and startling a deer that had wandered into view. Indignant, Jennifer hauled herself to a sitting position, ready to unleash an angry tirade. Then, realizing how ridiculous she must look, with the tips of her snowshoes sticking into three feet of snow, she began to chuckle, her hilarity building until the tears ran down her face. For several moments, the silvery sound of their mutual enjoyment filled the crystalline air.

"Hawk, help me up!" she scolded at last, extending a mittened hand to him. "It's cold down here, and I can't afford to catch my death!"

He was at her side in an instant, sobering as his large hand covered her small one. Though he had often assisted her in and out of the sledge, or helped her negotiate treacherous spots on the trail, this time his touch took her breath away, and she gasped in surprise.

"Maybe you'd better show me again, Hawk," she said in a tiny voice, the sudden hush amplifying her words.

Slowly, without taking his eyes off her, he circled in front of her. The tall figure was majestic, commanding, and his movements, even in the clumsy snowshoes, were fluid and elegant. She watched, mesmerized, until he came to a full stop. Her heart was pounding erratically, like the drumbeat she often heard in the village.

"The first lesson is always the hardest," he said quietly, his eyes eloquent with love. Then he gently coached her, showing her how to lift her feet and set down the snowshoes so they wouldn't trip her. Soon she walked beside him, hesitant, stumbling at times, but moving nonetheless. They had crossed the clearing and neared the woods when she stopped and looked at him with triumph in her eyes.

"You see, Jennifer," he said, her name on his lips like a warm caress, "I can teach you how to glide across the snow, but it takes two hearts beating as one to learn the most important lesson of all. I think God's greatest gift to me . . . next to the infant King whose birth we celebrate this day . . . is . . . you."

There was no sound at all under the great vaulted gray sky rimmed with snow-flocked trees—except her own sharp intake of breath.

Jennifer felt rooted to the spot, bound to earth, not by the contraptions she wore on her feet, but by the weight in her heart. Hawk loved her! Yet, how could she accept this gift he offered her? Their two different worlds were poles apart. If she dared believe that what he said was true, was Hawk himself God's special gift to *her*?

"I must leave you now . . ." he was saying, "to tend my traps and to hunt. I will not return until the moon is full."

And before she could protest, he gathered her hand in his and pressed it to his lips. Too soon he was gone, gliding quickly out of sight around the bend of the trail.

For the next few days, though Jennifer did not see Hawk, she could almost chart his activities by the schedule Pierre kept. He, too, had traps to tend—otter, mink, marten, fisher, rabbit, and beaver. The traps were checked every second day, and moved from place to place, depending upon the animal tracks.

If Pierre were not bringing home small animals from his traps, he was pursuing bigger game for their table. The forest abounded in deer, moose, fox, and wolf. She could envision Hawk, a sturdy buck draped across his shoulders, returning from the day's hunt. When a man killed a deer, however, he would often bring home only part of it at day's end. The women were sent into the woods the following day to retrieve the rest.

Both women were kept busy with the preparation of meat and hides, their tasks duplicated many times over in the homes of the Ojibway women. Watching Angelique, Jennifer learned how to tan hides for clothing, and dry meat that would last for many months. In the evenings, they sat by the fire, repairing the hunting togs that needed constant mending.

It was these hours that crept by for Jennifer. Gazing into the flickering fire, she was reminded of the changing lights in Hawk's eyes when he looked at her. She could almost track his thoughts by reading those gray disks—see his anger in their stormy depths, see his remoteness when they paled to the color of ice, see his compassion when they warmed to the hue of the sky, see his love when they blazed like coals. . . . How foolish seemed this love, how futile. A red man, a white woman . . . one molded by the primitive past; the other, forged by the shape of the future. What common bond could possibly meld their lives? Night after night, she wearied herself with these thoughts until the clock on the mantel told her it was time for bed.

On the second day of the year, Hawk came to the cabin before first light. Jennifer's joy in seeing him again was dulled by his pensive air. He said little, but packed her new snowshoes in the sledge for use later in the day, then bundled her securely in a fur rug.

Falling snow stung her eyes as Hawk drove the team toward the village. There was no sound except the crack of the whip, the yelping of the dogs, and an occasional sharp command from Hawk. No familiar landmark greeted her. The whole world was shrouded in white, and only Hawk's unerring instinct found the trail that had long since been obliterated.

When Jennifer entered the schoolhouse, she tried to ignore her uneasy feeling at the sight of Magidins' desk. She could still feel the pain of their last encounter, see the gingerbread cookie crumbled to bits.

Perhaps things would be different now. There was always hope.

She hung up her coat and returned to her desk to take out pen and attendance register, feeling Hawk's eyes on her.

"I will go now to check my traps. There have been problems. Many traps remain empty."

So that explained his uncharacteristic moodiness. Jennifer rushed to fill the silence, but could think of nothing to say.

"W—will you be coming for me later?" she stammered.

"At the usual time." He nodded briefly, then turned on his heel and strode out the door.

Shortly afterward, the students began trickling into the classroom.

"Good morning," she called, genuinely glad to see them after the brief vacation, but there was little response.

Magidins remained indifferent as well, returning her own cheerful greeting with a shrug of the shoulder and taking her isolated seat in the rear of the room. *I should be used to this treatment from Hawk's sister,* Jennifer thought, *but why are the other children so grim?* Looking at the rows of unsmiling copper faces, she sensed that their stoic expressions served to hide some unspoken concern.

Though it was past time to start class, several desks were still empty, and Jennifer realized that none of the older boys were present. She opened her book to record the attendance.

Mani's older brother, Wajki, or "The Younger Man," rarely missed a day of school.

"Is Wajki ill, Mani?"

"No, Miss Jenny. He go trapping. He go . . ." Mani mumbled a few words to Ajawac in Ojibway, then took her seat.

"Ajawac, what has Mani said?" Jennifer asked.

"Mani say there is trouble. Wajki say neighbor tribe steal from traps. Today, Wajki and his friends want stop them." She gestured toward the other empty seats.

Alarmed, Jennifer thought of Hawk. He must be in danger and had not wished to trouble her.

"Thank you, Ajawac." Looking at Mani, she said, "I'm very sorry to hear this. Would you like to say a prayer for the . . . students who couldn't be here today?"

Mani nodded. As the young girl prayed for the safety of her brother and the other boys with him, Jennifer added a silent petition for the Lord to watch over Hawk.

All morning, as the children stumbled through their recitations, the snow continued to fall. By the time the children were ready for the first recess, several new inches had accumulated. Fearing for Hawk, it was a struggle for Jennifer to keep her composure.

Ajawac, who had stayed inside to study her spelling, broke her anxious reverie.

"Why sad, Miss Jenny?"

Jennifer managed a tiny smile. "It's nothing, Ajawac. Come with me," she said, rising and moving to the back of the room, where her new snowshoes waited. "Let's join the others outside."

"These ver' pretty," Ajawac said, ignoring Jennifer's suggestion as she pointed to the black thunderbird. "You worry about Hawk, no?"

Jennifer laid a hand on Ajawac's shoulder. "You are wise, Ajawac. Yes, I am worried about Hawk, but it is best to keep busy. Come, join me outside. You can give *me* a lesson."

Soon, they were making their way along the edge of the promontory. The gusty northeast wind pelted them with a constant barrage of fine snow. Ajawac stopped, turned her face to the wind, and pointed toward the gray clouds obscuring the Huron Mountains to the northeast.

"My father say much snow coming. When dark clouds, wind come over mountains, bad storm. For three days."

"In that case, I'm even more thankful Hawk made my snowshoes and taught me how to use them," Jennifer commented. "There was already too much snow to go any distance without them." As she finished speaking, the sun peeked through the cloud cover to reveal a glimpse of the mountains and light the shimmering waves of crystal flakes. "Look! Maybe your father was wrong. Perhaps the sky will clear soon."

Ajawac shook her head. As if on cue, the brightness dimmed and clouds again shut out the direct rays of sunshine. "More snow come. Much more."

Throughout the afternoon, Jennifer watched the proof of Ajawac's prediction through the frosty window. The wind picked up, whipping the snowflakes into mounting drifts. She could see the trail to the wigwam village filling with snow. Soon, the smaller children would have a difficult time getting through. Jennifer dismissed her students early, urging them to hurry straight home.

The room emptied quickly, except for Ajawac, who remained at her desk, head down, copying spelling words over and over again on her slate board. Jennifer walked to the back of the room and sat at the desk beside her.

"Look, Miss Jenny. I nearly finish lesson number one hundred." She held her slate board up for Jennifer to see.

Jennifer scanned the girl's work. In the spelling book, each lesson was followed by several sentences making use of the assigned words. Ajawac had carefully copied five times the sentence reading, "A miraculous event is one that can take place only by the agency of divine power." Jennifer nodded with approval.

"You're doing very well, Ajawac, but don't you think you should be going home now? The trail is drifting over."

"No, Miss Jenny. I stay with you until Hawk come. I finish spelling lesson."

"But, Ajawac, he doesn't know I let the children go early. He won't be here for at least another half hour."

Ajawac shrugged. "I have snowshoes. I not worry."

Jennifer wanted to argue, but decided against it. Hawk would see Ajawac safely home.

Jennifer moved to the stove and added another stick of wood, then went to stand by the window. The snow was falling more heavily than before. It was difficult to see beyond the cliff. She removed the tiebacks from the curtains and let them hang down, closing off the view, then returned to her desk to make up individual lessons for some of the younger girls who were having difficulty in arithmetic.

Though she worked steadily, Jennifer's thoughts often traveled to Hawk. A half hour passed; forty-five minutes, and still he had not come. Jennifer glanced at Ajawac, hard at work in her seat. *The weather has slowed Hawk down,* Jennifer told herself. *He'll be here any minute*. She forced her thoughts back to her work, checking Magidins' paper. Hawk's sister had completed another lesson in geography, answering every question correctly and with surprising insight. She would have to remember to praise her for it, though she knew no emotion, even pride in achievement, would register on the girl's face.

Ajawac stirred from her desk. Jennifer watched as she pulled back the checked curtain, scraped away a circle of frost, and peered out. From her desk, Jennifer could tell daylight was fading with the lateness of the hour. A chill crept over the room. Jennifer put away her pen and inkpot, then joined Ajawac by the window.

"It's time to go home, Ajawac. I can't wait any longer for Hawk. In another hour, it will be completely dark. I must leave now if I'm to make it to LaFontes' before nightfall."

"You not go alone. I go with you, Miss Jenny."

"No, Ajawac. You are kind, but I can't let you come with me. I'll see you to your lodge, then continue alone to Angelique's. I'm sure I won't have any trouble. It's only a mile."

From the look on Ajawac's face, Jennifer expected an argument, but a moment later, her expression changed to one of complacency. "Yes, Miss Jenny."

A few minutes later, Ajawac and Jennifer stood outside the schoolhouse door, their snowshoes laid out on the ground before them. Jennifer had wrapped every inch of her skin in wool except for a small area surrounding her eyes. The wind had picked up considerably since noon recess, she realized, as she squinted toward the forest, hoping to see some sign of Hawk.

The stiff breeze tugged at her coat and pelted her half-closed lids with sticky granules of snow. She brushed the moisture from her eyes with the back of her mitten, then fastened the buckskin thongs of her snowshoes about her feet. The branches of the hemlock trees in the woods behind them groaned. At least the wind would be at their backs.

"Are you ready, Ajawac?" Jennifer shouted, preparing to lead the way.

"Yes, Miss Jenny," Ajawac called back, the wind quickly diminishing the sound of her voice.

The footprints of the children who had left an hour earlier had almost vanished from the path between the school and the lodges. Snow drifts obliterated portions of the trail as Jennifer plodded ahead.

After several minutes of strenuous effort, Jennifer and Ajawac arrived outside Sope's lodge. Ajawac reached out to her teacher, placing a hand on her arm.

"Stay with me tonight, Miss Jenny, *please*. Do not go LaFontes'."

Ajawac's touching plea was tempting, but Jennifer knew Angelique would be pacing the cabin, looking out the window at frequent intervals for signs of her return. Jennifer could feel the warm fire in the common room, taste the hot chocolate her hostess would pour in a mug to welcome her home, smell the venison soup cooking with dried plums—a meal so rich it had been renowned for its ability to revive the strength of voyageurs.

A sharp gust of wind pounded her back, urging her forward. "Thank you, Ajawac, but I must go. It isn't far now. I'll be all right." She removed the girl's hand from her arm.

With a wave, she turned to the trail leading across the village. There, the snow had been packed down with footprints, and progress was easier. When she left the clearing and headed into the woods on the west side, the path was half-filled with drifts. Already, her toes were beginning to feel cold. She wiggled them inside her boots each time she lifted a foot, trying to encourage the circulation. Inside her mittens, she abandoned the knitted thumb which kept that finger isolated and cold, and tucked it alongside the other four fingers for warmth.

Small tree branches had broken off in the wind and lay strewn across the trail. With difficulty, Jennifer managed to stoop down, loosen them from the deep snow, and toss them aside. This made progress slower than she had expected.

As the trail curved toward the shoreline of the bay, the wind became more wicked in its assault, the snow more blinding.

172

Branches creaked overhead. Daylight would soon be gone. She had expected to be home by now. Instead, she had another half mile of difficult going.

Jennifer forced her tired legs onward. Growing stiff with the cold, she began talking to herself, encouraging herself to move first one foot, then the other. A huge oak tree loomed ahead. She could stop there to rest, sheltered from the breeze. She headed for the west side of the tree and leaned against its trunk. *I can't go on,* she thought, breathing hard from her exertions.

Just as quickly, she contradicted herself aloud. "I *must* go on. I have no choice." She wiggled her fingers and toes, curling them, uncurling them again and again until she felt the rush of warm blood once more. The wind seemed ever stronger, the sounds of branches cracking, louder. She brushed the snow from her shawl and shoulders and pushed ahead, talking to herself.

"Right . . . left . . . right . . . left . . ."

A huge gust of wind howled through the trees, taking her breath. Behind Jennifer, a loud crack split the air. The earth trembled. In the eerie stillness that followed, Jennifer heard a moan. An animal? A person? *Hawk?*

She shuddered at the possibility. She started to turn around. There was barely room between the trees to do an about-face with the clumsy, long snowshoes. Inch by inch, she turned toward the east, toward the wind that now pelted her face with icy crystals. Protecting her eyes with her mittened hand, she could barely make out a downed limb in the distance. There was enough daylight left to highlight its considerable girth. It had fallen from the oak tree where she had rested only minutes before.

The howl of the wind now took on a human cry—louder more anguished.

"I'm coming!" Jennifer shouted.

She struggled against the fierce gusts, holding one arm against her forehead to protect her eyes from the blinding snow. As she approached the downed branch, she could see mangled snowshoes. From a distance, she could not distinguish the owner. That person remained hidden from view, partially buried in snow from the weight of the limb.

"Please, Lord, don't let it be Hawk!"

chapter
14

"AJAWAC!"

The Ojibway girl groaned.

"What are you doing here?" Jennifer crouched beside her, then broke off the small twigs scratching Ajawac's face and brushed the snow away. The heaviest portion of the limb had landed across the young girl's thigh. Her leg lay twisted at an odd angle.

Ajawac grimaced as she made an effort to move. "I worry about you. I follow."

"Lie still, Ajawac," warned Jennifer. "I'll get you out of here." She hoped the promise was not an empty one.

Jennifer took off her snowshoes and laid them aside, then forced her way between the smaller branches until she reached the heaviest part of the limb. Pushing against it with all her weight, she tried to nudge the branch, but it was anchored firmly in the packed snow that had fallen earlier in the season. She knelt in the new-fallen powder. Using her hands, she scooped away the snow alongside the tree limb where Ajawac's left leg was pinned. She decided if she dug deep and removed enough of it, she might be able to slide Ajawac from beneath the giant limb. It was her only prospect. In the worsening storm, it would take too long to find someone to help her move the branch.

Jennifer battled the fine, dry powder, working rapidly to scoop the snow away, but the uncooperative flakes slid back in place nearly

175

as fast as she removed them. Her fingers were growing cold and numb.

Ajawac moaned. Her words were unintelligible.

"You'll be out of here soon, Ajawac," Jennifer comforted. "Be patient a little longer—"

The sound of a hatchet on wood startled Jennifer. She looked up to find Magidins standing a few inches from Ajawac, hacking furiously at the tree limb.

"Magidins! What . . . how . . . ?"

Wrapped in a blanket that reached the ground, only the girl's arms were exposed as she chipped away tiny pieces of wood with a small hatchet. Beside her lay her backpack of tools and provisions. Without explanation, she continued pounding against the hard wood. Jennifer moved between Ajawac and Magidins. Turning her back to the flying splinters, she was able to keep them from hitting the trapped girl's face.

Ajawac lay shivering. Her lips had already turned blue. Jennifer took the girl's cold hand and rubbed it vigorously to restore circulation.

A few minutes later, long before Magidins could have worked her way through the branch, the hacking noise ceased. Jennifer assumed Magidins needed a rest. Turning around, she was about to offer to take over when she realized the branch lay severed at Magidins' feet.

"How did you manage that so quickly?"

Magidins pointed with her ax head to the center section of the branch. It was hollow, rotten. "Now I cut other side. Then, we lift." Magidins explained.

The girl was clever. She had accurately assessed the situation and gotten right to work. Chopping through the branch on either side of Ajawac's legs would leave a short, lighter-weight piece that could be easily removed.

"Let me do it while you take a rest," Jennifer offered, scrambling to her feet.

Magidins hestitated, then handed Jennifer her ax. She knelt in the snow beside the injured girl and began rubbing Ajawac's hands and arms, as Jennifer had, to keep her warm.

Jennifer struck the tough oak as forcefully as possible. The wood was harder than she expected. She attacked the branch more vigorously. Suddenly, the hatchet cut through the rotten core. With a few more strokes, she split it apart. The Lord was surely with them, she realized, as she thought how much longer it would have taken to cut through a solid, healthy branch; how many more precious minutes could have been spent exposed to the stinging, dangerous wind.

Together, she and Magidins lifted the freed section of limb from atop Ajawac's thigh and removed her snowshoes. Magidins knelt beside the twisted leg, took off her mittens and reached beneath Ajawac's clothing to probe the thigh. The injured girl winced, but did not cry out.

Looking at Jennifer, Magidins said, "Hold Ajawac's ankle. Pull."

Jennifer hesitated, wondering how much more pain Ajawac could bear.

Magidins fixed a stern look on her. "Do as I say. Then Ajawac feel better."

Kneeling in the snow, Jennifer grasped Ajawac's left ankle and pulled as hard as she could. As she watched Magidins work, she realized Hawk's sister was lining up the pieces of Ajawac's broken bone. At Magidins' signal, Jennifer slowly let go.

Using sturdy oak splints and the belt from her dress, Magidins braced Ajawac's thigh, talking to her quietly in Ojibway. Jennifer massaged Ajawac's arms and hands while Magidins worked.

When the leg was bound, she asked Magidins, "Do you think together, we can carry Ajawac? We're a little more than halfway to LaFontes'."

Magidins shook her head. "LaFontes' too far. Ajawac freeze."

"The village is a little farther, but we've already broken the trail," Jennifer observed.

"Trail not good. When I come, snow ver' deep. I dig trench." She lifted her cedar shovel. "Then put in branches." She pointed to the hemlock branches bowing in the wind overhead. "We lie down, cover with blanket, more branches." Magidins indicated the blanket on her back. "Ajawac lie in middle. We keep her warm. It is only way. I learn it from my father. We walk through bad storm after sugarbush one year."

The howling of the wind had become a scream. It was absurd to think they could spend the night huddled together without freezing, but Jennifer realized she must trust Magidins.

"I'll help you dig the trench, Magidins."

"Stay with Ajawac. I find good place." She headed off the forest trail and was soon out of sight.

A few minutes later, Magidins returned, dragging a large hemlock bough. Together, she and Jennifer positioned Ajawac on the soft branch. Stepping into her snowshoes, Jennifer helped Magidins pull Ajawac to the leeward side of a large white pine, then they dug a deep trench wide enough to accommodate the three of them. When this was done, Jennifer tossed hemlock boughs Magidins cut from a nearby tree into the bottom of the trench. The shelter was soon lined to Magidins' satisfaction, then she and Jennifer positioned Ajawac in the center.

"Take off snowshoes. Lie beside Ajawac," Magidins told Jennifer. "I put snowshoes here." She gestured to a nearby tree. "If someone come, they see snowshoes, they know we be near."

Again, Jennifer trusted Magidins' judgment. She watched as the young girl propped her snowshoes against the tree, then began inserting evergreen boughs into the snow along each side of the ditch so they overlapped above. This accomplished, she threw more boughs and twigs on top, then crawled into the shelter and spread her blanket over Ajawac and Jennifer.

Surrounded by darkness and the sweet, clean fragrance of the hemlock boughs, Jennifer listened to the wind moan through the trees. Though the sound alone was enough to bring on a chill, Jennifer realized she was snug and dry in Magidins' makeshift shelter. Beneath her, the layers of springy hemlock supplied a soft mattress to cushion her from the snow. The blanket and tree limbs overhead sealed out all drafts. Except for an occasional hunger pang, she could convince herself she was comfortable.

On the opposite side of Ajawac, Magidins shifted her weight. Jennifer wondered why she was squirming, disturbing the blanket so carefully tucked around them. Then she heard Magidins speaking in Ojibway to Ajawac, offering her something to eat. Ajawac tried to refuse but Magidins insisted, and the injured girl chewed on the piece of dried meat.

Jennifer felt a hand groping over her, then heard Magidins say, "Take. Eat."

"I'm all right. You've been working harder than I have. You should eat it." Jennifer gently pushed Magidins' hand away.

"Eat," Magidins insisted, pressing the dried stick of food into her mitten. "I have more."

As Jennifer chewed the cured venison, she was overwhelmed with a sense of God's presence. He had sent Magidins just at the right time. His hand had provided shelter and food. He would surely bring them through the night. *And Hawk, dear Lord,* she prayed silently. *What about him? Will you be with him as well?*

She had been so busy with Ajawac that her fear for him had been temporarily overshadowed.

"Magidins, do you have any word of Hawk? He told me he was going to check his traps this morning, and he would be back at the usual time. I waited an extra hour for him, but he didn't come. Do you suppose he had trouble with the neighboring tribe?"

There was a long pause. Just when Jennifer had decided Magidins was not planning to speak, the girl replied, "Hawk still gone. He send no word."

Another long silence ensued. There were a hundred questions begging an answer, but Jennifer refused to press. Magidins was an independent young girl, bright and resourceful. She had proven that. Jennifer would just have to wait until she was ready to share more information.

"Those with Hawk not return, either. All caught in storm," Magidins added reluctantly.

Jennifer relaxed a little. Having observed Magidins' skill in seeking protection from the fierce elements, she had no doubt Hawk knew how to take care of himself, but what if he were hurt? If he were injured, facing the storm alone as Ajawac had been. . . . The thought was too horrible. She pushed it out of her mind. *I must trust Hawk to the Lord. It's all I can do,* she thought, but her apprehension remained, making her realize how much she cared for him.

As she mentally reviewed the afternoon's events, Jennifer couldn't help wondering why Magidins had gone out in the storm. She could have stayed warm and dry by the fire in her mother's lodge, yet she had gone down the trail toward LaFontes', equipped with a hatchet, cedar shovel and food.

The question consumed Jennifer, and she had to know the answer. "Magidins, where were you going when you found Ajawac and me?"

Another long silence. Jennifer thought of the possibilities. Only the LaFontes and a few Ojibway families lived on the trail west of the village. Neither destination made sense.

"You answer own question," Magidins admitted.

"You came looking for us? But *why?*"

"What I tell Hawk when he come back? That I let you die? No. I tell him I help you."

Magidins' answer struck Jennifer like a lead ball. The one person she would have expected to rejoice in her difficulties had risked her life for her. Perhaps Magidins had changed, or perhaps this part of her had been there all along, buried under bitterness and resentment.

Ajawac moaned softly and Magidins comforted her, murmuring in Ojibway.

The three lay quietly for some time. Jennifer listened to the wind, wondering whether the storm would last three days as Ajawac's father had predicted and, if so, whether their crude shelter could protect them through the next day . . . and the one after that. . . .

Jennifer sensed that Magidins was awake, though Ajawac was

180

sleeping restlessly beside her. A verse from the Scriptures came to mind: "If two of you shall agree on earth as touching any thing that they shall ask, it shall be done for them . . . for where two or three are gathered together in my name, there am I in the midst of them."

"Magidins," she whispered, "would you pray with me that we will survive the storm and get Ajawac to safety?"

Again, there was a long silence before Magidins spoke. "You pray. Kitchi Manitou, Great Spirit, angry with me. He punish me and Ajawac. We bad."

"I know some of your people still believe in the spirits of Kitchi Manitou," Jennifer said, choosing her words carefully, "but your parents have been Christians for a long time. I know Hawk has accepted Christ as his Savior, and I thought you had, too."

"Sometimes, I believe in God, Jesus, Holy Spirit like Brother Bentley teach. Tonight, I believe in evil spirit, Kitchi Manitou. He live under sea. He know I do bad thing, Ajawac do bad thing. He punish us. He send storm, hurt Ajawac. He teach us lesson."

Ajawac stirred. "No, Magidins," she mumbled. "I pray long time ago. Jesus forgive me. He know I cause trouble at school. He know I play with stove. He know you tell me do it. He forgive me. Kitchi Manitou cannot hurt me."

"If Kitchi Manitou not hurt you, why branch fall on you?" Magidins demanded.

"I . . . was in wrong place," Ajawac managed to reply, though it was evident she was experiencing great discomfort. She shifted her weight, then said in a voice heavy with pain, "I pray with you, Miss Jenny. Great Father in Heaven . . . thank you for Magidins. She help us good. Some day, she understand you better. . . . Please keep us safe tonight, Father. Amen."

"Amen," Jennifer added, deeply moved. "Thank you, Ajawac. Our Father could not have failed to hear your words."

"Miracle. Like spelling lesson. Remember, Miss Jenny? Magidins find us. Miracle."

"Yes, I remember. Try to rest. Save your strength."

The shelter grew quiet while Jennifer's thoughts ranged back to

181

that first day of school. Now she understood . . . everything. The schoolhouse, filled with smoke and soot, had been Ajawac's doing. Magidins had convinced her friend to close the damper of the stove. When Hawk questioned his sister about it, she had responded truthfully. She had not committed the act literally. But she had masterminded it. Now, her conscience was pricking her.

"Magidins," Jennifer whispered, trying not to disturb Ajawac, "it doesn't matter what you have done. If you are truly sorry, ask Jesus to forgive you, and he will. I will help you pray, if you want."

"No," Magidins answered curtly.

Jennifer suppressed her urge to talk of God's love and the sacrifice of his Son on the cross for the forgiveness of sin. Silently, she prayed Hawk's sister would overcome her confusion before it was too late.

As the wind continued its unrelenting assault on the forest, Jennifer again wondered how long the three of them would be able to endure the storm. Her silent prayers continued until she fell into a light sleep. In her dreams, she saw Hawk's face—the gray eyes warm with compassion.

Jennifer's next awareness was of snuffling and snorting. She envisioned the long snouts and sharp pointed teeth of famished wolves pacing outside the shelter. The wind had subsided, and she was certain the vicious creatures had ventured out of their own burrows, intent on satisfying their hunger. Just as she was wondering how three young women could protect themselves from a pack of ferocious animals, she heard someone call out.

"Jennifer! Magidins! Ajawac! Are you in there?"

She recognized Hawk's voice, then the yelping and barking of his wolf-like sledge dogs.

"We're all here, and safe, Hawk! Thank the Lord, you've found us!"

The roof of the shelter shook as the hemlock branches were peeled away, one by one, gradually admitting the pale morning light. As soon as Jennifer could crawl from the shelter, Hawk wrapped his arms about her.

"You were ever in my prayers," he said, crushing her against the thick blanket he wore as a coat.

"And you, in mine." For a few moments, Jennifer reveled in the security of his strong embrace, then leaned back to gaze into the clear eyes, now filled with relief. The strong jawline, the prominent cheekbones, the rugged nose were there before her, no longer a vague image in her mind.

Cradling her face in his hands, Hawk brushed a kiss on her forehead, then looked deep into her brown eyes. "This moment is answered prayer."

The joy she felt flooded over, spilling out through her tears. "I thought I might never see you again, but our Father was gracious."

Hawk held her, murmuring words of endearment. "I should never have left you, but there was trouble in the woods. I hoped you would stay in my mother's lodge. When I arrived home, she told me you, Magidins, and Ajawac were not to be found."

"Magidins saved my life, and Ajawac's. You can be justly proud of your sister."

"Praise God." There was both fervor and reverence in his voice.

Though several inches of new snow had accumulated overnight, Hawk had broken the trail to the village, making travel on snowshoes easy compared to the previous day. With Ajawac cozily bundled into the sledge, and Magidins and Jennifer following behind, Hawk led the way to the village.

Word of the rescue spread quickly, and, by the time they arrived, the entire village gathered round, babbling in excited welcome. "Miss Jenny! Miss Jenny!" Small children hugged her unabashedly, while the older students, like their parents, offered a more reserved greeting.

Canodens took Jennifer into her lodge. There, she warmed herself beside the lodge fire and sipped hot tea. Though she credited Magidins with saving her life, and praised her to her father and mother, Hawk's sister remained reticent. It was as if she believed herself unworthy of recognition for her deeds. Jennifer could see admiration in the eyes of her parents as she recounted Magidins' skill in freeing Ajawac, setting her leg, and building the shelter. Jennifer learned Canodens had begged Magidins not to venture out in the storm.

"Last night, I sure Hawk die, husband die. All night, I pray Magidins not die, too," Canodens explained. "But God hear my prayer. All safe now. He use Magidins!"

The chief stood at the back of the lodge, an unmistakable look of pride on his face. Stepping forward, he took a seat by the fire and studied the flickering light of the flames. Jennifer waited, certain that, when he was ready, he would begin to speak.

In Ojibway, he told of the trouble with the neighboring Indians. As Hawk translated, Jennifer learned that the trouble had begun the previous summer, on the day Hawk had come late to the mission to see her and discovered she had fallen while trying to rescue her mother from the cliffside. In the summer, the neighbors had been poaching from Ojibway bear traps. This winter, they had taken smaller animals.

"Our men wanted to fight. My son spoke to them of peace. When they heard his words, they agreed to meet with the leaders of the neighboring tribe. We will place a rock where the Silver River flows into Huron Bay. It will mark forever the dividing line between our lands."

When Hawk returned Jennifer to the LaFontes' cabin, there was much embracing and many exclamations of relief, both in Ojibway and in French. Pierre could not do enough for her, bringing her fur robes to line the rocker he had made for her, warming stones to place at her feet. Angelique served venison soup in her finest china bowls and pressed Jennifer to take a second hearty portion.

Hawk stayed long enough to share a bowl of soup. When he rose to leave, Jennifer accompanied him to the cabin door. As they stood in the secluded entryway, he took Jennifer in his arms.

"I wish you were always by my side as you are always in my heart," he said earnestly. "Last night, I feared you would die because of me. If so, I could not have forgiven myself." The gray eyes clouded with pain. "Jennifer, I speak of . . . love. There is love between the Creator and the ones he has created. I have known that love for a time. Now I know another love. That of a man for a woman."

Her heart could not contain the surge of joy she felt, and she gave herself over to the feelings, not daring to think beyond the precious moment they were sharing.

"And I love you, Hawk," she murmured over and over. "I love you!"

In the wintry weeks to follow, Jennifer found herself enjoying her teaching more and more. No longer did she dread facing Magidins each day. The bright young girl willingly participated in question-and-answer periods and helped translate difficult words and phrases for the younger children, taking over these responsibilities while Ajawac recovered at home.

Magidins devoted herself not only to her own studies and to assisting Jennifer in the schoolroom but to tutoring Ajawac, as well. Each week, when Jennifer called on Ajawac, she was delighted to see that her student was healing rapidly and was progressing in her studies on a par with those who sat in the classroom every day. Jennifer left, shaking her head in wonder. Though Magidins said little about her friend, Jennifer knew that Hawk's sister was responsible for another small miracle.

Only one dark cloud remained to be dispelled. Magidins refused to enter into a discussion of spiritual beliefs. Jennifer had hoped to reach her through the daily Scripture reading, even using illustrations from nature and paraphrasing the formal English to simplify the deep truths. But Magidins either arrived too late for the morning reading, or otherwise sidestepped a confrontation. Once, attempting to draw her into a meaningful study of the Scriptures, Jennifer asked her to translate a Bible verse in Ojibway to the younger children, but Magidins quickly found a polite excuse to decline. In all other ways, she had become a model student.

February's short days produced an abundance of heavy snow and overcast skies. Except for recess periods, Jennifer saw little of the daylight hours, going to school in the darkness of early morning and leaving as dusk began to settle over L'Anse in late afternoon. She might have traveled home during the last sunlit hour of the afternoon had she and Hawk not engaged in lengthy conversations in the schoolhouse. Often, he would help her tidy up the classroom after the students had been dismissed, talking of his daily activities as they worked.

Their conversations, while long, were carefully constructed to avoid the subject that was at the forefront of their thoughts. Ever since the day of her rescue, Hawk had spoken of many things, but never again of love. He told her of the furs he and others from the village had found in their traps, how many marten, beaver, fox and rabbit had been taken since the peace treaty with the neighboring tribe. Jennifer reported on the progress of her students, repeating some of the comical translations and rejoicing over their improved skill in English. Occasionally, the conversation would drift to their feelings about the differences in their cultures, careful probings Jennifer sensed would eventually answer an important question neither dared yet ask directly. Though they loved each other, could they build a future together?

As the vanishing daylight dimmed the schoolroom, Jennifer often ended such serious discussions by exclaiming in mock horror, "If we don't leave right this minute, I'll miss dinner, and Angelique will send me to my room hungry!"

Hawk always laughed, but lurking beneath his smile, Jennifer sensed the apprehension that, when the school year ended, they might part, never to meet again. It was a concern she shared.

March began deceptively, with a sunny, mild day. As the snow started to melt, falling off the school roof in sheets, Jennifer noticed an air of anticipation in the classroom. During recess, when she walked about the schoolyard on her snowshoes, she caught portions of the children's excited Ojibway chatter. Soon, it would be sugarbush time!

Angelique and Hawk had both warned her there would be several days of poor attendance once the maple sap started running. When she resumed class following lunch, Jennifer devised an exercise in English for the younger students. Beginning with Mani, she asked them to tell her about sugarbush.

"We go to the woods, Miss Jenny. We make *sisibakwatagon*." She looked to Magidins for a translation, then repeated the words the older girl supplied. "We make sugar snow."

"And how do you make this *sisibakwatagon*, or sugar snow?" Jennifer asked.

With help from her young friends, Mani explained how to pour thick sap, heated to boiling, over clean snow. As it cooled, the sap was twisted about the fingers to make various shapes, and when it was no longer soft enough to mold, it could be chewed.

The afternoon went quickly as Jennifer guided the children's learning, using a sugarbush theme. When Hawk arrived at the schoolhouse following dismissal, Jennifer was in high spirits.

Taking her coat from its peg, she joined him at the door. "Let's leave for Angelique's right away. It's been a long time since I've seen a sunset."

Hawk was quiet, his expression contemplative. "We must talk. It is important. It cannot wait."

chapter

15

JENNIFER STEPPED INSIDE THE CLASSROOM and sat down at one of the desks in the back row.

Hawk dropped lightly beside her, taking her hand in his. "Next week, village lodges will be empty. Many families will go to sugarbush. Only old women and babies will stay behind. There will be no children to teach. I've spoken to my mother and father. They invite you to go with us to our sugar camp."

Jennifer beamed with pleasure. "Oh, Hawk, I'd love to go!"

He remained solemn. "Jennifer, sugarbush means hard work. I will explain. Perhaps you will not want to come."

She chuckled. "I'm not afraid of work. You should know that by now. Tell me about sugarbush and don't leave anything out. I want to know everything."

Hawk explained how important sugarbush season was to the Ojibway—a celebration of the coming of spring as well as a time to put by food for the coming year. The men would collect sap from the trees in barrels and pour it into large kettles. The women would boil the liquid day and night, stirring it into granules when it thickened.

Hawk and his father would also fish through the ice for pickerel while Jennifer helped his mother and sister dry the catch. She would be expected to work alongside Canodens and Magidins.

When he finished his explanation, she cocked her head. "Well, you haven't frightened me away yet. As a matter of fact, I can think of nothing I would rather do. When do we leave?"

"You sound like one of your small students," he said, his lips curling upward. "They welcome sugarbush."

"Hmm." She made a wry face. "Probably eager to have a vacation from school and me."

Hawk raised a brow. "You put words in my mouth." He slid from the chair to retrieve her coat from its peg.

As they stepped outside the door, Jennifer noticed the sun was still setting over the frozen, white bay. Intense reds and pinks painted the western skies as the rim of the flaming scarlet ball fused with the horizon. At the lookout, she caught another glimpse of the descending crimson ball, and through the trees, its soft rays reminded her of a flame, like the flame of love flickering in her heart.

At the end of the week, Hawk came to fetch her and take her to his mother's lodge. From there, they set out on foot for the maple forest.

The sledge, driven by the two men, was piled high with poles and birch bark for a temporary shelter, cooking utensils, and food which had been prepared days in advance. Canodens, Magidins, and Jennifer followed, carrying the smaller utensils.

They walked for five or six miles before reaching the camp. It was situated in a stand of maples near the shoreline. Here, the forest floor had been cleared of underbrush.

Three other families who shared the camp had arrived earlier, and the fragrance of boiling syrup mingled with the aroma of wood smoke and coal-broiled venison wafted through the air. Jennifer noticed a small enclosure for the storage of the birchbark containers positioned next to a larger structure, where the sap was boiled.

She helped Canodens and Magidins erect their temporary shelter of birch bark laid over interlacing poles, then learned how to insert spiles into the sugar maples, using an odd-shaped iron ax. While Hawk and his father went ice fishing, the women took bags of cedar filled with wild rice, makuks of dried blueberries and cranberries, and dried potatoes and apples from a cache near the camp where they had been stored the previous year. There was fresh pickerel for dinner, along with cooked vegetables and sauces made from the blueberries and cranberries.

For the next two weeks, Jennifer worked in the out of doors from early morning until nightfall, breathing in the fresh air and exercising muscles she had not known to exist. Though she fell, exhausted, onto her rush mat most nights, her sleep was dreamless and deep, and she awakened each morning with a sense of exhilaration.

Most days were spent drying the extra fish caught by Hawk and his father and making grain sugar and cake sugar. Grain sugar was made by stirring the boiling sap until it crystallized. Cake sugar required less effort, as it was boiled without stirring, then poured into wooden molds prior to crystallization. This became Jennifer's favorite type of maple sugar, because it produced such lovely gifts when molded into flowers, stars, squirrels, and rabbits.

A third type of sugar provided entertainment for the children. This was the gum or wax sugar, or as Mani had explained to her in class, "sugar snow." Jennifer often came upon groups of children huddled over the snowdrift, taking pieces of the cooled, pliable maple candy and twisting it into shapes limited only by their imaginations.

Aside from fishing, Hawk and his father tended to collecting sap, pouring it from the makuks into barrels and bringing it on the dog sledge to replenish the cooking kettles. As Hawk had warned, the women boiled sap day and night. Sometimes, they worked the whole night through. At such times, Hawk stayed beside Jennifer, and they shared moments of quiet conversation which were impossible during the daylight hours while the camp bustled with activity.

When the maple syrup became thick and dark, the Ojibways collected the "last run of the sap." This syrup, along with the dried fish would provide sustenance during the garden-making season following sugarbush.

Though her hands were always busy, there were moments for reflection as well, and Jennifer found herself comparing her former lifestyle to that of the Ojibway women. Though she had considered her lot superior to theirs, she was forced to reassess her opinion as she observed their contentment and the skill which they brought to each task. Too, her body was growing stronger—toughened by the hours of hard labor and nourished by simple food and fresh air. She had never felt so free, so much in harmony with nature. Suddenly, she realized that she could not be so happy anywhere else in the world. Hawk's presence at that moment confirmed her thought, and she smiled to herself. She was being presumptuous. He had not asked her to share his life. . . .

Spring had made great advances by the time the Ojibways returned to their village at the end of March, as had Jennifer's appreciation of Hawk and his family.

On the way to the LaFontes' cabin, he paused at the rocky promontory overlooking the bay and Jennifer stepped out of the dog sledge. Clearing the snow from the top of a boulder, he scaled it in a graceful move and reached down to pull Jennifer up beside him. The afternoon was waning, and the golden sun was lowering over dark patches of thinning ice on the bay. They sat in silence for several moments, admiring the sunset.

With a gentle hand beneath her chin, Hawk turned Jennifer's face toward him. "I don't look forward to returning you to your home. Will the day come when we no longer say good-by at the LaFontes' cabin door?"

Jennifer's pulse quickened. "What are you asking?"

His large palm cupped her face tenderly. "I am asking you to be part of my world, Jennifer, part of me."

"Are you asking me to marry you, Hawk? Because if you are, the answer is yes! As long as you are here, I never want to leave L'Anse!"

His eyes shone silver in the fading light as she melted into his arms, hearing the quickened pace of his heart echoing her own joy.

"You make beautiful bride, Jenny!" Angelique was ecstatic when she heard the news. "You wear dress of white doeskin—like moccasins." Angelique pointed to the lovely gift Jennifer had received from Ajawac. "Brother Bentley marry you and Hawk. Or maybe Brother Woodworth, if you wait 'til July!"

"Angelique, Angelique!" Jennifer shook her head, laughing. "I'm sure Hawk will want to speak to his family before we make definite plans."

The woman ignored her, ticking off the details. "They be pleased. You see. In July, your mother and father come with Woodworths. Hawk can fetch from Hancock. Wedding be big celebration!"

"First, I must write to Mama and Papa. I hope Papa will be able to take time off from his work at the mine."

"Write them now," Angelique urged. "I mail letter tomorrow." She brought Jennifer a pen and writing paper, then left her alone to compose her thoughts.

Classes resumed at the mission school the following morning, on the first day of April. The students were more subdued than usual and Jennifer could tell they were experiencing the same let down she had felt on her return from sugarbush.

Though spring had made its first intrusion on Keweenaw country, bringing warmer breezes to melt the ice and snow, by mid-week a storm dumped several inches of fresh snow. The heavy new layer disappeared quickly, leaving muddy ground outside the council lodge.

Along the trail, however, where the sun filtered through the hemlocks, melting and refreezing produced perfect conditions for snowshoeing. Jennifer remembered her first efforts to walk on the clumsy contraptions, and laughed to herself. Now, she glided with the ease of a native.

By the following week the ice on the bay which had become too treacherous for icefishing, broke in two with a resounding crash. Excitement rippled through the village as children and adults alike ran to the shore to see the jagged line of water extending from the mission on the west shore to the village on the east. The south winds pushed the frozen chunks out into the lake, widening the gap between the two huge pieces of ice. From these, smaller cakes of ice broke off and began moving toward the lake, but a change in wind direction brought them back again, to break against the shore.

Toward the end of April, other signs of spring appeared. The soggy earth burst with bright green skunk cabbage and fuzzy hepaticas, arbutus and wood anemones, violets and marsh marigolds. In the air, sparrows and robins added their songs to the calls of crows and gulls.

In the village, children adopted the young of the forest. Baby skunks were seen running in and out of several lodges, while other families cared for baby beaver and raccoon. While they worked, young mothers propped their babies in cradle boards. Several students reported the births of new brothers and sisters and invited Jennifer to their lodges after school to admire the newcomers.

Before the first of May, she received a letter from her parents. Her mother wrote:

> I thought last summer you and Hawk be meant for each other. I be glad to know the two of you will share the future, no matter what it may bring.

Her father penned a brief note at the bottom of the letter which touched her deeply.

> My dearest JennyMae,
> I be glad you found love at L'Anse. I look forward to giving you to Hawk in marrig.
> It be almost a year since you went away. So much has changed!
> I know why the Lord took away the store. He had new work for me. I've told many men from the bal about Christ. Several have professed converson.
> I will see you in July.
>
> Love, Papa

On the first weekend in May, Hawk took Jennifer across the bay to visit the Bentleys. When he asked Brother Bentley to preside over their wedding with Brother Woodworth in July, the normally staid minister embraced Hawk as if he were his own son. Sister Bentley insisted they celebrate with a cup of her finest tea served in delicate china cups.

By the third week of May, Jennifer was anxious to conclude her duties in the classroom so she could prepare for her wedding. Canodens had offered to make her a bridal garment of white doeskin, so she was not burdened with sewing, but there were utensils to make in order to equip her household for married life.

On fair weather days, Jennifer visited Canodens' lodge after dismissing the students. There, she made baskets or makuks. If the weather was rainy, she went to Angelique's to weave yarn bags.

In spite of wedding preparations, she and Hawk still set aside a few minutes at the end of each school day to talk. Jennifer always welcomed the sight of her tall Ojibway brave as he entered the classroom late in the afternoon. He would bring the chair from the corner and sit beside her while she straightened her desk.

One sunny day during the last week of May, Hawk's tall shadow fell across the floor of the schoolroom. Jennifer looked up, sensing an uneasiness in him.

"From the look on your face, something is wrong," she concluded, a frown marring the smooth marble of her brow. "I hope there hasn't been more trouble with the neighboring tribe."

"No trouble with them," he answered, though he remained at the door.

Giving him time to weigh his words, Jennifer rose from her desk to stroll to the open window. "I'd like to spend some time at your mother's lodge before I go to Angelique's. The weather is perfect for outside work."

Hawk strode across the room, his eyes darkening with concern. "Today is not a good day to stay in the village. The Bentleys wait for you at Angelique's—with an important message."

A dart of anxiety rippled through her. "Is it Mama . . . or Papa?"

Seeing the pain in his expression, she reached for him, feeling that her legs could no longer support her. "Papa is dead . . . isn't he?"

He pulled her to him, crushing her against his chest. "I'm sorry, Jennifer," Hawk whispered into her hair. "A timber fell. He felt no pain."

Numb with shock, Jennifer's eyes remained dry as she forced her brain to think through the next logical steps. Her mother would need her.

"I must go to Mama," she said, releasing herself from Hawk's embrace.

Hawk nodded. "Tomorrow I will take you to her."

Jennifer moved mechanically about the room, tidying her desk, straightening the bookcase, putting away chalk and erasers. Hawk withdrew to the doorway and stood waiting.

A few minutes later she stood beside him looking over the rows of desks, knowing it would be a long time before she returned to the little log schoolhouse on the promontory.

As he locked the door behind her, she tried to shut out all thoughts of the children who would miss the last few days of the school year.

Jennifer remained quiet as Hawk led her down the forest trail toward Angelique's. She was too deep in thought for conversation, and while she could read the compassion in his face, he made no attempt to console her further.

Once again, her world had turned upside down. There would be no July wedding, no visit from her parents. Instead, she must leave L'Anse as quickly as possible, perhaps forever. And there was nothing anyone could do to change it. Not even God.

When Jennifer stepped inside Angelique's door, the teary-eyed woman embraced her. "Oh, Jenny, my sweet Jenny," she sobbed.

Despite the loving display, Jennifer held herself stiff and erect. The older woman ushered her to a chair in the common room and set about pouring her a cup of tea. Flanking her were Brother and Sister Bentley, murmuring warm expressions of sympathy.

"God loved your father, Jennifer." The kind countenance of Brother Bentley swam into view. "His work on earth was done, and he took him home."

"Of course," Jennifer replied, her words infused with an acceptable tone of reverence. At least for now, she was able to hide her anger that her father was not allowed enough time on earth to give her hand in marriage, to come to know Hawk, or to learn about her new life in L'Anse.

"The funeral was yesterday," the good man continued. "I'm sorry you couldn't be there, but it takes time to transmit messages. You can leave for Hancock tomorrow morning at sunrise. Hawk, Gray Wolf and Red Wing will take you in the Montreal canoe, so there will be plenty of room for your trunk. If this calm weather holds up, you'll arrive by early evening."

Sister Bentley leaned forward to touch her hand. "I do hope you will return to us soon." Her drooping lid could not diminish the sincerity in her pale blue eyes.

Jennifer answered, "I shall try," though in her heart, she wondered.

"Send a letter when you are ready to come back, and we shall have Hawk fetch you," Brother Bentley instructed.

"I will." Again, the words spoken seemed not her own, but what was expected under the circumstances.

The Bentleys stayed awhile longer, then she accompanied them down the slope to the dock to bid them farewell. When she returned to the cabin, Hawk was waiting for her on the front lawn.

"Please, Hawk, go now. I want to be alone."

He nodded in understanding, though Jennifer could see that she had wounded him. Without a word, he turned and disappeared down the trail.

That evening, Jennifer's thoughts roiled as she packed her trunk. Her worst fears had been realized. Her father was dead, and she would never see him again.

She traced the progression of events, reliving the horror of the

JENNY OF L'ANSE BAY

fire, the narrow escape from the burning apartment above the store, her anguish at losing everything except the clothes she was wearing. *Why had God allowed the fire?*

A feeling of desolation flooded over her, filling her heart with an unhappiness she thought she had laid to rest forever. Now, it came back, slithering into her memory like a snake, poisoning her mind with the deadly venom of resentment. She felt angry, betrayed by God.

It didn't matter if she had found contentment with Hawk, for now she must be parted from him. She didn't want to think about the proud Ojibway who loved her and had asked her to be his wife. She must be with her mother, the dear, sweet woman who deserved none of the sorrow being dealt out to her. Her mother would find lonely days ahead, and would need her daughter nearby to console her.

Jennifer felt she must cut herself off from L'Anse. Formal mourning would require a year. Then, she could reconsider marriage, but it would be too late to pick up the pieces left behind at the Ojibway village on the bay.

The thought of being near Hawk for a day of travel only sharpened her sadness, knowing she must part from him. It would be easier to say good-by to him on the dock in front of the LaFontes' cabin . . . and never look back.

Angelique's eyes were rimmed with red when she woke Jennifer for breakfast the following morning. She served her in the common room, then returned to the kitchen. When Jennifer finished, not tasting a bite she swallowed, she carried her plate and cup to a tearful Angelique. The kind woman was rolling a piece of birch bark around portions of smoked fish, parched corn, and lumps of maple sugar.

"For you and the others," she explained, tying the bundle with a thong.

Jennifer went through the motions of gratitude, accepting the package and kissing the older woman's cheek.

At the sound of the front door, both women gravitated toward the common room to greet Hawk. He crossed the room quickly, assessing Jennifer with a grave look.

"Are you ready to go?" he asked, his voice solemn.

"My bag and trunk are by the bed."

When Hawk had left the room, Angelique put her arms around Jennifer. "I keep your room ready. Hurry back."

Moments later, Jennifer stood on the dock and looked back at the cabin she had called home for the past ten months. Angelique was waving to her from the front doorstep. Woodenly, Jennifer reached up to return the salute, then turned to get into the canoe.

Pierre, who had delayed his early morning fishing to see her off, helped to steady the Ojibway craft as she stepped in. "*Au revoir,* Jenny. It is pity you must go." He shook his head regretfully.

"*Au revoir,* Pierre," she answered. Settling onto the fur robes in the center of the canoe, she added, "Be sure to catch lots of fish for Angelique."

"But of course," he answered, his lips nearing a smile. Shaking a finger at Hawk, he admonished, "Keep Jenny safe!"

Hawk nodded, stepping into the stern of the craft.

As Red Wing and Gray Wolf paddled away, Jennifer did not look back. Instead, she leveled her gaze on the western shore, where at last she saw the Bentleys waving a last farewell from the mission dock. Jennifer waved back, thankful when the craft had progressed far enough along the shoreline so these familiar sights were behind her.

The pink sun was still rising over quiet bay waters. Unlike her trip to L'Anse, it appeared the weather would be fair, waters calm, the breeze light.

There was little reason for conversation in the canoe. Jennifer kept her back to Hawk. She had already built a brick wall around her emotions for him.

They stopped for food and rest several hours later at the Portage Entry. The sky remained clear and sunny. A gentle breeze blew at their backs. A few Ojibway words were exchanged between Hawk and his crew as the canoe slid onto the sandy beach, and Jennifer understood them to say they would make Hancock before nightfall.

Hawk offered a hand to steady Jennifer as she stepped from the boat, and for a moment, the familiar feel of his strong fingers around hers threatened to crack the stoic barrier she had erected. How she loved him, how she wished she could remain always by his side . . . but she quickly banished those thoughts before her eyes welled with tears again for what could not be.

Jennifer spoke only when necessary, serving Angelique's lunch to the men as they stretched out on the beach, thanking Hawk when he helped her into the canoe again after their rest.

Hawk seemed to understand her need to remain apart. He had made no attempt to engage her in conversation during the trip, nor to sit beside her on the beach. Their relationship had been reduced to nothing more than the exchange of common courtesies.

As the canoemen once again took up their paddles, Jennifer's mind was filled with questions about the future. Only fifteen miles separated her from her mother. By early evening they would be reunited. Though her mother would have been able to continue running the store had she been widowed in Eagle River, Jennifer feared that now she would soon be out of funds. Perhaps there was a way to help her mother earn a living.

Hours later, when the dock at Hancock came into sight, there had been no satisfactory resolution to the problem. And now, seeing the familiar harbor town, memories flooded back. Hard as she tried, she could not eradicate thoughts of the first moment she saw Hawk. She recalled running away from him because she didn't trust his fragile-looking craft, then his coming after her and literally sweeping her off her feet.

As they approached the shoreline, Jennifer caught sight of Tim Hocking. He stood near the foot of the Tezcuco Street hill waving wildly. She lifted her hand in response, and the boy took off up the street. Jennifer knew it would be only minutes before a carriage came to fetch her and her trunk.

Hawk landed the canoe several yards past the main dock at Tezcuco Street. Though a ship was unloading cargo at the foot of the hill, most of the activity along the waterfront had ceased, giving a measure of solitude to the scene. Gray Wolf and Red Wing disappeared the minute they finished tying up, and Jennifer realized they had purposely left Hawk alone with her to say good-by.

She had been dreading this moment, but as Hawk helped her onto the dock, she renewed her determination to face their final parting without tears.

"There is little time, Jennifer, and much to say." Hawk turned her toward him and tilted her chin, forcing her eyes to meet his.

"There is *little* to say. I must remain with Mama for the next year. You must return to L'Anse. It's over between us, Hawk. The only appropriate words are 'good-by'." Her harsh tone, intended to prevent any sentimentality on Hawk's part, became a self-inflicted wound as a look of anguish flitted across his features.

"This is not good-by," he gently argued. "You have agreed to marry me."

"How can you want me?" she demanded. "I'm not worthy to be anyone's wife. I'm angry, resentful. I blame God for taking away my home, my father . . ."—her tone softened—"and now you. I'm not fit to love or be loved." Jennifer turned away as a tear slid down her cheek.

"Time will heal your wounds. You will love again. I will wait for you."

At Hawk's tender words, Jennifer longed to feel his arms around her once more, but there was no time. She saw her mother alight from a carriage at the bottom of Tezcuco Street, saw the wave of a lace-edged handkerchief.

When she turned to face Hawk again, he was reaching into the canoe for a buckskin pouch. From it, he extracted a piece of folded foolscap. Gray Wolf and Red Wing appeared to fetch her trunk, then Hawk took her by the elbow and escorted her along the dock toward Tezcuco Street while the others followed closed behind.

"Keep this." He handed her the paper. "Open it later."

Jennifer nodded, slipping it into her skirt pocket.

As they approached the ship at the main dock, someone shouted derisively, "Injun lover!"

Horrified, Jennifer looked up to see a grimy longshoreman.

"Stay here!" Hawk ordered, unsheathing the hunting knife at his waist. With the stealth of a panther, he mounted the gangplank, his weapon poised to strike.

The greasy dock worker stood firm halfway up the ramp, his feet spread apart, his hands on his hips. His expression of contempt turned to one of surprise when Hawk spoke to him in perfect English.

"Apologize to her. Now."

chapter

16

TWO BURLY COMPANIONS APPEARED at the top of the ramp behind the man who had issued the insult.

"Come on ahead, redskin," jeered the one on the left.

Hawk flashed his knife like a whip of dancing light, positioning himself to advance.

"No, Hawk!" Jennifer shouted, running toward the ramp. "It's not worth fighting over!" She moved up the gangplank and grabbed his wrist. He flicked his arm, releasing her hold.

"Stay back," Hawk warned, his voice edged with steel. He moved forward with the grace of a wild thing, the silent gliding step of a hunter, and the skill bred of years of stalking.

The first longshoreman crouched, pulling his own knife from his belt. "Y'd better listen t' yer white squaw. Ya take me on, y'll never leave Hancock alive. I'll see t' that." Behind him, his cohorts wielded cudgels, braced for the attack.

"Hawk, *please* put your knife away," Jennifer begged, backing away from the men, her heart pounding frantically.

The next moment blurred with action. The stevedore stabbed at Hawk. The copper-toned Indian jumped back, evading the thrust of his knife.

Strong arms plucked Jennifer from the gangplank, setting her on the dock beside her trunk. Then Red Wing and Gray Wolf joined their companion, knives unsheathed.

The first longshoreman lunged forward again. With a powerful burst of strength, Hawk twisted into him with his shoulder, throwing him over his back into a sprawl near the bottom of the gangway.

"Ha! We ain't finished yet!" taunted the man on the left, swinging his cudgel menacingly. Gray Wolf sidestepped him. With a yell and a mighty kick, he knocked the longshoreman's feet out from under him, sending him rolling down the plank to join his injured companion.

The third stevedore, confronted by Red Wing, turned and disappeared into the hold of the ship.

When the two burly dockhands who had landed at the bottom of the gangway at last melted into the dark alley between the two buildings, Hawk turned to Jennifer. "As long as I am here, you are in danger of insult. We leave immediately."

Tim Hocking jumped down from the driver's seat of the carriage and ran to retrieve Jennifer's trunk from the canoe before it slid out into the water.

Hawk stood in the stern, lifting his hand in a gesture of farewell. It was only then that Jennifer allowed the tears to come, spilling down her cheeks. She stood for long moments, watching the craft glide past and beyond, down to the first bend of the waterway. It seemed that a part of her heart went with it, and she couldn't help wondering if she would ever feel whole again.

Turning, she saw her mother standing by the carriage. Belle Crawford was outfitted in black from head to toe. Jennifer looked into the sad eyes, then threw her arms about her mother, inhaling the fragrance of lilac.

"Mama, I'm so happy to see you again." She could not tell whether her tears were for her father or for the tall man she had sent away. Shaking with sobs, she laid her head on her mother's shoulder. "Whatever shall we do without Papa?"

"Hush, darlin'," her mother soothed, stroking her long hair. "Your papa be with the Lord now, and we mustn't be wishing him back."

When they parted and Jennifer had wiped her eyes with her handkerchief, she noticed a top-hatted gentleman waiting nearby. "I'm sorry, Mama." She sniffed. "I didn't realize someone else was with you."

"Jennifer, this be Mr. Pierce." Belle introduced them as she dried her tear-stained cheeks.

"Pleased to make your acquaintance, Miss Crawford." With a wide, sweeping motion, the gentleman doffed his hat and bowed low.

Jennifer extended her hand tentatively. "My pleasure, sir."

"Mr. Pierce drove me to the Hockings' this morning," her mother explained. "He be one of the new owners at the Cliff, a widower from the East. Your father invited him to our worship services several weeks ago, and he's been attending ever since."

"Thank you for bringing Mama to meet me, Mr. Pierce." She gave him an appraising look.

"Glad to be of service, though I'm extremely sorry about your father. He was a good man Now, if you'll excuse me?" He tossed his hat on the seat of the carriage to help Tim load her trunk.

Tim, who had grown as tall as Jennifer since she had seen him last, took the driver's seat up front, while Mr. Pierce held the door and helped her inside. As she settled on the seat beside her mother, she tried to force her thoughts away from the disturbing incident at the dock.

Jennifer rested her head against the diamond-tufted satin of the cushioned seat. Though this was an elegant carriage indeed, she preferred the fur-lined canoes of the Ojibways. Still, it must be quite expensive with its gracefully scrolled silver-plated irons and the pearl-and-silver-inlaid panels. Only a very wealthy man could afford such a coach, and she wondered if it belonged to Mr. Pierce.

The man took the seat facing Jennifer and her mother. "A pleasure to finally meet you, Miss Crawford. I've heard for weeks of your brave entry into missionary service among the Ojibways. You have earned my greatest respect for your chosen work. May I also say that your father was respected by all who knew him at the Cliff."

205

"That's very kind of you, sir. He—he was the best man I ever knew," she stammered, thinking now of Hawk, "and I loved him very much."

Belle touched her daughter's hand. "There be much to tell you over dinner, but I'll wait until we get to the Hockings'. Mary be ready to serve dinner the instant we arrive."

In the few minutes it took to ride to the Hockings' Quincy Street home, Jennifer noted some disturbing changes in her mother. Belle's blond hair was now streaked with silver, and the tiny lines radiating from the corners of her eyes had deepened. Upon closer inspection, she saw faint smudges of fatigue.

The carriage came to a halt beneath the Hockings' portico. Though Jennifer was vaguely familiar with the Hockings' home from her visit there ten months earlier, it felt strange to enter a frame house once again. So accustomed was she to bark-covered wigwams or rough-hewn log structures that the refinements of painted clapboard seemed foreign to her.

She had barely gotten over the contrast when Tim Hocking escorted her to the elegantly-set dining table, seating her on a carved mahogany chair. Mary Hocking, assisted by her niece, Lily Ashforth, served her guests plates heaped high with beef roast and baked potatoes, spring peas and flaky dinner rolls.

Though the atmosphere was properly subdued, Jennifer noted a look of anticipation on her mother's face.

After the blessing, she was the first to speak. "Jennifer, you may remember Lily from our last visit with the Hockings." She looked at Lily Ashforth. "She been helping out with their millinery and fancy goods business since she came from Cornwall. She's quite the one at hat-making. In fact, Lily and I, we be going into business together in Eagle River."

"I'm . . . happy for you," Jennifer managed, stunned by the news. "How did this come about?"

"Mr. Pierce, he been planning for some time to open a business in Eagle River. So—" she took a deep breath—"when he built a new store with living quarters above, he be needing a tenant. Well

. . . with Lily's hat-making, and my experience in general merchandising—"

"—and your lace-making and sewing skills," Lily added.

Belle nodded. "Between us, we think we can make a go of a millinery and fancy goods shop like the one Mary and Jonathan own here in Hancock."

"What about your boarders in Clifton?" Jennifer asked.

At mention of the mining community, a momentary look of anguish passed across her mother's features. "Someone else be renting the company house in Clifton and took on the boarders. I moved to Eagle River already, and Lily, she be coming with us tomorrow."

While details were discussed and advice given for the opening of the new business, Jennifer tried to accustom herself to the idea of living with Lily and her mother over a store belonging to someone else. Changes were happening so fast in her life that it made her head spin.

Following an early breakfast the next morning, Mr. Pierce drove the carriage to Eagle River, stopping first at Clinton Crawford's gravesite. As Jennifer and her mother knelt by the mound of fresh dirt, their loss became even more real. Though Jennifer knew her father's spirit soared in the heavens with his Maker, she couldn't help feeling angry he hadn't been allowed more time to wind up his affairs on earth. Notably, with his daughter.

Beside her, her mother wept silently into her handkerchief, and Jennifer's resentment over their loss surged anew. *Lord, why have you taken Papa from us when we both needed him so much?* God's timing seemed unreasonable, unacceptable, inexplicable. She hated seeing her mother suffer.

She rose to wander to the adjacent grave, the resting place of her beloved Grandma Jen. Several years had passed since her last visit to the gravesite. Though her grandmother had seen hard times in her long life, she never let her troubles defeat her. Jennifer wished for the same inner strength.

As her mother touched her shoulder, she turned to look into a face marred by deep lines of sorrow. She consoled her mother with a hug, then walked with her to the carriage.

Though the atmosphere inside the coach was subdued as they continued into Eagle River, conflicting emotions battled within Jennifer. Thoughts of her recent loss were pushed aside. In their place emerged memories of happy days before the fire, at war with the bitter feelings she had experienced at her departure. Reminiscences of Crawford's General Merchandise flooded back as the carriage pulled onto the street where the store had once stood.

Though John Senter's fuse company stood solid by the dam near the bridge at the outskirts of town, and the County Courthouse a little farther down on the opposite side of the street looked just like Jennifer remembered it, Eagle River had changed. New buildings had been erected on the site of the old. Jennifer mentally checked off the establishments. Mr. Austrian had rebuilt on his old location and expanded onto the adjacent lot where Mr. Retallack's tin store had once stood; Joseph Loth's saloon was in operation once again, as was Mrs. Clemens' brewery. Jennifer was not surprised. Alcohol had always been a weakness of the miners.

The next lot had belonged to her parents, and she was not prepared to find a tall white building with two large display windows—almost identical to the one her father had owned.

"Well, Jennifer, what do you think?" Lily asked. "There be more work to do before your mother and I can open, of course," she explained as the carriage came to a halt.

For several moments, Jennifer remained speechless. She looked from the building to her mother's face. Belle had stopped weeping. The sight of the new store seemed to be having a medicinal effect on her.

"Mama, why didn't you tell me Mr. Pierce had built on Papa's old lot?" she asked, a note of surprise in her voice.

"I thought it be best to let you see for yourself." Her forehead wrinkled with concern. "Your father sold Mr. Pierce the property several weeks ago. I hope you aren't upset."

"No . . . not upset . . . just surprised."

The worry lines disappeared as her mother continued. "Mr. Pierce built the store as soon as Papa deeded the lot to him. He asked me then to manage it and Papa wanted me to take the offer, but all was well with my boarders in Clifton, so I declined. Then, after the accident, I knew I'd be needing more money than two boarders bring in, and Mr. Pierce still needed a tenant. I couldn't run a shop like this alone—you'll be going back to L'Anse one day—so I asked Lily if she wanted to go into business with me. That's when we agreed on a millinery and fancy goods store. Let's go inside."

Though the shop hadn't been completely furnished, it showed remarkable potential. Jennifer felt increasingly abandoned as Lily and her mother discussed how they would display their merchandise.

By contrast, the upstairs rooms had been transformed into comfortable living quarters. The lace curtains at Jennifer's bedroom window, the huge pine wardrobe and blue carpet almost made her believe she was in her old room again.

Mr. Pierce and a neighbor brought up her trunk, saw to the unloading of Lily's belongings, then discreetly left. By the time Jennifer had unpacked, her mother and Lily were at work downstairs in their shop. She helped them for a while, and though they made a point to ask her opinion on the arrangement of racks and shelves, she felt her contribution was not really needed.

An hour later, she set out for a walk along the beach. As she ambled along the shoreline, she realized she had little missed its familiar white sand and driftwood whatnots, for she had filled the void with another place. This cherished scene along the shore of Lake Superior had been replaced by the view of the mission on the west coast of L'Anse Bay and the graceful arc where land met water at the bottom of the inlet.

She did not look forward to a year of mourning. Surely, she couldn't expect Hawk to wait for her to return to L'Anse. Love, if not reinforced, would dwindle and die. She could write Hawk letters, but there was no use. Real communication between a man and a woman in love didn't take place on paper. It meant looking into each other's eyes, seeing the affection in a loved one's face, feeling the gentle touch of his hand, hearing whispered words of endearment.

No, there would be no letters from Jennifer to Hawk, no promises of her return, nor did she expect to hear from him. She must lend emotional support to her mother through the difficult days ahead, even if she *wasn't* needed in the shop.

It seemed as if a year had gone by, yet it was only the end of June. The past month in Eagle River had brought all of the sorrow Jennifer had expected, and some surprises as well.

The Eagle River Millinery and Fancy Goods shop was doing well. Both Belle and Lily worked long hours without complaint: Belle, fashioning gowns which were close-fitting in front but wide at the back according to the style Empress Eugénie had made popular; and Lily creating spoon bonnets, small-brimmed confections of ribbon, lace and netting that had become the latest rage in headgear. Except for her black attire, Jennifer's mother showed few outward signs of grieving during the day, and this had been surprising.

Nighttime, however, was another matter. Jennifer would listen for the sobs to begin, then go to her mother's room where she spent countless late-night hours.

"I'm so glad you're here, Jennifer," her mother would say, mopping the tears from her cheeks. "I miss your father so after I close my bedroom door each night. I look at his side of the bed and expect him to be there, but all I find is a smooth bedspread, and it makes the tears come. I'm sorry, Jennifer. I didn't mean to be waking you."

"That's all right, Mama. I'm glad I can be of some comfort."

Jennifer would sit in the rocker next to her mother's bed until she had fallen asleep, then return to her own room and sleep late each morning. By the time she rose, Lily and her mother would have put in an hour or two in the shop. Jennifer went down by mid-morning to offer her assistance, but it was rarely needed, and the day would stretch out endlessly before her.

Idle hours gave her ample opportunity to walk the beach and reflect on recent events, to ponder why the Lord had brought about these unwanted changes in her life. Though she regularly attended church services and prayer meetings led by Brother Woodworth in the Eagle River schoolhouse, she felt farther from God than she ever had before.

By the second week of July several nights had passed without a tear being shed in Belle's room. When Brother and Sister Wood-worth invited Jennifer to join them on their trip to L'Anse, her mother urged her to go, saying her darkest hours of grieving were over, but Jennifer declined, refusing even to send a message to Hawk or to any of her other friends in the Ojibway village.

On the evening prior to the Woodworths' departure, her mother joined her as she walked the white sand beach. "I don't understand you, Jennifer," her mother said, picking up a moss agate and dropping it in her pocket. "What could it hurt to visit Hawk, or at the very least, write to him?"

Jennifer stiffened. For weeks she had been trying to push memories of Hawk from her mind, but it was a losing battle. Just when she thought she was making progress, they managed to resurface even stronger, giving rise to anger and frustration.

"Mother, a year of mourning is a long time, " she said with a sigh. "I've told Hawk I didn't expect him to wait for me. He'll find someone else. Maybe he already has."

"Hawk's love for you be stronger than that. Besides, sharing the gospel with his people be more important than the rules of polite society. If you can serve the Lord best as Hawk's wife, I wouldn't think you disrespectful not to wait the full year before marrying, nor would your papa if he be here. Maybe it be time for you to return to L'Anse."

Jennifer forced a smile. "I'll give it some thought."

When the Woodworths returned in early August, they brought greetings to Jennifer from the Bentleys, but no word from Hawk. She was disappointed, but relieved. Though a part of her yearned to ask about Hawk, she refrained from inquiring. Besides, she reasoned, the Woodworths would have told her of any important news.

As summer faded into early autumn, bringing cool Lake Superior breezes, business at the Eagle River Millinery and Fancy Goods grew brisk. Mr. Pierce stopped by often as he had from the very first, but Jennifer detected a subtle change in his interests. No longer were his visits strictly business. He was clearly taken by Belle. At first, Jennifer resented his attentions to her mother, feeling that Mr. Pierce was infringing on the memory of her father. Yet, he was a kind, considerate man, quite handsome, really. And her mother seemed happiest when he was in the shop.

Nor did Jennifer feel she had been influenced by the fact that Mr. Pierce had recently given her a locket for her birthday—an exact duplicate of her Grandma Jen's, the precious memento destroyed in the fire.

Jennifer had promised her mother she would consider returning to the mission at L'Anse, and though the words had been spoken out of obligation, she truly had given the advice much thought. Sadly, thoughts were all she had been able to muster. For weeks, she had been unable to pray. The unwanted changes forced on her during the past year and a half had mounted like bricks in a wall held together by the mortar of resentment. As a result, an imposing edifice stood between her and her Lord, casting a long shadow over her spiritual well-being.

By mid-October, two weeks before the Ojibway school should start, Jennifer finally admitted to herself she longed to be with her students, longed to see Angelique and Pierre, and most of all, longed to be by Hawk's side once again. But she also realized it would be a mistake to return. Her teaching hadn't been effective, and most of the students had not understood the spiritual message she had shared.

If she returned to L'Anse, she wouldn't be able to share her love with Hawk, nor God's love with her students. She had cut herself off from both of them. Admitting this to herself brought feelings of remorse. She had let adversity win. Fingering the locket at her throat, she realized her Grandma Jen, a woman of great fortitude, would have been disappointed in her.

This feeling persisted until late one October night when, unable to sleep, Jennifer made her way to her mother's room.

"You be sick, dear?" Belle asked, propping up on one elbow. "Come here and let me feel your forehead."

"I'm not sick, Mama—at least, not physically. I—I just wanted to talk."

Belle sat up in bed and patted the space beside her. "Of course, dear. Tell me what be on your mind."

Jennifer perched on the edge of the bed. "I'm not sure how to explain, but I feel as if I've lost touch with God. For several days I've tried to pray, but . . ." Her throat tightened with emotion.

". . . you can't find the words?"

Jennifer nodded, her eyes blurring with tears of frustration.

Belle wrapped her arm about her daughter's shoulders. "Go ahead and cry, dear. Lord knows I've shed my share of tears. It will make you feel better."

Unable to hold back any longer, Jennifer yielded to the compulsive sobs that racked her. When her tears had subsided, she blew her nose into the handkerchief her mother offered and began telling of her anger toward God and how it had increased until she had felt cut off from him.

When she finished, her mother took her hands in hers. "Jennifer, do you remember when you be a very small girl and learned the Lord's Prayer . . . a few words at a time?"

"I remember." She nodded, recalling how she herself had taught the Ojibway children the familiar prayer, encouraging them to use this model when they found it difficult to pray.

"Let's try saying it that way again." Bowing her head, Belle began, "Our Father which art in heaven . . ."

Lord, thank you for reminding me that you are my heavenly Father, and that you are with me even though my papa can't be.

By the time she had come to the phrase "Give us this day our daily bread" and had considered how the Lord was even now bringing this prayer to pass through her mother's new business, Jennifer was convinced anew of God's love and provision for them.

"For thine is the kingdom and the power and the glory, forever, Amen," she finished, on a note of triumph.

For a long moment she sat quietly, tears of joy coursing down her cheeks. Then she turned a radiant face to Belle. "Thank you, Mama," she whispered. "Thank you."

"Don't thank me, daughter. Thank your heavenly Father, who is never more than a prayer away. We may turn our backs on him, but he is always ready to forgive and welcome us home to him if we ask."

"I know, Mama. I've always known, but the wall I had built in my mind shut him out." She rose, kissed her mother good night, and floated back to her own room, hugging to herself this newfound joy.

Throughout the next week, Jennifer's spirits lifted more each day as she read her Bible and opened her mind to the will of God again. From the depths of despair, her Father in heaven raised her to new peaks of joy, secure in his love. She thought again of L'Anse, and wondered if she could offer enough love to her students to make a difference in their lives.

She pondered this as she straightened the clothes in her wardrobe one morning. There, at the back, was the skirt she had worn home months ago from L'Anse. She had put it away to don her black mourning clothes and had not taken it out since.

She ran her hand over the blue fabric, remembering that day. It had been difficult enough leaving Pierre and Angelique and the Bentleys, but when it was time to bid Hawk a last farewell. . . . She stifled a sob.

As her fingers brushed across the pocket, she realized there was something inside. Her heart thudded as she recognized the folded foolscap Hawk had given her on the dock at Hancock. With trembling fingers, she sat on her bed to open it.

A line at the top in Hawk's handwriting explained that he had helped his sister compose the letter, but the thoughts expressed were her own. At the bottom was Magidins' signature.

Jennifer read eagerly:

Dear Miss Jenny,

You are like sister to me. Sister of Ojibway, sister in spirit.

Hawk say you very sad. I am sorry. Please come back. Marry Hawk. He make you happy.

Now, I tell you some things. When you first come L'Anse, I not like you. Hawk like you. My mother like you. My father like you. I get angry.

I like Miss Simpson. She good friend. I not want anyone to like you.

Then, Miss Simpson die. I get angry. I turn from God. I stop praying. I believe again in Great Spirit, Kitchi Manitou. I not need white man's God.

I make new friend. Ajawac treat me nice. I treat her bad. I tell her, close stove, or I not be her friend.

Ajawac care about you. She want you like her. I get angry. I not listen to you. Still, you treat me nice.

You read Bible verse every day. I try not listen. I come school late. No matter. God talk to me.

The snowstorm come. I fear Evil Spirit. He make bad weather. I see Ajawac follow you. I worry. I come find you.

I worry when Ajawac hurt. Maybe she die. Maybe we all die.

You help me save Ajawac. You pray. You ask God help us. You say I not cause snowstorm.

Later, I know you speak truth. I know Evil Spirit cannot hurt me. I pray to God. He forgive my sins. I love Jesus. Son of God die for me.

Now I ask you forgive me. Come back to L'Anse. Today your heart sad. Ask God make you happy again. He will. Just pray.

I love you. Hawk love you. Our village need you. Hurry home.

Fondly, Magidins

Jennifer wiped her eyes. Hawk's sister had come to know the Lord as her personal Savior! What a blessing! Except for Ajawac,

Jennifer had felt that all her efforts to persuade the Ojibway children of his reality had been in vain. Now this message told her otherwise. Her heart warmed anew with a deep sense of longing to return to the Ojibway village on the bay.

She got out pen and ink and wrote to the Bentleys, asking if they still needed a teacher at L'Anse. Perhaps her position had long since been filled. Perhaps she had forfeited her place there—both to share God's love with the children and to offer Hawk her own. Still, no matter what the reply, she would accept it with the peace and knowledge that her heavenly Father would show her his plan for her future.

Her most ardent prayer—a selfish one, she knew—was to be reunited with Hawk. Her memories of him, her love for him had heightened with the passing of time and the renewal of her faith. She couldn't help wondering whether he wanted her back, but she was certain she would soon know the answer.

On a cool, crisp day in October, Mr. Pierce's plush carriage delivered Jenny to the Hancock Textile Company on Water Street. List in hand, she stepped down, her entrance through the front door of the shop setting the bell a-jingle.

The supplies she had come to collect, neatly packaged, were waiting for her. She paid the clerk from her small reticule, then turned to finger a length of black bombazine. If the letter she had posted to L'Anse was not favorably received, she would be needing some more mourning clothes.

Looking up, she gazed out on the busy harbor, a wealth of emotion overtaking her. Here, she had last seen Hawk, had sent him away, certain she would never see him again. She recalled the ugly scene with the dock hands on the occasion of their parting, and her eyes stung with hot tears. Would it always be so—white man hating red, red man mistrusting white? How she longed for the day when there could be harmony between the races, though in her heart she knew that as Hawk's wife, she would have found little acceptance in this town, or any other.

At that moment, a birchbark canoe skimmed into view, and she almost stopped breathing. Moving to the window for a better view, she watched the craft glide to a full stop. The tall figure of an Indian leapt lightly to the dock and tied up. She blinked, trying to bring the image into sharper focus. He was wearing fringed buckskin breeches and a blanket draped over his shoulders, Ojibway fashion. But there were many Indians in Hancock at this time of year. Already, she had seen some of them, had even spotted some Ojibways through the window of the carriage as she rode into town.

It was not until he turned his strong profile to her that she knew. Hawk.

Leaving her purchases, Jennifer flew out the door, the tinkling of the bell accompanying the music in her heart.

"Hawk! Hawk!"

At her joyous cry, he drew himself erect, looking in the direction of her voice, but he made no move to meet her. She slowed her steps, an icy knot of fear spasming in the pit of her stomach. Perhaps he had left a wife at L'Anse, no longer loved her. . . .

As she approached, trembling, his lips curved in a welcoming smile, and his feet took wing.

"Jennifer!" Her name on his tongue was sweet. "Heart of my heart. My own Jennifer. I was coming for you."

"Oh, Hawk! How did I ever believe I could live without you?" Caught up in his embrace, she buried her face against his broad shoulder, shutting out the sight of a liveryman looking on in contempt, then turning his back and purposefully moving away.

"I need you, Jennifer," he murmured into her hair. "The children of my village need you. You must come back with me and be my wife . . . be the companion of all my days."

"I was so afraid you had . . . that you didn't . . ."

But when at last she lifted her shining face to his, the smoky pools of his eyes told her all she needed to know.

ABOUT THE AUTHOR

DONNA WINTERS loves to explore history. With her husband, Fred, who has taught American History for sixteen years, she enjoys visiting various restored villages and historic sites. "We go with our tape recorder and camera loaded, trying to capture a slice of America's past which I can share with my readers or Fred with his students."

The Winters live in a small midwestern farming village, a town so small they can walk their dog around the entire community in less than an hour every night. "I love a slow pace and quiet life," she explains. "It's perfect for creating romances."

This is Winters' second novel for Serenade/Saga Books. Her first was *Elizabeth of Saginaw Bay*.

A Letter to Our Readers

Dear Reader:

Welcome to Serenade Books—a series designed to bring you beautiful love stories in the world of inspirational romance. They will uplift you, encourage you, and provide hours of wholesome entertainment, as thousands of readers have testified. That we might better contribute to your reading enjoyment, we would appreciate your taking a few minutes to respond to the following questions and return to:

> Lois Taylor
> Serenade Books
> Zondervan Publishing House
> 1415 Lake Drive, S.E.
> Grand Rapids, Michigan 49506

1. Did you enjoy reading *Jenny of L'Anse Bay?*
   - ☐ Very much. I would like to see more books by this author!
   - ☐ Moderately
   - ☐ I would have enjoyed it more if _____

2. Where did you purchase this book? _____

3. What influenced your decision to purchase this book?
   - ☐ Cover
   - ☐ Title
   - ☐ Publicity
   - ☐ Back cover copy
   - ☐ Friends
   - ☐ Other _____

4. Please rate the following elements from 1 (poor) to 10 (superior).

☐ Heroine   ☐ Plot
☐ Hero   ☐ Inspirational theme
☐ Setting   ☐ Secondary characters

5. What are some inspirational themes you would like to see treated in future books?

_____

_____

6. Please indicate your age range:

☐ Under 18   ☐ 25–34   ☐ 46–55
☐ 18–24   ☐ 35–45   ☐ Over 55

Serenade / Saga books are inspirational romances in historical settings, designed to bring you a joyful, heart-lifting reading experience.

Serenade / Saga books available in your local bookstore:

#1 *Summer Snow*, Sandy Dengler
#2 *Call Her Blessed*, Jeanette Gilge
#3 *Ina*, Karen Baker Kletzing
#4 *Juliana of Clover Hill*, Brenda Knight Graham
#5 *Song of the Nereids*, Sandy Dengler
#6 *Anna's Rocking Chair*, Elaine Watson
#7 *In Love's Own Time*, Susan C. Feldhake
#8 *Yankee Bride*, Jane Peart
#9 *Light of My Heart*, Kathleen Karr
#10 *Love Beyond Surrender*, Susan C. Feldhake
#11 *All the Days After Sunday*, Jeanette Gilge
#12 *Winterspring*, Sandy Dengler
#13 *Hand Me Down the Dawn*, Mary Harwell Sayler
#14 *Rebel Bride*, Jane Peart
#15 *Speak Softly, Love*, Kathleen Yapp
#16 *From This Day Forward*, Kathleen Karr
#17 *The River Between*, Jacquelyn Cook
#18 *Valiant Bride*, Jane Peart
#19 *Wait for the Sun*, Maryn Langer
#20 *Kincaid of Cripple Creek*, Peggy Darty
#21 *Love's Gentle Journey*, Kay Cornelius
#22 *Applegate Landing*, Jean Conrad
#23 *Beyond the Smoky Curtain*, Mary Harwell Sayler
#24 *To Dwell in the Land*, Elaine Watson
#25 *Moon for a Candle*, Maryn Langer
#26 *The Conviction of Charlotte Grey*, Jeanne Cheyney
#27 *Opal Fire*, Sandy Dengler
#28 *Divide the Joy*, Maryn Langer
#29 *Cimarron Sunset*, Peggy Darty

#30 *This Rolling Land,* Sandy Dengler
#31 *The Wind Along the River,* Jacquelyn Cook
#32 *Sycamore Settlement,* Suzanne Pierson Ellison
#33 *Where Morning Dawns,* Irene Brand
#34 *Elizabeth of Saginaw Bay,* Donna Winters
#35 *Westward My Love,* Elaine L. Schulte
#36 *Ransomed Bride,* Jane Peart
#37 *Dreams of Gold,* Elaine L. Schulte

Serenade/Saga books are now being published in a new, longer length:

#T1 *Chessie's King,* Kathleen Karr
#T2 *The Rogue's Daughter,* Molly Noble Bull
#T3 *Image in the Looking Glass,* Jacquelyn Cook
#T4 *Rising Thunder,* Carolyn Ann Wharton
#T5 *Fortune's Bride,* Jane Peart
#T6 *Cries the Wilderness Wind,* Susan Kirby
#T7 *Come Gentle Spring,* Irene Brand
#T8 *Seasons of the Heart,* Susan Feldhake
#T9 *Ride with Wings,* Maryn Langer
#T10 *Golden Gates,* Jean Conrad
#T11 *Sycamore Steeple,* Suzanne Pierson Ellison
#T12 *Captive's Promise,* Jeanne Cheyney
#T13 *Jenny of L'Anse Bay,* Donna Winters
#T14 *Gallant Bride,* Jane Peart
#T15 *Destiny's Bride,* Jane Peart

Serenade / Serenata books are inspirational romances in contemporary settings, designed to bring you a joyful, heart-lifting reading experience.

Serenade / Serenata books available in your local bookstore:

#29 *Born to Be One,* Cathie LeNoir
#30 *Heart Aflame,* Susan Kirby
#31 *By Love Restored,* Nancy Johanson
#32 *Karaleen,* Mary Carpenter Reid
#33 *Love's Full Circle,* Lurlene McDaniel
#34 *A New Love,* Mab Graff Hoover
#35 *The Lessons of Love,* Susan Phillips
#36 *For Always,* Molly Noble Bull
#37 *A Song in the Night,* Sara Mitchell
#38 *Love Unmerited,* Donna Fletcher Crow
#39 *Thetis Island,* Brenda Willoughby
#40 *Love More Precious,* Marilyn Austin

Serenade/Serenata books are now being published in a new, longer length:

#T1 *Echoes of Love,* Elaine L. Schulte
#T2 *With All Your Heart,* Sara Mitchell
#T3 *Moonglow,* Judy Baer
#T4 *Gift of Love,* Lurlene McDaniel
#T5 *The Wings of Adrian,* Jan Seabaugh
#T6 *Song of Joy,* Elaine L. Schulte
#T7 *Island Dawn,* Annetta Hutton
#T8 *Heartstorm,* Carol Blake Gerrond
#T9 *After the Storm,* Margaret Johnson
#T10 *Through the Valley of Love,* Shirley Cook
#T11 *This Band of Gold,* Georgia Dallas
#T12 *Candle,* Mary Harwell Sayler
#T13 *Love Is the Key,* Irene Brand